Let Them Fall

Book One of
The Children of the Gods

Meg Wilson

Acknowledgements

Cover Layout design by Gaetano Pezzillo

Cover Model - Joslyn Winters – twilitesmuse.deviabtart.com

Cover Background Photography - at-stock.deviantart.com

Editing by Carly Tenille – www.carlytenille.com

Thank you to all who helped and guided me through
this very long and arduous process,
especially my husband
Daniel.

This novel is a work of fiction.

For you my dear Persephone,

our little warrior xo

Prologue

The Pit - Present Day

'Do you believe she will fight?' whispered Kingston as he stared out onto the burning horizon. Tristan, his current demeanour composed, turned his head towards his friend.

'Yes. I believe she will,' he answered with quiet calm. 'She is fulfilling a prophecy that was fated to her before time itself. An absurd and damning fable that was written in the stars by those unforgiveable witches. The same witches who thread time and torture souls for their own enjoyment, as you know. Only the Gods would know why she holds them in such high esteem, especially since it was they who condemned her in the first place!'

He turned his head back towards the line of shadows outstretched before them. His heart pounding in his ears, hoping that what he had just said would not come to be. For she was not just his enemy. It would not be that easy. She was his light when darkness took him, which, since he had first met her, had happened often. She was that someone he had entrusted his whole heart to centuries ago. She was the only one he had ever loved in all of his existence and she knew that. He anticipated she would use it to her advantage this very day. Quietly, he whispered her angelic name, hoping it would summon her somehow. 'Aurora,' he breathed, 'don't do this'. She had betrayed Tristan not long ago and that cavernous wound she had carved into his soul still bleeds. She had asked for his forgiveness, though he wasn't sure how he could. The wound was too deep.

Kingston looked to his friend and for a moment, he imagined the Fates twisting their thread of despair around Tristan's soul, tighter and tighter until the thread would finally break. They had known one another a long time, fought beside each other in the many wars of men, protecting mortals, and for what? Kingston was at a loss as much as his brother in arms was. They had been slowly losing their faith in the Gods, bit by bit, as doubt wrapped itself around them. Tristan had trained Kingston to become the Guardian that he was today and he would do anything to repay that. But the one thing he knew he couldn't do was the one thing that Tristan required most, and he didn't know how to help him, not with that. Kingston saw that Tristan was lost in her, his mind belonged to Aurora as well as his heart. He would never admit that every piece of him was drawn to her, the commander of their enemy. All he could do was stand by Tristan's side in what could possibly be their final battle together. If the rumours were true about her, then it would be a magnificent one at that. Gripping the handle of his weapon that hung just above his waist, Kingston turned his eyes onto the field of warriors that stood in the distance before them.

'They're not too shabby,' he said attempting to change the mood.

'Meaning what exactly?' asked Tristan.

'Well, for a mixture of mortals and the Fallen, I'd say she has outdone herself by bringing them all together. Not even *they* could do that,' he replied and looked up towards the Heavens.

Tristan forced a smile at his friend in response. Aurora was something of an enigma to them, the Gods, their creators. Not to Tristan however. He knew who she was, what she wanted, and he understood that she would do anything to get it, even if it meant his own destruction and the total annihilation of humanity. They had been waiting in this place for hours now, forming rows like cattle to the slaughter, prepared to fight to the death if the need arose. In the command brief the Gods had ordered that only a small company of warriors would be required to quell this small nuisance, and that this very battle would be a mere speck of dust within the sands of time itself. Tristan glanced sideways down the line of Angels and Nephilim and knew it wasn't enough, and wondered why they were worth so little to their creators. A *speck of dust* he reminded himself, *that is all that we are to them.* Closing his eyes, he reached back within his memory to Aurora's last touch. The yearning that he had felt when he looked deep within her emerald eyes clawed at his wounded heart bringing him back to the present again where the air was still, but the smell of sulphur wound its way around them like coils of blackened fog. Its stench strengthening with every inch it gained. It was a putrid reminder of the

Demons lingering below. The Pit was a place where no Angel would choose to enter willingly. However, there was something down there, locked away, deep within the scorching vaults that Aurora wanted and nothing, or no one, would stop her from getting it. Not even Tristan.

He glanced back towards his own warriors, Nephilim Watchers, the descendants of Fallen Angels who have chosen a life of servitude in the protection of mortals. They were young but strong of mind. Even with their show of fearlessness, he could see the unease deep within their eyes. This would be their first battle against such a force. They were used to one-on-one combat, not legions of warriors all at once. All he could do at this moment was give them a convincing smile and hope that it lifted their spirits. Tristan may be their commander but he wasn't one of them. Unlike them, he was a true Angel, a Guardian, their Guardian Angel for want of a better term. Kingston and he were both Guardians, sent to train and protect the Watchers. At first it was a punishment, but after some time had passed, they grew to enjoy it and actually cherish their time on the mortal plain.

Unnerving silence took hold of all of them as Tristan glanced back towards his brother in arms. 'Is there something else you wish to say?' said Tristan, as he turned his gaze towards the enemy.

'Do you think she will fight *you*?' asked Kingston, his voice a soft murmur.

Looking up into the night sky he said, 'she has not come here for me brother. She wants *him*'. Looking away from the stars above, he focused his glance to the burning pit behind his troops of Nephilim.

'If I get in her way, however, she will have no other choice but to fight me.'

Kingston followed his friend's gaze towards the flames.

'She will not get to him, nor you. The Valkyrie will stop her in her tracks. With the Three leading the way, we will win this night.'

Grinning at his naive friend, Tristan gripped his broad shoulder in his left hand.

'Do you really believe a company of Seraph Warriors or even three Archangels are going to stop her? After everything we have seen her do! Do you think she will allow them to stop her from getting to him? Don't be so naive brother, she has a plan, a plan she forged long ago through many different timelines. She will see it through no matter who stands in her way,' said Tristan, letting go of Kingston's shoulder and resuming his gaze on the horizon.

'There's movement,' said Kingston, excitement growing in his voice. 'Look there, it must be the Warlords.'

Tristan's eyes followed Kingston's and saw the movement within the shadows, at least three or four miles in front of them. The centre ranks parted and one at a time, the enemy Warlords emerged. Styx, a tall nymph-like Fallen Angel with porcelain skin and ebon hair came first. She was Commanding Officer of the Fallen, and once a true friend. She chose to side with Aurora's father during the Fall and had lost her wings in the process. Second, was a mortal known as MacGregor. It was rumoured that Aurora had found him on the battle grounds of Culloden, looking Death in the eyes when she found him. She offered him a deal, to serve her or perish with the rest of his Scottish brethren. Obviously, he decided against the latter. He was a burley sort of being, with fiery locks of amber hair tied behind his head and a stern look upon his aged and unshaven face. He led the *Unknown* forces of her army, a mixture of mortal kith and kin of those she had met throughout the ages across Europe. Even with her diverse mix of races, they were all armoured in similar garb with coppery chest plates, helmets and brown leather bodices. The only differences were their commanders. Instead of copper, they wore gold with blackened leather. The most majestic looking, thus far, and third Warlord to take up his position was Balthazar, Aurora's Second in Command and most trusted adviser. He was a cunning creature of darkness that could take on the form of any living thing within the realm. His classical looks and sun-kissed skin won him the minds of many and his crystal-like eyes mesmerised the soul. Tristan could see straight through them however. He had known Balthazar a long and arduous time. He had kept Aurora from him all of these years, taken her as a child. He had at first thought Balthazar had brutally murdered her foster family, the family Tristan had left her with as an infant to guide and protect her and to ensure her power was kept hidden from creatures such as him. But he was wrong. Balthazar hadn't murdered them, something else did that, but he did take her. Balthazar had saved her life in the end, not Tristan. He didn't fulfil his promise to her father and his failure became his curse. It was as though the recent torment she had put him through was her vengeance for his failure. He could almost understand that; however, he knew the truth, he knew she loved him, and he loved her. Curiously, the enemy turned swiftly inwards, facing someone or something he could not see.

'What do you think is going on over there?' asked Kingston. Tristan tried to focus more, but there were too many enemy warriors standing between them and what they were themselves looking so intently at.

'I could not tell you. You know what I do brother.' Was all he said. Then they heard a great roar from the enemy, and just as swiftly as they had turned inwards, in a moment they were facing out again. Tristan saw a glitter of light break through the cracks of Aurora's vanguard. The legions dispersed like dominoes and he saw *her* glide through to stand in front of her Warlords. She was as perfect as the last time they had spoken. Clad in ancient golden armour, with her braided silver hair held tight behind her shoulders. She held no weapons but for the scythes that rested on her back, with something else that held what looked like arrow heads. She was what humans would describe as elf-like, or a mythical Viking Queen, which made her stand out among her people. Proof that she was very much from the Archangel bloodline. She was not only beautiful but also majestic, a creature from a child's storybook. Tristan was painfully in awe of her. His heart ached at what she had done to him. He tried to look away, to focus on the battle that would begin at any moment but their eyes had met. She mouthed something to him, a message to him alone. It wasn't until he realised what it was she had said that he felt a searing pain rip through his chest. He looked down and saw the shaft of an arrow imbedded in his armour. The glowing head now neatly tucked inside his heart. He put his hand to the bloody mess beneath his breastplate and looked back at Aurora in shock as he fell to his knees. She placed a bow back into the hands of one of her warriors and unsheathing her scythes, she bellowed a war cry to begin the carnage.

Kingston held his friend in his arms wishing that there were something he could do to save him. The problem was he had no idea what the daughter of Lucifer had done to him. He pulled the arrow out of Tristan's chest. The tip was gone, no longer on the arrow but not within Tristan's body either. This was a new weapon that they had not seen before. Tristan spoke but Kingston could not comprehend him.

'Quiet my brother. It'll only cause you more pain.'

But Tristan needed to say it aloud, to make sure he hadn't dreamt it.

'Did you see what she said?' he gurgled as blood slowly dripped from the corners of his mouth.

'I didn't. I didn't see anything.' Looking down at his brother, he leaned in to hear his whisper.

'She said ....' and Tristan closed his eyes.

Chapter One

Before the Fall

Lucifer and Corvis observed the novices from afar, assessing the adequate Seraphim from the inadequate ones. The Seraphim who had completed their training were nearly equal in strength and ability to him and his siblings, the Archangels. Not exactly *equal*, but just close enough that if any of them were to fall out of line, there would be other Angels strong enough to correct them. Of course, the Valkyrie, an unbiased security force of Seraph Warriors and the High Guard, the protectors of the Gods, had to be in groups of at least three, or they could be overpowered by just *one* Archangel. The High Guard itself was run by the Archangels, therefore, an alternate force within the Kingdom was required to match it, hence the creation of the Valkyrie. Obviously, this was just a precaution, they would never be required to attack or defend against the first children of the Gods, so the Valkyrie's first priority was to investigate celestial criminal activity within the newly created realm of mortals. The Archangels were highly favoured by the Gods, especially Lucifer, he could do no wrong in their eyes. He was the perfect son. The Seraphim, on the other hand, are first created as Lower Angels. Only specific Angels of a certain calibre make it to the elevated heights of the Seraphim.

However, if they fail the first stage of Seraph training, they have the option of becoming a Guardian of mortals or working as Sentinels within the Pit, confining those created by the Gods who were a mistake, most however, choose to be Guardians. Therefore, perfection was key for the Angels who would strive to become a Seraph Warrior.

Lucifer was far from *perfect*. He had only come to assess this particular Seraph training session because there was one member of the troop he specifically wanted to join his Guard. And, if he had left it all for Celeste to decide, it was likely only one or two out of the twenty in front of him would rise to the next phase of the training. Celeste was a hard woman, fantastic trainer and brilliant strategist, but severe in attitude and remorseless in her instruction. To this very day, he could not believe she was the twin sister of the woman that he loved. However, Lucifer saw Celeste as the favourite of the Gods, because she was everything he was not; righteous and unforgiving. He couldn't care less about their wants or needs. He was a *self-centred arrogant arse* according to his sister Uriel. The Archangels were required to command the armies of the Gods and fight on their behalf. Lucifer refused and left that task to his brother Michael. Lucifer would fight for no one unless it benefited *him* in some way. Normally, insubordination would be punished, especially if it was towards the creators but, as usual, he got away with it. He was their greatest warrior and he knew it, so did Celeste, which is why she despised him. There was a deep and unforgiving hatred that burned in her eyes each time she had to look and speak to him. He was her superior, so naturally, to her dismay, she was forced to do this daily. He rather enjoyed it though, watching her squirm. Of course, the outcome was that she took her anger out on the novices, unfortunately for them. Balthazar, her Second, didn't even bother trying to calm her down. Like Lucifer, he disliked Celeste, but loved her sister, albeit in a different way than Lucifer did. If Celeste had any idea about the connection between her sister and Lucifer, it would be the end of everything he knew. She would destroy everything that he loved, even if it meant destroying her sister in the process. The twins were the opposite of each other, one was cruel, while the other was kind, but Pandora did have her flaws like many other Seraphim, Lucifer knew that. But she was nothing like Celeste.

Corvis laughed a little when he saw her quickly glance in their direction. He was a member of Lucifer's High Guard. Somewhat of a privilege. Just because Lucifer wouldn't fight a war for the Gods, didn't mean he wouldn't be their protector. He was, after all, the Commanding Officer of the High Guard. The sisters Celeste and Pandora, who also instructed the training that would lead them to either fail or pass today's trials, jointly led the Valkyrie, his opposition. Right now, Lucifer and Corvis were looking for new members, *one* in particular.

'So, boss, are you going to torment her today?' Corvis asked Lucifer as he looked away from Celeste's violent eyes.

'I would like to say no this one time, but just being here is probably causing her some discomfort already. I think I'll be good today. I wouldn't want to make this morning's drill practice more difficult than it has to be. As I said, just being here is starting to burn a fire under her, which isn't turning out well for poor Christian over there. She's really going at him for not lacing his armour correctly,' said Lucifer, smirking.

'He's not getting over *that* anytime soon,' said Corvis.

'No, he is not. I wonder where Pandora is this fine morning?' he asked casually.

'I believe she has the morning off, said something about going for a walk.'

'Very well. Keep a good eye on Tristan. His skills as a warrior are promising.' Corvis did as he asked, watching Tristan's swift movements with the sword as he sparred with his partner. Corvis was a master swordsman, which he guessed was why Lucifer asked him to join him this morning in his hunt for their newest member of the Guard. Though there was one other novice that had caught his attention; Styx he believed her name was. Her movements were as graceful as the wind. He had seen her before, walked passed her in the garden, but as she was just a Lower Angel, they never really had a reason to talk. This gave him an opportunity to introduce himself to her, and possibly challenge her. Or, have her combat Tristan. At least then they could truly see who was worthy of the position within the Guard. Lucifer was just about to walk over to Celeste when Corvis stopped him.

'I have a suggestion,' he said. Lucifer looked curiously at his brother in arms.

'Go on,' he said, raising an eyebrow.

'Perhaps we should hold a trial? You see, I believe there is more than one novice among this lot that could join our ranks. But if you're only looking for the one, I think we should have Tristan combat Styx. In observing them, I noticed she was equal to him in skill, if not better in some aspects. Neither of them knows why we are here. Would it hurt to test them both?' asked Corvis.

Lucifer smiled, 'No I guess it wouldn't hurt, not me in any case. Though, we could make this a little more interesting for the two of us?' he suggested, rolling a gold coin backwards and forward along the top of his knuckles of his right hand.

'I'm in. Let's say ten gold coins each, winner takes all,' beamed Corvis.

'Agreed,' smiled Lucifer.

'Celeste, can you come over here a moment?' yelled Lucifer, grinning ear to ear.

*

Tristan had been training since dawn to ensure Celeste passed him onto the next phase of training where you could be chosen for either the Valkyrie or the High Guard. Becoming either was difficult, as they were where the elite soldiers of the Gods were placed. But it was the High Guard that gave you any real honour among

Angels. Especially since there were so many Angels within the Kingdom. Being selectively chosen from the many highlighted that you were indeed the cream of the crop. He had been working hard to get to this point but he knew the others with him this day had also been working just as hard. Especially Styx, his competition, and friend. She reminded him of Celeste but somewhat kinder and with a personality. He knew, if he was ever put up against her in combat, she would probably win. He wouldn't admit it and he wouldn't go down without a long hard and drawn out fight but he knew deep down, she could end him. Unfortunately for him, battle came naturally to her. He was more of a protector, which is why he was first chosen to go into Guardian training. It was he who requested to be transferred to the Seraph. He wanted to do something different, something unpredictable. Guardian training was predictable. What hadn't been predicted was that he had passed the first phase of Seraph training and was now up to the third of four phases. Number one was basic; learning discipline, defensive and attack moves as well as strategy. Two was their initial training in the two different directions Seraph instruction could lead you. Three was everything you have learnt thus far, with challenges included to lead you to the next phase, if you passed. The fourth and final phase was where you would ultimately end up, the Valkyrie or the Guard. Both Styx and Tristan wanted the Guard. Seeing Lucifer and Corvis show up at their final test meant that they had that chance. Tristan watched Celeste eye the novices to see which ones she was going to partner up next for the final trial. He had been sparring with Demeter for the past hour and knew he wouldn't be partnered up with her again. His calibre of fighting was stronger than Christian's, so that was a no go. There were many others like Nateri or Odin he could be partnered with but there was just the one that he knew he was equal to, if not lesser than on occasion. Lucifer called Celeste over to him and they spoke for a bitter moment. Time always seemed to go too slow in these particular settings. After what had looked like a painful transaction for Celeste, she walked straight over to Styx and then called on Tristan. *I knew it*, he thought to himself as he walked over to face his doom.

*

Lucifer attentively watched Tristan and Styx in their contest, praying to himself for *his* guy to win. He wasn't a fan of losing. They were both quite agile and smooth in their movements, it was honestly the best fight he had watched in a long time. Styx favoured the double dagger, while Tristan worked with a short sword. Styx had cut Tristan's armour a number of times so far, while Tristan had relieved her of one of her daggers, knocking it out of her hand. It stuck out of the ground metres away from them. She changed from weaponry to hand-to-hand combat seamlessly and Tristan adapted just as easily, ridding himself of his own weapon. They were an equal match until she got the better of him with an armbar, leading Tristan to give in to her reluctantly before it ended in a break. He had lost. Lucifer had other thoughts however, to his dilemma. Corvis slapped him on the back in enthusiasm.

'Fantastic! Shall I go inform Styx of her prize?' he asked with a grin.

'What prize would that be brother?' Lucifer looked at him puzzled.

'The one where we offer her a position in the Guard. Was that not our deal?' goaded Corvis.

'Not in the least. All you asked was that we hold a trial and have the two compete against one another. At no point did you suggest we offer her a place in the Guard if she were to win. All I owe you is a bag of twenty gold coins,' he said, unperturbed.

'Blast you! You knew what I meant. How can we not offer her a position after that fight? She was brilliant! Do you think her inferior to the rest of us?' Corvis argued.

'Okay, okay. Calm yourself brother, and no, I do not believe her to be inferior. I may not have promised what you suggest but may I make a different suggestion?' he offered.

'I'm all ears brother,' said Corvis, eagerly.

Lucifer walked over to the two exhausted Angels sprawled out on their backs on the ground. They both looked up at him and rose to stand as quickly as they could, almost knocking each other to the ground once more.

'My Lord, apologies. We didn't realise you were there,' lied Styx hurriedly.

'Relax, both of you. What you just did was impressive. You should be very proud of yourselves,' said Lucifer, beaming. 'I would like to offer both of you the chance to become part the greatest group of Angels our realm has ever witnessed. Would either of you be interested in joining the High Guard?' asked Lucifer, sensing Celeste's disgust from behind him at what he just offered.

Both Styx and Tristan looked at one another, and then back at their superiors. They were absolutely dumbfounded. Lucifer answered for them. 'So, I'll take that as a yes then. Be at the Circle at midday. If you're not there, you know where you'll be staying,' he finished. He nodded goodbye to Celeste and Balthazar and both he and Corvis left the training grounds.

Chapter Two

Fledglings or Friends

Tristan and Styx made their way to the Circle after training, expecting the rest of the Guard there waiting for them. There was no one in sight. They stood alone in the garden pondering what to do next. It had been an hour since Lucifer, their new commander, and Corvis, their Sergeant in Arms, had offered them positions within the High Guard. They felt exhilarated at the thought of becoming one of them. Hearing movement beyond the garden's walls, Styx breathed out a sigh of relief when she caught a glimpse of Lucifer's golden hair shining in the light of the sun that beamed down upon them.

'Finally they have come,' said Styx smiling. What was an empty garden was now filled with warriors listening to their leader's words in great anticipation. Hanging onto everything he said, Tristan and Styx were pointed out within the crowd and everyone turned to face them.

'Here we have two Lower Angels named Tristan and Styx ready to further themselves by joining us. They will be challenged in more ways than one, won't they brothers and sisters?' he yelled, a roar of laughter echoed throughout the garden in reply.

Lucifer faced the new members as he continued, 'we will strip you down to nothing but the bare flesh and bones that the Gods gave to you. If you thought the last three phases were difficult, you have no idea what lies ahead. Fledglings, welcome to your new Hell.' In silence, Lucifer turned and left the garden. Tristan and Styx stood frozen in the midst of the horde that surrounded them not knowing whether to move or stay put. At last, Corvis moved towards them sending orders to the other warriors to move out of his way. Reaching the two fledglings, he offered them both a welcoming gesture of placing his right hand on his heart. 'Welcome. I hope that little speech hasn't frightened you too much,' he said, grinning. 'He tends to overdo it sometimes, loving the sound of his own voice as all Archangels do. Well, follow me and I will show you both to your new sections.' Corvis gently ushered Styx through the crowd beckoning Tristan to follow behind them. The way Corvis brushed his hand against her back lead Tristan to believe there was something more than just a superior and subordinate relationship between the two. Shaking the thought out of his mind, as that would be forbidden, he pushed his way through the other warriors to trail behind Corvis as ordered and made his way to his new beginning.

*

As time passed, the days and nights for Tristan became one and the same. Though, he couldn't say the same for Styx. She had become distant, almost as if they had never known one another. For months now she ignored him in the halls and on the training grounds, and when he finally had the stomach to confront her, she acted as if he was nothing to her. He even had the gall to challenge her, which she coldly accepted. To his dismay, she was still just as brilliant with a sword as she was when they had trained together under the gaze of Celeste and Pandora. The fight was as long as the sun rising and falling beyond them, until she finally caught him with the light in his eye and knocked him to the ground sending him into a deep slumber. Tristan woke up to the sun beaming directly onto his face through the open windows of what looked like his quarters.

'Good morning sunshine,' said a familiar voice.

Tristan struggled to open his eyes through the blaring sun and the searing pain that shattered his senses. Slowly, forcing himself to rise, he started getting dressed.

'I said *good morning*! You know it is rude not to take part in pleasantries,' said the voice, now annoyed. Tristan looked at Lucifer bewildered, it wasn't the sun blaring down at him at all. Lucifer stood at the base of his bed rolling a ball of fire between his hands.

'What happened? How am I here in my room? What are you doing?' he asked.

Lucifer looked him over.

'Styx beat you, then brought you here. This?' he asked looking down at the rolling flames. 'I'm just hiding our conversation from prying ears and eyes.'

'Besides that last part not making any sense, is that all of it?' asked Tristan curiously.

'Yes, that is it. No twists, or hidden messages or veiled speech. Your friend, with whom you challenged, won the fight, again. Though, you are probably wondering why she has been so withdrawn from you of late?' bated Lucifer, changing the subject. Tristan glared at his commander, and sat back down on his bed. 'Corvis?' he asked.

'Yes. It is very much a private matter that is none of our business,' stated Lucifer, hiding his humour.

'It is forbidden,' said Tristan, looking down at the ground in shame at the thought of it.

'Which is why she has kept away from you. If you were true friends, she wouldn't have the need to do so,' said Lucifer, blatantly.

'She could have her wings stripped! Do you not give a damn about that?' he said quietly through gritted teeth so no other could hear. Lucifer sat down beside him then.

'Would you condemn their love? Force them to work side by side for eternity knowing that they are both drowning silently in torment because of one damned rule our creators have forced upon us? No, you would not and nor would I. For one thing, it would make me a hypocrite,' he said, amused. 'One day Tristan you will find that same sacred connection with someone. A love so strong not even the Gods could take it away from you. In time, you will understand. Just let them have this now while they have time remaining, because every moment we have in this unforgivable realm counts.' Sighing deeply, Tristan looked at his commander and friend and forced a small smile in response.

'So, no harm done then?' asked Lucifer grinning. 'Come on, get up. Let us not speak of this subject again. Corvis and I are heading to breakfast. Join us. Balthazar and Pandora will be there too, so it will be just like old times for you,' extinguishing the flames he grinned, slapping Tristan on the shoulder. Lucifer was just like that annoying older brother that constantly teased and abused your trust, but who would always be there for you if you required it. That's what he was to Tristan, he didn't quite understand why and he would never ask. It was just the way it was. Lucifer was his mentor, probably one of the best he ever had, besides Pandora. A part of him missed her guidance. He looked up at Lucifer who was now standing and offering his hand. Tristan grabbed it.

'Yes fine. As long as Styx stops treating me like I am a wounded mortal she can trod on,' he uttered.

'Tell her that yourself,' said Lucifer motioning towards the door as it opened. Styx was standing on the other side waiting for them. 'Let's go you two,' said Lucifer, leaving the room behind him.

Chapter Three

As Beautiful As a God

The morning splendour that was laid out in all its glory on the breakfast table reminded Pandora's stomach that she didn't need to be anywhere until midday. As they neared the end of breakfast, she decided she'd go for a walk out under the beauty of the sun. Saying her goodbyes, and shooting Lucifer a serious glare that said *don't follow me*, she stood and left the hall. Normally, she would walk along the sand dunes and watch the clouds float by her. She would pretend she was on a deserted Island in the mortal realm below until a member of the Valkyrie patrolling their assigned route interrupted her solitude. This seemed to always be right when she thought she could float away on the puffy white clouds below. Of course, the Gods were watching, even using her own warriors to spy on her. The bond of trust was slowly diminishing daily between Angel and creator. Lucifer was right. As the Gods fed on all the evil within the world, it not only sustained them, but it was changing them too. All of those dark prayers and evil souls stained their minds, slowly turning them against their own children. Still no one challenged them. There was no one brave enough. Not one Angel among the many, not even Lucifer would cross that line for a taste of freedom. Her warrior bowed her head in respect as she walked by. Pandora waved her off and decided on a different route, just letting the path guide her. Reaching for her chest, she began to play with her rosary, the highest honour given to an Angel by the Gods that hung permanently around her neck. They had been given to her for her unequal dedication to her subordinates and for her performance against the Tyrants during the creation of the human race. The Tyrants were a mistake. They were the siblings of Archangels but malicious and unpredictable. They could not be controlled; therefore, a creation the Gods would rather forget, locking them away for eternity within the Pit after one of the bloodiest battles they have ever known. Remembering those times, she made her way through the burning brush. This gift of fire, known as the Incendium, was a maze of crimson leaves and everlasting burning branches. It was so precious to the Gods that only the Seraph and Archangels were privileged enough to be allowed to see or go near it. On this morning, it had steered Pandora towards the training grounds. She hadn't meant to go there as her sister Celeste and their Second in Command Balthazar were running the morning training session. It seemed the maze of flames had led her there for a reason.

'The rumours were true, she is a beauty. As beautiful as a God perhaps?' said a voice behind her.

'Yes, yes. As beautiful as a God, indeed. No wonder he can no longer lead,' said another.

Unsheathing her long sword, Pandora whipped around to confront the owners of the strange voices but there was nothing to be seen.

'What is this? Who are you?' she demanded.

'Strong too. The will of an ox and stubborn as a mule,' giggled a third voice.

'Who are you? I order you to reveal yourselves at once!' yelled Pandora.

'Order? Order? She orders us! Should we let her see?' said the first.

'Does she really want to see?' asked the second.

'Oh yes, let her see!' said the third.

Burning with anxiety, Pandora raised her blade before her, waiting patiently for the strangers to reveal themselves. Three figures emerged from the flames. They were dressed in nothing but leaves covering most of their bodies, except their legs and arms. The three women stood before her, with skin of green and eyes of fire. Their hair was the only thing that one could use to tell them apart. One had auburn locks entangled with twigs that hung past her shoulders. The other had hair as black as a raven's back, twisted on top of her head with thorny vines. The third had hair like water, glistening hues of blue and green flowed down her back and touched the ground beneath her.

'Why do I not know you?' Pandora asked.

'Because we have never met. If you had met us, you would know us. Now you do, because now we have met,' laughed the blue-haired one.

'We are sister seers of fate, readers of your path. You will birth greatness, with motives of pain she will release us from our chains,' sang the raven-haired woman.

'Stop talking in riddles. Just tell me what you want, now!' demanded Pandora.

The three looked at each other with perfect fluid movement.

'Ooh burning anger just like her sister. A sister not like us, she will betray. Look here, a gift for you, to choose your fate. They will make you Fall and she will help them and this will only take one and not all.' The auburn-haired woman took a silver rectangular box from somewhere and passed it to the raven-haired one. She took a step forward, an inch away from Pandora's touch.

'Do not open until it is time, for you will know when you see the last crow.' Stepping forward, she placed a hand on Pandora's stomach. 'She is strong and stubborn like you. They will not rest till dawn no longer exists.' Stepping back, the raven-haired woman retreated into the Incendium, taking her sisters with her. Pandora didn't move. Holding the box in one hand and her rosary in the other, she stood silent for what seemed like days. Taking a deep breath, she looked down at the innocent looking container. It had some weight to it but the strange bird woman told her not to open it, yet. She lowered her other hand to her stomach. *Could I be?* She thought to herself. It had never happened before, but then, two Angels had never fallen in love before. So, anything is possible. Thinking back to what that strange woman had said, 'to choose your fate.' *What did that mean?* Her mind became a jumbled mess of question after question. She felt she needed to get away, that there was some reason she needed to move away from this place as quickly as possible. That reason was walking straight towards her, prompting her to turn around and head back towards the sand dunes.

*

Lucifer told Corvis and Tristan to ready the Guard for some midday training. He informed them that he would join them in a moment, for he needed to be somewhere else for now. Corvis gave him a bewildered look then headed off towards the garrison quarters with Tristan in tow. Lucifer could sense Pandora from a mile away. He followed her trail to the Incendium, just another reminder that the God's were superior to them. He saw her spot him and turn quickly away, pretending not to see him. She looked pale. Lucifer wasn't going to make it so easy for her. Stretching out his golden wings, he lifted himself off the ground, landing right in front of her with a smug look on his face.

'What are you doing?' she gasped. 'They'll see us!'

'Not here Pandora. They can't see through the flames, ironic, isn't it? It's why I stopped you before you left the path. It's just like the Circle, another place where

31

we can be together away from them,' he said walking towards her, driving her back towards the flames.

'Oh, it's ironic?' she spat sarcastically, rolling her eyes and trying to look unshaken.

'You know why. Don't you?' She shook her head in response. 'Well, it's ironic because they created it. Funny that a creation of theirs should defy them the ability to see, is it not? It seems the flames can think for themselves,' he said, looking into her emerald eyes.

*

Pandora stopped moving once they were completely covered by the burning brush, which was not hot in the least. She could feel her heart beating faster and faster the closer he was to her. She still didn't understand why he had this effect on her. After thousands of years working opposite one another, never really speaking, she now felt that she would starve without him. She needed his touch against her own skin. It was very confusing for her to feel desires such as these. They were new ground to her. It made her mind swim and her heart ache in agony whenever they were apart, which was most of the time. These feelings towards him that had begun not long ago, she believed it was the same for him. As soon as she was granted approval to touch the Flame, the world around her erupted from black and white to perfect colour. Her mind felt open and free and she could now breathe in the fresh air that surrounded them for the first time in centuries. She could see other Angels around her more clearly, she could see the Guardians caring for their early human protégées and the great and empowering Archangels, who beamed down their golden light over the Kingdom. She no longer saw everyone with a condemning eye, like that of her sister Celeste. She assumed that must've been the moment for both of them. She wondered if it were the same for any of the others with access to the Flame. She would never dare ask anyone else though. The only reason she knew Lucifer felt as he did was because he made the first move. A risk, but a rewarding one he always said. Access to the Incendium was limited to those directly under the Gods, and for good reason too. Pandora couldn't imagine if everyone felt as she did, it would be utter chaos. Especially now after her unexpected visit just a moment ago.

*

Lucifer couldn't understand how she could still doubt his feelings for her. The first moment he had laid eyes on her was the best moment he had ever been privileged to have. The fact of the matter was, he had held these feelings a lot longer than she had. The Archangels and Tyrants were granted freewill upon their creation by the Gods; their first mistake. This was not given to any other creature of the Gods, until their next and final creation, mortals. They had failed with the Tyrants and after locking them away in the dungeons of the Pit below, they tried again, but on a lesser scale. Mortals were only created to feed the Gods, to sustain their life. Emotions from the mortals created a life source for them, which they drank to survive. It didn't last long. Emotions of peace were not enough for them, so they offered them fire from the Flame. In granting them this gift, they gave the mortals every sensation at once, fuelling the God's life source once more. When Pandora was invited to see the Incendium, she was so mesmerised by it that she held her hand out and touched it. Lucifer saw her transform in a second as she promptly withdrew her hand. That's when she caught his eye and blushed. Right at this moment though, she wouldn't look him in the eye. Something was wrong.

'Pandora, please don't fight me, I can tell something is not right. Who knows what could happen to any of us, at any stage. I've been waiting a long time for you to actually see me, please tell me what's wrong,' he begged graciously.

Pandora looked away for a moment, then back into his eyes. 'What do you mean, you've been waiting a long time?' she prompted, changing the subject.

'My siblings and I were granted the freedom you see now, from the time of our creation. It has nothing to do with the Incendium, not for us,' he said, smiling at her.

'Well, that explains everything. How you're always the fool and you are always up to some kind of mischief for one reason or another. If only Celeste knew,' she laughed, becoming more at ease. 'But why haven't you said anything before?'

'You were still adapting. Besides, if Celeste knew she would only be more annoyed with me,' he grinned.

'Yes, I guess she would be,' Pandora smiled back.

'Enough talk of *Celeste*,' he said, holding out his hand to her. 'Instead of diverting me, again, tell me what the matter is? I can see it in your eyes and you're trembling,' pressed Lucifer, still holding out his hand in trepidation. Pandora looked at it for a short while, then slowly lifted her own to meet him. At her touch, Lucifer felt tingles where her fingers grazed the inside of his palm. Their eyes met in blissful awareness, and he sighed in relief.

Chapter Four

The Fall

'Death is not extinguishing the light; it is putting out the lamp because dawn has

come.'

Rabindranath Tagore

The atmosphere within the palace walls was suffocating. Pandora was struggling to

surface out of her quiet demeanour when she reached the Hall of Divinity for the

morning's orders. She leant out a steady hand to push open the entrance door, when

someone grabbed her shoulder from behind.

'Excuse me!... Luke what are you doing?' she gasped as she turned to face Lucifer.

His black robes were torn and his face was as pale as winter's touch.

Covered in ash and sweat, he lowered his voice to a whisper, 'Pandora, they know.

We must leave. We must leave now!'

Without one word of a question, she took his outstretched hand and they ran

towards the exit of the Small Chambers. As they reached the darkened door, four

members of the Valkyrie stepped out of the shadows, blocking their path of escape.

'Where will we go?' she asked desperately as they turned quickly down another passageway.

'The dunes or maybe the Flame. Yes the Flame, it's our only safe way out of here,' he shouted over his shoulder. They had almost reached the exit when Lucifer's brother Michael flanked by more Valkyrie appeared through the oak door. They were trapped. They stopped, realising they were surrounded and had no way out; no escape.

'We... I have to fight. Stand behind me,' he said sweeping his robes to one side and taking out his blades. Pandora knew that just one Archangel and the leader of the Valkyrie could not face off against another Archangel and a whole troop of her own guards, not in her state anyway. Looking at Lucifer's back as he stood his ground, she noticed something on his armour, something small and insignificant to an Angel outside the High Guard. An engraving of a bird.

'Luke, what kind of bird is that? On your shoulder?' she asked him nervously.

He looked down in confusion, 'It's a crow, why?'

Pandora subconsciously placed her hand over her stomach. She felt her heart try to leap from her chest when, without warning, Celeste stepped out in front of her warriors. Staring at Pandora, with a look of pure murder. She marched towards them a smile of triumph suddenly transforming her darkened face.

Pandora, taking a deep breath and still holding her stomach, felt her sister's betrayal cut through her as easily as a knife would through her back. She lifted her other hand and gripped Luke's shoulder, silently telling him to surrender to their fate. She could see from her sister's remorseless glee that they were unmistakably alone.

*

Forced forward, step by step, the High Guards lead them to their fate. They begrudgingly marched towards the Trinity's throne. Lucifer knew his warriors were just following orders. That didn't mean it hurt him any less, nor them. His heart sank deeper and deeper the closer they got to the end of the line, especially since his own brother helped to take him there. Michael would not be lenient towards them. He was proud and lawful and Lucifer knew what he had done was against their laws, but he did it anyway. He had fallen in love with Pandora. And now, he had caused her demise and that of their unborn child. Once she had told him of the child, he tried desperately to think of a way out of the Kingdom, if only to save them, but he could think of nothing. The Flame was all he had thought of, but that portal was still a mystery to him. The Angels only used the dunes to move to the different realms of men, but they were constantly patrolled. He did not have enough time to think, to gather those loyal to him. Pandora shook him from his reverie as she whispered into his ear, asking him where he had been, and how they had found out.

'The Trinity met with me last night, after I left you. They questioned me about our relationship. I gave them nothing of course, but they knew it all anyway. They said I was free to go, but as I left the Hall, Celeste and a section of Valkyrie came out of nowhere and attacked me. They ordered me to comply and be taken into custody. Obviously, I tore them down. I have been looking everywhere for you ever since. Where have *you* been?' he hissed through gritted teeth.

'I was at the Flame, trying to figure out what to do, with *her*,' she said looking down at her stomach. Lucifer didn't know whether to be happy or sad knowing it was going to be a girl. 'How do you know?' he asked.

'I can hear her thoughts. It's strange, almost as if her mind has already grown to be able to comprehend me. I feel as if at any moment, she could be in this world with us, but I'm so frightened Luke. I don't know what to do,' he could see her anxiety start to weigh her down as her shoulders fell. Against popular mortal belief, Archangels were the highest order, below the Gods, next to the Seraphim. Pandora being the latter. However, they were all Celestials, higher beings to mortals. After the failure of the Tyrants and the human children, the Trinity created new decrees. One of which condemned any relations between Angels in order for them to have complete control over their creation. Even after their own failure, they deemed any celestial other than the Trinity unfit for the creation of life. Lucifer and Pandora broke this statute as they slowly fell deeply attached to one another, just as the mortals had done when they were awakened by the Flame. Before the Fall of the humans from the garden, or as it is known to the Celestials, the Circle, Pandora was simply a warrior of her people, and Luke their leader. The Trinity were the creators of mortal and the immortal alike. However, against mortal belief, there was not one God, there were six. The Trinity, Isrea, Titus and Chaos were the Higher Powers. They and the lower Gods, Gaia, Nubis and Hecate, formed the High Council. The Ancient Greek stories spoke of them as Titans, and their *children*, the Angels, were the Olympians. The difference was, they had not usurped the Old Gods, and they served them still, to this very day. They are as old as the universe itself just like their sisters, the Elementals also known as the Fates, who lie in the hierarchy between the Gods and their children. They were created from the same beginning, however, the Gods had matured at a more advanced rate, leaving the Fates to be nothing more than servants to their more formidable siblings. The Trinity refused to let their sister's existence be known to the world, especially to their children. If they had known them to be more than just small stories from insignificant mortals, and knew exactly what the Fates were capable of, then the Trinity's control over the Kingdom would end, and they couldn't have that.

*

Tristan and the other High Guards were summoned to the Hall of Divinity where the throne room was located. This had never occurred before, having everyone within the hall at the same time, not in his time at least. Standing at attention, his troop of guards stood in three ranks along the left-hand side of the hall, facing inwards. The Trinity Throne stood dead centre. While on the right stood the Valkyrie, in the exact same alignment, opposite the High Guard. In the rest of the hall sat the subordinate Angels, Guardians, Sentinels and Lower Angels alike. It was completely crowded. Glancing sideways, Tristan caught a glimpse of someone leaving as the hall's doors opened on the opposite side, letting in the Archangels, followed by the Trinity themselves, and the rest of the High Council behind. Gasps could be heard among his fellow Angels. The Trinity had not shown themselves to them in over a century. Only the Archangels were privileged enough to speak with them if required. Even being a part of the High Guard didn't grant you access to them, unless they sought their protection. He watched them enter the throne room. One by one, they glided across the marble floor and took their positions on their thrones, the door closing behind them. The mother, Isrea, sat within the high arched chair in the centre, while her two brothers Titus and Chaos sat on either side of her. Gaia, Nubis and Hecate sat to the left of them, with the Archangels, Uriel, Raphael and Gabrielle standing beside them.

Where was Lucifer and Michael? Thought Tristan. Tristan glanced to his left and right, and across at the Valkyrie. There were members on both sides missing too. He moved his eyes back towards the Trinity, the mother waved her hand and the great doors opened once more. That's when he saw them, their arms bound in light behind their backs, being escorted towards the front of the hall. Lucifer, his mentor, and Pandora, his previous commander treated like mere slaves.

*

Once they had reached the Hall of Divinity, Zachariah met Celeste at the door and they took point, ushering Lucifer and Pandora through the great doors and entering the hall. Michael followed behind with the rest of the guards who had apprehended them. Again, Pandora glanced sideways at Luke, his eyes were staring blankly forward. She could feel her hands start to tremble. Zachariah must have noticed as he loosened his grip on her arm. She could feel his apprehension towards their present situation. He was one of her best warriors and a loyal friend. Normally, she would show her defiance or strength in a situation that made her vulnerable, but because of her current physical situation, all she could feel was terror. Terror at what was about to occur. To the Trinity, what she carried, was an insult, it was unnatural. Her heart began to sink. She felt like the walls were starting to cave in on her. Luke brushed up against her and she looked at him. His eyes were full of hope for just a second before turning to face their makers. A look of defiance, that she herself could not muster, now dominated his form. She couldn't bear to look anywhere else. She could feel the room, full of her kin and those who were merely friends or acquaintances, leering at them. She followed his gaze forward as they were stopped and made to kneel before the Trinity.

Neither the mother nor her brothers moved when Lucifer and Pandora were placed before them. It was as if they had not even entered the room. The mother spoke first. She moved now, standing. Her voice, like honey, was sweet and flowed effortlessly through the hall.

'Lucifer my son, you have been brought here before the court accused of breaking the law of liaison that you made an oath to protect upon its creation. Your brother Michael has informed us of your actions against the court. You were summoned to us before these proceedings and questioned, to which you lied, not only to your brothers and sisters, but also to your makers. You have become unruly and rebellious and your actions have caused the downfall of a great warrior, as well as your own.' She glowered in Pandora's direction but not once looked directly at her as she had spoken her words.

'You have been found guilty of forming a relationship beyond the natural order with the Valkyrie's commander, Pandora, First of the Seraphim. How do you plead?' she ordered.

Lucifer said nothing to this accusation, but merely smiled at them, winking. Ignoring him, Isrea's brother Titus, spoke. He was not as intimidating as his sister, more frighteningly calm, especially in a time of great concern such as this. 'Pandora, you are the Commander of the Valkyrie. How did you come to be in this situation?' he requested, looking down at his perfect finger nails on his right hand, appearing as though he would rather be somewhere else. She took a breath and was about to answer when he cut her off.

'I am greatly saddened by your actions and in your weakness to give in to such depravity.' He stopped for a moment and whispered something into his sister's ear, who whispered something in kind back. He turned to look at Pandora once again. 'You are no longer pure. You are a disgrace to your name and position. You will be stripped of your wings, of your command, and sent to the Pit to live out eternity. As for the *thing* that grows inside of you, well, the *Fall* will deal with that.' There was a slight lift in the corner of his mouth and her heart felt as if it had been ripped into two. It was nauseating. A gasp echoed throughout the hall as Pandora stood in shock. She had just lost everything she had worked for her entire life, in just one ruling. She didn't know what to say. All she could do was stand there and stare at them, completely blank of any form of emotion. She had no idea what was going to happen. This was something she had never once thought to expect. This was the worst possible outcome.

'*The thing that grows inside you...the Fall will deal with that*'. She was not a *thing* and nothing would harm her.

Pain surged through Lucifer's hands as his fingernails pierced his palms. His heart ached the more Titus insulted and belittled Pandora. His patience becoming less and less as his fury raged within him. Michael held his brother's chains now and tugged them whenever he felt his brother was about to become more challenging, which sent a blow up his arms and down his spine. Michael knew at any moment Lucifer could break free, so he kept close by, just in case. The comment about the *thing* growing inside of Pandora, made the golden chains crack slightly. Lucifer had to do something to save her, he just didn't know what. All he could do was lie through his teeth and maybe, her life and the life of their unborn child could be spared.

'She had nothing to do with it. Nothing. I swear to you on my soul that this was all my own doing. I forced her and manipulated her. She could not stop me. She's just a Seraph. Her mind is nothing in comparison to my own. It was easy. I was bored and needed someone to play a game with. She was my plaything, nothing more. If you must punish someone, punish me.' He forced his face into the most earnest of looks. He could almost hear Pandora's heart quicken. *Please Pandora don't you believe it*, he thought.

All the Gods looked like they were about to burst into laughter in disbelief at Lucifer's plea. Titus looked to his brother and sister. The ruling would not be final until the third spoke. That was how it worked. It was then that Chaos declared whose side he was on. His eerily charming voice, which drew in everyone who could hear him, was unnerving. Lucifer looked at all of the Gods, attempting to decipher their faces into something that he could comprehend. They were all so calm, which agitated him to no end. It was strange to him, as if they knew this was coming for a lot longer than he had first thought, they had been ready for this. Chaos looked to his wife, Gaia, who regarded him with grief in her eyes. With a heavy heart, he breathed in a long sigh before casting his own thoughts aloud. 'My son, what you have said, even if it were true, which, I believe it is not, does not change what will come to pass. You may have manipulated her, but the fact remains that you were able to manipulate her in the first place. What you have said is true, her mind *is* weak. This Angel has lost her way and will never again find her way home to us. You, my son have rebelled against us too far this time to be forgiven. By way of punishing her, it seems fit to finally bring guilt to your ever-deceitful soul. This is your doing Lucifer. Because of you, an innocent child must die,' he said with brief emotion. Pandora's heart froze as her mind tumbled through memory. *'Only one may live' and I must make the choice. They had known my fate all along.*

Chaos snorted as he continued. 'Both of you have shamed this court, so shall you both be condemned for eternity. Lucifer, you will not be stripped of your wings. No. I have a purpose for them, but you will no longer be named my heir. You are no longer worthy of that honour. You will Fall and be condemned to the darkness you so promised to defend us against.'

The Gods echoed together, 'So it shall be, let them Fall.'

Michael stepped out in front of his brother and Pandora, unsheathed his sword and started dragging it along the ground, trapping the two within a temporary circle on the marble floor, crafting an Angel trap. Their chains were released but they couldn't escape. The blade of an Archangel was made from pure Featherstone, the only weapon that could kill another Angel. A Featherstone blade was created from the petrification of Angel feathers. Their most beautiful attribute could be transformed into their ultimate downfall. An Angel could give a feather to another, understanding that they would have complete control over them. If the feathers were taken against an Angel's will, then only the Gods could control them. And if the feathers were petrified, any control ceased, but the Angel who holds the stone, can take the life of any Angel if they so desired. The words, *let them fall* repeated themselves over and over within Pandora's mind. *Let them fall, let them fall, let them fall.* She felt panic rise up within her. They had been presented with no chance for forgiveness, nor any form of mercy. She could no longer fight the tears that had begun to fall down her face as she pressed one hand against her stomach and gripped Lucifer's with the other. He had taken it as soon as the chains had fallen to the ground. He gave a look, which Pandora recognised. She made a move to stop him but he was too quick. He released his golden wings and tried to fight the Angel trap his brother had imprisoned them in. In doing so, he gave Michael the chance to take one of Lucifer's feathers by force. He clipped one of Lucifer's wings with the tip of his blade. As the feathers fell, he caught them on his sword and quickly manoeuvred them out of the Angel trap. Picking them up, he took one last look at his brother.

'Celeste, Zachariah, hold out Pandora's wings,' he said, smiling at Lucifer. Celeste made a move towards Pandora but Lucifer had already wrapped his wings around her.

He reached both his arms around her, shielding her from those who would harm *them*, as it was not just Pandora that he was now protecting.

'I don't know how to stop this. I can't stop them from hurting you. What would you have me do?' he begged.

She looked into his beautiful violet eyes and whispered, 'Nothing my love. We can do nothing. Let them take my wings, all I need is strength for her. As long as I have you to hold onto, that is all I require. But there is something you can hide for me. Take this.' Pandora remembered what the sisters had said and retrieved a small rectangular box out from within her wings and handed it over to Lucifer.

'What is it?' he asked, taking it and hiding it within his own wings.

'I do not know. It is for when we are down *there*. I am to open it when I believe it is right to do so. But never mind that now. As I said, there is only one thing I need you to do after they take my wings,' she said, taking his hands into her own.

'Anything,' he said, gripping her hands tight.

'Hold me, hold us tight?' she asked, tears brandishing her cheeks.

'I'll never let go,' he said. Lucifer felt his wings parting against his control. He looked up and saw Isrea holding a feather that Michael had taken from him, her eyes glowing with cruelty, she only needed the one.

'Let go of Pandora. You will stand back and do nothing but watch as the wings of your beloved are ripped from her flesh,' she ordered Lucifer and he reluctantly did as she had requested.

'Michael, Gabrielle, take them,' spoke Titus as he pointed to Pandora's pearlescent wings. Dread flowed through her now, wrapping her arms around her waist, she closed her eyes. Taking a deep breath, she felt the tearing pain sear down her back and screamed.

*

The Trinity stared down upon them both with their golden eyes as they ordered, one last time, the condemned Angels fate.

'Let them Fall.' And fall they did. The circle entrapping them, opened up like a doorway into darkness. Gripping one another as the air stung their flesh, they struggled to keep conscious. The burning pain from Pandora's torn flesh ripped through her body as they fell. Endless agony tore at both of their minds as they struggled to keep hold of one another. Lucifer would never let her go. He swore it to her, and so, his grip became unyielding. They were in agony as the burning air continuously stung their skin. The only thing that didn't cause pain was their embrace. Lucifer knew he couldn't let her go, if not for the sake of Pandora, but for the child that grew within her. The only thing stopping them from being torn apart, were his wings. He was forbidden to fly, but he wasn't forbidden to wrap them around his love, protecting her from the brunt of it, mostly.

Pandora looked up at Lucifer. Both of them had wretched tears stinging their cheeks but that didn't stop her from smiling at him. As they fell to their prison, she tried not to scream, she had already done so when her wings were ripped from her back. She shivered at the thought. She couldn't see anything through Luke's wings but she didn't mind all that much. She needed something to take her mind away from the torture. Each breath felt like shards of glass stabbing at the inside of her throat. But she had to keep breathing. Their one hope for redemption or even freedom was growing inside of her. She had to survive this. That was her choice.

Pandora closed her eyes for a moment but was shaken by Lucifer. He couldn't let her fall asleep. She needed to be prepared for their landing. Forcing her eyes open again, she looked back up at Luke. She spoke to him in what sounded like a whisper within the intensity of the wind that was trying to suffocate them. 'Protect her,' was all she could muster. She couldn't fight the pain anymore. It felt like months since they had been falling through the Angel trap. It could've been years for all they knew.

*

By the time they fell through the portal, through the salivating mouth of the Pit, and landing on the unsteady ground, the child inside of Pandora had grown and was ready to embrace their crumbling world. Taking Lucifer's hand, Pandora placed it upon her stomach. He gripped her hand so tight the pain shot through her arm and she nearly let go, stopping, she reminded herself he was a lot stronger than she was and his own pain probably blinded him to that.

'Give these to her,' whispered Pandora, placing her hand on her rosary that still hung delicately around her throat. They had forgotten to take them. Knowing what the Fates had told her, there was no point in her saving herself by using them. The rosary were more than just beads, they were a gift that could be used to turn time.

'What do you mean? You can use them! Go back and save yourself at least! Why hadn't we thought of that earlier? I'm such a fool!' he said, with pleading eyes. Shaking her head she told him she could not. 'There is no point and I am not strong enough now. They are for only one to use, we have no idea how they would affect the child! There will only ever be one outcome in all of this and she needs you to survive,' she said, breathing heavily.

'You will survive this. You have to survive this. All of this would be for nothing if you don't,' begged Lucifer, clutching her hand tight.

'No, I won't Luke. Only *one can live*, the sisters told me I had to make the choice of *who*. Give me the box. Get it for me please?' she asked.

'The sisters? Do you mean the Elementals?' he inquired, reluctantly.

'Yes, I guess so, I don't really know exactly as they didn't actually say. I didn't tell you before, but these three women, wait how do you know…' she groaned in pain.

'Stop, rest, you need your strength,' pleaded Lucifer, as he placed the unopened box in her hands.

Pandora laid half on the molten rock and half in Lucifer's lap. His arms wrapped around her as she struggled through the sharp pains. She looked up into his violet eyes, tears were streaming down his face. She could feel his heart breaking with every drop. She took his hands and placed them on the top of her stomach once more.

'She is both of us. Our little Angel. The three women, they told me she would be great. We must give her the chance to, to save us all,' she cried.

'How did you see them?' he asked, frustrated.

'They came to me through the Incendium,' she struggled to say.

Lucifer knew at once who she was speaking about. They were the triad sisters of the Trinity, information he had come across by accident as a young and inquisitive warrior. The reason as to why he had become so rebellious to his much beloved creators. Once he had found out that they had locked up their own kin for power, he swore to himself he would never fight their wars again. The Trinity had no honour, and their lies filled the lives of everyone he loved. He had watched the sisters through the Flame, knowing it was they who blocked the view of the Gods. He had held this one secret tight, not telling a soul so that the Fates would grant his love sight to see the world as he did. Now, he feared that was the wrong decision.

'Seers and spinners of fate. We cannot trust them. This is all my fault. They are the God's prisoners! They will say and do whatever it takes to become free again,' he panicked.

'We can't take the chance not to Luke!' she screamed. Writhing in pain, she opened the box. Inside was a small vile and beside it laid a slightly curved dagger. She assumed the vile would take the life of their unborn child and the dagger, her own. Looking back at Lucifer, she picked up the dagger, made from Featherstone and had a crimson gem at the end of the handle. They both wondered who they had taken this one from, as neither had seen a Featherstone dagger embedded with a gemstone before. In the end it didn't matter to Pandora, she would still use it to save their child. She placed the blade above her heart, assuming that's where it would claim her soul.

'What do you think will happen? Where will I go after? Into nothingness?' she asked, her eyes welling up. Lucifer didn't know how to answer her. He had never taken the life of an Angel before.

'I, I can't do this without you,' she said, her eyes begged him.

Lucifer felt an unbearable pain disperse throughout his body, he was in shock, his mind stuck on the dagger in his love's hand. He could barely breath. He looked into her eyes again, they were pleading him. *She would do it anyway, or fail, either injuring herself or worse most probably kill the child and herself,* he justified. He had to do it or she would never forgive him. He could never forgive himself, no matter which path he walked. He knew, as much as she loved him, she would never choose herself over the child. She was selfless like that. *Who knew a member of the Valkyrie could be selfless?* he thought. Forcing a smile, he cradled her head in his lap. Her face was as pale as frozen water, any minute it could crack with the pain that intermittently tried to break through to the surface. This world was nothing without her, but there was nothing he could do to change her mind. He felt like such a fool. He strained to pull his eyes from hers, but compelled himself to, to look around them and see their prison. They had done this on purpose, the Gods, imprisoned them in this small insignificant golden cage together. Forcing him to watch her die.

He noticed then that both of their wrists were clasped in iron. She whispered his name, and slowly moved the dagger to his hand. It glared at him. It's bronze glint shining from the fire in the torch not far from their caged door. The three-sided blade that the three sisters had graciously provided Pandora not long before their Fall. They knew what was about to happen, and yet, they let it go ahead. No warning was given to either Pandora or their nephew. Cowards. They would allow the death, no, the murder of one of their own, with no remorse whatsoever, forcing Lucifer to take her life. His eyes flooded with loathing, not only was he condemned, his heart was too. He heard a voice within his own head, *either they both die or only one*. He could see her eyes beseech him, his soul crumbled away the closer he got to taking the dagger and doing as she wished. She writhed in his grasp.

'It's the only way my love. Please, please do it. Let her live. It hurts so much. Make it stop. Make it stop!' she screamed, her eyes bursting with tears.

He took the blade firmly into his grasp but struggled to lift it. It hovered over her chest and he began to sob, his hands shaking. *How could I destroy the only being that I have ever loved? The only one that has ever truly loved me in return?* These questions raced through his mind, over and over until it ached.

Taking a breath, he pressed his lips to hers and whispered in her ear, 'I love you'. Without further hesitation, he forced his hand down upon her beating heart. She gasped and let go of his other hand, her flesh slowly disintegrating into dust from the wound. It crept over the rest of her body like a flame, leaving her to disappear into the air around him. He couldn't look away, not now. This memory will live with him for eternity. Reminding him again and again of his weakness. He wasn't able to protect her from the senseless pride and vicious cruelty of the Gods. With their daughter's help, he hoped he would rise again and meet them in battle. Whether in justice or revenge, he would destroy them all. For now, however, all he could see was Pandora turning to ash in front of his eyes. Unknowingly, she had taken her rosary with her, shattering the string the tiny little beads had clung to in an instant, the beads disintegrating just like her flesh. Looking down to where she had laid, he heard a little squeal. Beneath the ash that laid below his feet was a tiny little thing, a child, her eyes opened wide, staring right at him. Her eyes were an emerald green, just like her mother's. Slowly, he took her into his arms. His tears streamed down his face and onto her forehead. She frowned at him, which made him choke with laughter and despair. He ripped a strip off what was left of his robe and wrapped her inside, he thought it might comfort her, and it did.

Time passed slowly while he gazed at his daughter until out of the darkness came a *tap tap tap.* Startled, he looked around and saw a single rose gold bead, roll across the ground. Lucifer picked it up and placed it inside the wrap with his daughter, safe within a pocket that was still attached. At least one had survived.

Looking at her once more, he sighed. 'What do we do now?' he asked. Her face shifted with a tiny grin, aware of his question. Suddenly, she shifted her head in the opposite direction, hearing what her father had also heard. A noise in the darkness beyond their golden cage. They were not alone.

Chapter Five

Friend and Foe

Tristan and Styx hastily made their way out of the Hall of the Divine, knocking into others, they rushed to the only place they knew where the Gods could not hear them speak, the Incendium. Even though they were not allowed to be there, they went anyway. Reaching the burning brush, they stood in silence thinking of a way to save their mentors.

'I don't care what they did. They are the greatest, most noble Angels that I know. They made me who I am! We can't let them be treated like this. They couldn't even defend themselves! Is that how we are all to be? Cowering under the eyes and judgement of the Gods. Looking over our shoulders, not being able to trust our brothers and sisters for the rest of our lives! I hate them! I loathe them! They have destroyed the bond we have with one another. How could Michael do that to his own brother and Celeste, to her own sister!' screamed Styx, gasping for air.

'Calm down! Just breathe!' Tristan yelled back at her.

'Calm down? Calm down?' she repeated.

'Yes! We can't think logically when we're both yelling hysterically at one another! We have to think. We need a portal to the Pit. That's the only way, but what then? What do we do once we have them? The Gods see all! We don't have the Flame blocking them down there,' said Tristan pacing. 'We need a plan, a good, robust plan. One that we can all walk away from unscathed. What about Corvis?' he asked. Styx gave him a long hard look. 'What about him? He's just like us, he could not stand against them. It's not his fault!' she yelled justly.

'No, that's not what I mean. Would he know of another way to help them?' asked Tristan. Ashamed, Styx shrugged her shoulders in response.

After a moment of painful silence, strange voices from within the Flame echoed around them.

'Protect the child, not the rest,' said the voice. Styx and Tristan looked at each other. Staring back into the Flame, three women strangely dressed and not at all like Angels or Gods in the least emerged.

'Who are you?' asked Styx taking out her sword. Tristan did the same.

The three women simply smiled at them in response.

*

Corvis stood within the hall, his body in shock at what had just occurred. Suddenly, he was knocked into consciousness by two young guards, who flew past him with disregard as they exited the hall. He decided to follow them. Styx and Tristan led him to the

Incendium. They were not allowed to be there, especially after what they had just witnessed. Breaking rules should've been the last thing on their minds. He understood that they looked up to Lucifer and Pandora, nearly every Seraphim did. But they had broken their oath and had been caught. The oath that they had all made to each other under the eyes of the Gods. He knew he too broke that promise daily with his own thoughts of Styx, his love. They were a lot more careful in their treachery, and it helped having Lucifer support them, which is why he trailed Styx and Tristan slowly as they reached the Flame, staying close, so he could hear them. What they had all just witnessed was unjust, his brother and friend had been given no mercy, no voice to ask for clemency or redemption. That could've been Styx and him in their place. He felt ashamed with his lack of courage. It wasn't long until he heard the two younglings fiercely figure out a plan to save his brother in arms. He just stood there, trying to justify to himself that not doing anything was the right thing to do. He heard other voices then, snickering at the young warriors from within the Flame. Plucking up the courage, he stepped out from the shadows.

'Yes. Who are you indeed?' he asked, weapon poised towards them.

Tristan and Styx stood nervously as their instructor addressed the three women. Not knowing if they were about to be in trouble for mutiny against the Gods or if he was actually thinking of joining them because Styx was now a part of it.

'You have joined them, yes you have. In their quest to save the one,' said the women, echoing each other.

'Who is the *one*?' asked Styx curiously.

'She is, the one born in ash, drenched in tears, she will destroy and conquer but only with your help. She will redeem seven in fire, bleed one, destroy another and drain the last. Reborn will she be again and again till she finds the key,' spoke the sisters.

'Okay, well that doesn't help at all,' said Styx, growing frustrated.

'She speaks of the child,' said Corvis looking at Styx. 'Pandora would not have let the child die. Did you speak to her before their punishment?' he asked the Fates, who smiled in return.

'That we did, of course we did. Give her a choice, to live or let live. Featherstone was our gift which she graciously took,' they answered.

'You gave her Featherstone! You treacherous beasts! Why would she take her own life?' screamed Styx, readying her sword to swing at them. Corvis stopped her.

'It was her or the child my love. What would you do?' he said, turning to face the three women.

'Assuming Lucifer had to go through with it, knowing that Pandora would not be strong enough. How would you know the child would survive?' he asked the Fates.

'We know, we saw, she breathed life in the thread, her mother's thread stopped. She is special, special indeed. You will take her, find her peace. Peace and quiet in a time with the children of those who had wished not to re-join their brethren Upstairs, those who had their own children roaming the Earth! Do not forget this, someone will come and breathe a great wind over her, destroying that peace. Protect her. For she will be great,' they said as they retreated into the Flame.

'Wait! Come back! How do we protect her?' asked Tristan. Looking to Corvis, the two young warriors waited for guidance. Corvis stared deep into the flame before him, thinking about what his next move would be.

'Are you with me or against me?' he asked them quietly.

'With you, you do not need to ask us that,' they echoed.

'We will need others, those who were, are, loyal to both Lucifer and Pandora. Styx, you need to find Balthazar, but be careful everyone is watching and I can't lose you too. Tristan, you and I will go to the Pit and save the child. You will take her somewhere, where none of us would care to look,' he ordered.

'How do we get in? What about the Sentinels?' asked Tristan.

'I'll take care of them. You just get the child and get out. I will leave a portal for you. Styx, once you have gathered those we can trust, take them through the Flame. I can feel its powers even now,' he said as he felt the Flame with both hands.

'What do you mean go through the Flame?' asked Tristan.

'Can't you sense it? The portal within? It has been here all this time and we never realised it! We will use this to our advantage. Though, if we are caught we will all be court-martialled for this, so ensure everyone is utterly sure they have made the correct decision,' he said, trying to remember his plan as he instructed it.

'But, what about you?' asked Styx.

'Never mind me. But both of you must understand, this could send us all into exile or the Pit. We could all lose our wings and our freedom. The others must understand this too.' He said.

'We understand,' they responded.

'Once you have gone through the Flame Styx, don't come back for me. Balthazar knows what has to be done, he will be at the dunes getting others to join, if you find him, you find our loyalists. Styx,' he took her into his arms, 'if you come back, they will do to you as they did Pandora and you will become the Fallen,' he finished with pain in his eyes.

'How do you know all of this?' she asked him, a puzzled look on her face.

'In truth, I have known this for a while now. I spoke into the Flame when I first fell for you and it told me that something else was brewing between others I loved. That's when I noticed Lucifer and Pandora meeting more than normal and there was a change in him. She transformed him. It could've only meant one thing, that there was more to their relationship than just mere friendship. So, I went to Balthazar, Pandora's closest friend. We agreed on a plan and left it at that,' he admitted.

'You spoke to the Flame? What do you mean?' she asked him.

'I, I can't explain it. I guess I was speaking to those strange women and not the fire itself. This has all been so revealing. Everything makes sense to me now,' he said.

'I knew I saw him leaving the hall before they brought Lucifer and Pandora in! You don't think Balthazar turned them in?' asked Tristan.

'Never. Balthazar owes everything to Pandora. She was *his* mentor. He would rather stick himself with Featherstone than betray her. He left because he was putting our plan into motion, he is not the coward that I am. I betrayed my brother by standing silent he needed me most. I may not be Lucifer's blood brother, but he and I are more like brothers than Michael and the others are to him. He trained me, mentored me and befriended me. I am as loyal to him now, as I ever was. I just wish I had the courage back in the hall to have stood up for him. I owe him everything and I failed him,' he said distraught.

'We all did. I was frozen in place. I had no idea what to do. Watching them tear Pandora's wings, I, I'm so ashamed that I just stood there and did nothing. And Celeste! Her own sister! I couldn't believe my eyes. Imagine the betrayal Pandora felt. I will come back for you Corvis, I will not leave this place without you by my side. I don't care if I become the Fallen, if my wings are ripped away,' confessed Styx.

'If you had not stood silent Corvis, this plan of yours would not be put into action. They would have overpowered Balthazar, and Lucifer and the child would be lost to us forever. You are no coward. It may be too late for Pandora, but we may have hope yet that the child still lives. I'll get her from the Pit, if Lucifer allows it, and put her somewhere safe. That is my oath to you Corvis,' swore Tristan, grabbing Corvis' shoulder guard and squeezing it a little.

'We'll go together as discussed, I'll distract the guards, you go straight to their cell. As soon as you have her, leave. I'll come for you when the time is right. Styx, do you know what you have to do?' he asked.

'Yes. Find Balthazar and everything will fall into place, and then come back and save

you.' She said as she gave him a kiss.

'We may or may not see each other again, or if we do, it will be under very different

circumstances. Here, take this.' Tearing branches off the burning brush he handed one to

each of them. 'This might help to hide you for a brief moment. I've seen Lucifer play with

the flames before, I never understood why until now. Good luck,' he wished them both as

they begrudgingly went their separate ways. Styx to find Balthazar, and Tristan and

himself through the Flame, their destination, the Pit.

Chapter Six

Dawn

'He that is taken and put into prison or chains is not conquered, though overcome; for he

is still an enemy.'

Thomas Hobbes

The Pit was darker than Tristan believed it would be. The only light came from the torch

he held and those few forged into the cavern walls, lit with red flames every ten metres or

so. He had no clue as to where to go, he was just following a feeling, an awareness that he

was being lead in the right direction. After the guards had been distracted, he and Corvis

had split up at least fifteen minutes ago, thinking that it would be easier to locate Pandora

and Lucifer that way. Now he was thinking it was a foolish idea. Especially, since this

was the very first time he had been inside the Pit, whereas Corvis had been down here

many a time, locking away malevolent souls from the different realms. He began to run

and finally came upon a number of locked doors he assumed were cells. He was hit in the

face by the smell of rotten eggs, stopping him suddenly, as it viciously tugged at his

senses and burned away at his airways. Corvis had warned him about what lay beneath

them, in the deepest depths of Hades. He remembered the stories, he did not need any warning about them. The Tyrants wreaked of evil, a sulphuric evil that blinded him for just a moment. Corvis had also told him that if you place a hand on the door of a closed cell, it will show you who is inside. Covering his mouth and nose with his free hand, he placed his other hand on the base of the cell's door closest to him. Nothing. He was at his sixth door when he heard Corvis' voice in the distance. Finally reaching him, he saw who he was talking to, or trying to talk to. Lucifer sat quietly on the ground, cradling what looked like a bundle of rags. He was rocking back and forth, either from pain or for comfort. Tristan believed it was both. There was a dagger lying at his feet, which Tristan assumed was used on Pandora. The world had now been filled with pain and desolation, but that little bundle of rags Lucifer held tightly within his wretched hands, was hope. Hope for change and hope for a peaceful future. Tristan notionally placed himself in Pandora's position, what would she do to ensure the child's safety? He knew he had to take her, to save her. How would he convince the one man in this entire universe, who had fallen in love with another Angel who sacrificed herself for their child that he needed to take the only thing he had left in this world. He had to take the child.

'Lucifer? You need to give her to me. On my honour, I swear to you I will take her somewhere safe, where she can grow up and live a happy and fulfilled life,' he begged. Lucifer stopped rocking and looked up at him, his eyes were red and his features were worn. For a newly made father, all that could be seen in his eyes was despair.

'I know that you're right, but I don't think I can let her go, not her too,' he cried quietly. Tristan's own heart was breaking at the sight of his most esteemed commander and Archangel in such agony.

'If I am able, I will get news to you of her, so you wouldn't truly have to let her go my lord. You would know she is safe,' he promised. Lucifer knew Tristan would be true to his word and with Corvis on his side, his little girl would be taken care of.

'What about you? This will not do you well in their eyes. You could lose your wings. How could you look after her then?' he questioned, looking back down at his tiny little girl.

'I know. I will take that chance, a hundred times. I will take it,' he said with such honesty that it could tear a Tyrant in two. Tristan placed the torch on the ground as Lucifer gradually made his way over to the crossbars of his golden cell and leaned his head down to kiss his child. He whispered something into her ear and gingerly, with slight hesitation, handed her over to Tristan, who wrapped her up in one of his outer layers.

'What do I call her?' he asked Lucifer.

'Ahh, well,' he sobbed. 'I guess if I am the 'light of day', then she is my dawn. Her name is Aurora,' he said, smiling at her little face, tears stinging his eyes. 'Please, don't let anything happen to her,' he begged.

Tristan looked into his eyes and with a stern voice, gave his word again, that he would protect her with his life. Corvis heard the Sentinels moving in their direction and told him to leave. Tristan gave Lucifer one final chance at goodbye with little Aurora and then ran in the opposite direction from the guards, transporting himself to the mortal realm with

Corvis' help where he knew he would find someone to help him. He just needed to figure

out which millennia would be safe enough for her. Walking through hidden but well

positioned portals throughout many different cities, he believed he found what he was

looking for. *Children of those who had wished not to re-join their brethren Upstairs,*

those who had their own children roaming the Earth! He thought to himself.

He would leave her with them, the children of Angels and men, the Nephilim.

Chapter Seven

Silent Night

Kiltimagh, Ireland - January 1839

'Humans were created without any knowledge of good and evil.'

John Milton

Aurora stood listening to the wind outside as it started to pick up and watched the old oaks sway violently, struggling to hold their weight against it. The missing melodies from the nests above the windowsill stood out hauntingly against the tormented storm. They were so beautiful to wake to at dawn every day, so peaceful. It was strange to think that what was normally a place of peaceful serenity was on the verge of chaos. She glanced behind her as she heard her mother's footsteps clatter up the narrow staircase to her room.

'Aurora sweetheart, we have to go,' she said desperately. She walked over to her daughter and stood beside her. Cora followed Aurora's gaze out the window into the molten sky above. Her right hand gripped the handle of a small brown suitcase she had packed urgently only moments ago.

Aurora's mother had come home in a panic, rushing around the cottage in a frenzy searching for her. Her daughter thought she was playing a game, she was only five years old after all, until she'd heard Cora scream her name in such a shrill the windows nearly shattered beneath their crumbling panes. She had been hiding in the corner of her father's study, attempting to read one of his ancient leather-bound books about fairies and other wild creatures. There was a profound sadness shadowing her mother's features and tears stained the corners of her hazel eyes. Her usually neat scarlet hair had fallen from its silver broach. Aurora noticed then that her dusty blue apron was splashed with a dark substance, like mud from the fields. But it had soaked into her garments, like a liquid, a dark burgundy liquid. Aurora had frozen as she realised it was blood. Her mother's appearance was dishevelled in a way that she had never before seen, her finger nails were caked in dirt and what she thought was dried blood.

'Mama, where's papa?' she had whispered, barely audible, leaning out of her father's age-old armchair. Cora's face had immediately changed and she ordered her daughter to go to her room and pack a bag with essentials only.

'We're leaving. You have five minutes. Go, hurry up,' she'd said with an urgent wave of her hand. Unquestioning, Aurora left the study and ran upstairs to her bedroom.

It only took her a couple of minutes to squeeze what little belongings she had into an old patchwork knapsack. She grabbed everything from inside her drawers; a pair of worn leather boots, her woollen doll she had named Lucy when she was but two years of age and her father's leather-bound book. With her knapsack in one hand, she placed the other on the decaying window sill and stared at the foreboding sky beyond. She felt useless not knowing what to do for her mother. A thunderous rumble from the skies above reminded her of the troubles outside. The twisted sky outside sent a chill down Aurora's spine. Something clouded her mind. There was something out there, something dark that was reaching out to her.

Aurora finally woke out of whatever stupor she had been trapped in. Bewildered, she stared at her mother, silent. Cora snapped herself out of her own thoughts and hastily grabbed Aurora's arm.

'We have to go. The storm is coming, you're...we're not safe here anymore, you need to trust me.' With that, she turned and pulled Aurora down the stairs and quickly out the front door.

Normally, Cora was very good at hiding her exhaustion but not this day. The dark rings around her eyes spoke the truth. Aurora glanced up towards the melancholy morning sky and saw the unnatural darkness growing thicker above them. The weather seemed to change quickly as her mother dragged her down their cobbled path. It was strange enough to have snow fall in her small corner of Ireland at this time of year, but it had already begun to melt as well! Looking back at their snow covered stone cottage, she felt her mother's grip tighten and pull her out of her stupor once more.

'Aurora please hurry we have to get to the church, now!' Aurora wasn't sure if she had understood her mother correctly. Had she said church? Why would they want to go there? How could they be protected from what was brewing outside within a bluestone building built centuries ago? Aurora's mind became clouded with questions as they hastened along the cobblestoned path towards the town's only place of worship. There was an overwhelming sense of confusion that filled the space between her and her mother. Her father was probably hurt or worse, dead, and her mother was acting mad! This was indeed too much for a mere five-year-old to rationally understand. However, this was her mother and a warm rush of trust and love flowed through her. She tightened her grasp on Cora's hand. Continuing to move along the path, they finally saw the bluestone building behind its stone archway. It had stood in this spot for many a century, staring out towards the moors and would continue to stand for many more lifetimes. They reached the threshold but Aurora stopped dead on the spot, there was something wrong.

'What's the matter sweetheart?' asked Cora, quickly.

'I feel something. It's too cold Mother and not because of the snow,' she shivered. Cora looked around them and with her opposite hand, reached for something from the side of her dress.

'It's fine darling, it's just because of the storm. Don't worry, I've got you,' she said looking down at her daughter smiling. Aurora forced a smile back at her mother and they continued to move up the muddy cobblestoned path that would take them into the main church building. She heard something shuffle behind them and glanced over her shoulder, but saw nothing but the empty commons. Turning her head back towards the dark horizon, she glanced sideways at her mother. Not one word passed between them as they walked the troublesome path towards the main hall of the churchyard. To distance her mind from the unknown noises that surrounded them behind the shield of darkness, she closed her eyes and held her mother's hand tighter than before. With her mind racing, she tried to think of a good memory. After a few steps, she remembered her parents telling her the tale of their meeting when they were young at this same location. Her father and mother had both sat her down by the hearth with tea and soda bread and told her their story as if it were from a storybook itself. They were in their fifteenth year and both had started to get into quite a lot of mischief. Tomas, her father, had accidentally bumped into Cora as they both had reached the church's gate at the same time.

Her mother had said 'He was all flushed. As red as an apple in springtime. He didn't say a word, he just looked at me with a terrified look upon his face. I giggled and said, "Excuse me, could you move please?" Your father's terrified look disappeared as quickly as it had appeared and he said...' 'Excuse me, *I* said to your mother, "Oh, well excuse me miss I apologise for getting in your way." And I winked at her and jumped the gate so that she could gracefully walk through it.' Smiling at the obscure memory brought her back to the present as Aurora remembered that her father was not with them. She then remembered the blood on her mother's apron and the look of despair hidden behind Cora's hazel eyes. She wanted to know what had happened and she wanted to know where her father was, but she couldn't ask her mother. She could feel the desperation in her mother's grasp. Just looking at her, at how much she had changed in just a day, terrified Aurora. Her mother was usually vibrant and full of life, but at this very moment it felt as if she was only just clinging to it, for her sake. After passing a number of newly dug graves, they had finally reached the door to the main hall. Their small village had seen a number of deaths over the past month, their causes unknown. Aurora's mother wouldn't explain them to her but she knew. She could see them, the dead that is. Of course, Aurora kept that morsel of information to herself, Cora wouldn't understand and neither would the townspeople. Being a simple kind of folk, they would probably burn her at the stake as a witch like in the old stories. However, she did believe the deaths to be her fault, that she was drawing something evil into their village. Being a child, she thought she should be scared, like any normal child would be, but she wasn't. She didn't feel danger from the dead. They smothered the town with their withered faces and white eyes. She felt sorry for them. She could feel their sorrow. They reeked of it. She believed they were stuck between worlds and would never find peace. From what she could tell, Aurora was the only one who could see them and she could never understand why. She told her father about them and he had believed her straight away. He said that it was their little secret. They promised each other with their pinkie fingers wrapped around the other that they would keep their secrets to themselves and Lucy, Aurora's ragdoll. Her father even told her not to tell her mother, that it would only upset her. So, as they reached the main hall door, Aurora pretended not to see the little girl standing in front of it, she was almost trying to stop them from entering. She thought her mother had enough to worry about, let alone hearing that her daughter could see the dead.

*

Cora unknowingly reached through the little girl's spirit and turned the handle to the main hall. She became more and more anxious as she moved closer to the tower, towards their safety. The weather seemed to follow them from their home all the way to the churchyard, which added to her anxiety. Over and over Cora screamed at herself inside her head, thinking she should've trained Aurora, or at best, she should've told her everything. This is the worst possible mistake she had ever made, to deprive her daughter the ability to protect herself. When Tristan had landed at their doorstep holding their soon to be daughter in his arms, they had made a vow to protect her with their lives. That they would give her a normal and mundane life, nothing from their world would interfere with hers, until now that was. Tristan had warned them that someday, someone would come for the child, but they didn't think it would be so soon. He had left a portal in the tower for her to get the child to him safely. She knew she had failed Tristan, and she had failed Aurora, but she still had time to save her, if only her. She just had to get her to the tower unscathed. The portal stone was only a flight of stairs away from them. This night would be the beginning and the end for Aurora, if Cora could get her out safely, as it would present to her the truth that the world she knows, is not the only truth to be told.

*

As they pushed their way through the doorway, Aurora felt an icy draft rip through her body. Doubling back, she saw a dark figure materialise in front of her. Her body went rigid as she realised who it was and gripped her mother's hand tighter.

'What is it Aurora?' asked Cora.

'Where is Father O'Conner Mother? Doesn't he normally greet people when he sees them enter the archway? Isn't he nosey like that?' prompted Aurora.

'Yes, yes, he is, and yes he does. That's strange. Perhaps he has actually gone to bed and not heard us entering the gate. Never mind that now though sweetheart, we have to get to the tower quickly.'

'What's up there that we need to get to?' asked Aurora, curiously.

'Never mind that, I'll tell you when we get there,' responded Cora as they ascended the spiral stone staircase. Aurora couldn't shake the image from her mind, the dark figure that lingered before them, as if it were trying to block them just as the little girl had. That was the second spirit to appear in front of them in a short moment of time. Aurora tried to shake it all from her mind, her mother wouldn't believe her if she told her, so there would be no point in saying anything. They finally reached the top of the staircase and Cora ripped open the door to reveal a sight so gruesome, even she let out a loud cry in shock.

*

Father O'Conner's lifeless body was crucified to a makeshift cross, his internal organs had slipped out of the wounds that had recently been carved into his abdomen. Blood was still dripping. Cora protectively placed Aurora behind her back and, reaching for the war hammer she'd been carrying, held it out at eye level, ready for an attack. They just had to reach the other side, but whoever their enemy was knew that, which is why they placed the priest in their way.
'Sweetheart, try not to look. Promise me you won't look at him,' she begged her five-year-old daughter.

'I promise Mama,' said Aurora, already breaking the promise as they slipped by the poor priest's body.

'It'll all be over soon my little dove,' she promised, trying to believe her own lies.

'Yes, it will,' said a strange voice.

Cora stopped in place, weapon out in front, her other hand gripping Aurora's arm behind her. Looking around the circular room, she could see nothing but the dark night and Father O'Conner's tortured body.

'You put an awful lot of effort into the priest Demon, what did he ever do to you?' she said to the darkness. She was attempting to be calm, for Aurora's sake.

Tilting her head towards where she spoke, she heard a slightly muffled laugh. There was one thing about Demons, this being a Greater Demon, or Tyrant as they were known to Celestials, they had a certain smell about them, a mixture of sulphur and faeces. The combination was so strong it could tear your nostrils apart. Cora hadn't smelt that fragrance in a long time, not since before the famine had begun. There was something about this particular Demon that made him special though, she knew as soon as she saw the snow start to melt that he was stronger than any average Demon. Her studies into Greater Demons or Tyrants had taught her that some of them had a gift of controlling the elements.

'How did you escape the Pit?' asked Cora.

'So many questions, so little time to answer. The priest did unpriestly things, temptation was too tempting for him, deserved was he of his pitiful outcome. Your husband too was a tasty treat. You will join him soon and she will join me. Now if you please, hand her over,' requested the Demon.

Feeling helpless at knowing she now faced a Tyrant, alone, she tried desperately to find a way to save her child. She ignored his comment about her husband, as it was used only to bruise her. She looked to Aurora though, who had tears in her eyes and clasped her head into her side lovingly. Tomas had gone missing in the early hours of the morning after they had released the sheep in the moors. He had not returned for breakfast, so she had gone out looking for him only to find some of his remains in the creek below the cottage. Looking back towards the rear of the room, she thought desperately for a way to save Aurora. They were so close to the portal stone and she knew exactly what was in the way of it. She needed a distraction for Aurora to get through to the Guardians. But there was only one possible distraction and so it had to be.

*

Cora was blocking Aurora's view of the creature with the voice that taunted them. Leaning forward and stealing a look through the gap under her mother's arm, she saw a glimmer in the distance. It was probably five or six metres in front of them,

80

not too far really, but in the dark, it seemed like miles away. She could feel Cora slowly stepping forward. Aurora assumed this was so she could see whoever or whatever it was, a Demon if that was to be believed, playing games with her. As they moved closer to it she could feel the temperature rising, strange that they were in a stone-cold tower. *Why would there be heat up in a cold stone tower*, she thought to herself. Aurora looked again, the glimmer had grown. They were very close now. She could feel beads of sweat slowly drip down her forehead. She tugged at Cora's arm.

'Mama, why is it so hot in here? What are we doing? Who is that?' she asked.

Kneeling down to face her daughter, Cora held Aurora's face in her hands. 'Aurora, there is something I have to do and there is something that you will have to do also. Okay? Can you see the glimmer of light in the distance? Just nod if you do. Good. When I say, you must run as fast as you can towards it, take it into your hands and close your eyes tight. Do you understand?' she asked calmly.

'But, but what about you?' she stammered.

'I'll be right behind you. I promise,' pulling Aurora into her arms, she kissed her on the forehead. 'When I say, you must run okay?' she said, desperation creeping into her voice.

'Okay,' promised Aurora, begrudgingly letting go of her mother's hand.

The creature stood before them shaded by the dusty night, but Aurora could see its soulless eyes staring down at her. They were red beady little things, the shape of tiny stones. She wasn't sure if she should be afraid of it or not, her mind was telling her she ought to be but she didn't feel frightened in the least. It was more fear of what was going to happen to her mother. She knew now that this monster had murdered her father, which enraged her. They stood in front of it, its putrid smell fermenting into the air around them. Her mother whispered in her ear before leaping into the air and landing on the creature. This was the moment that fear finally struck Aurora. She stood frozen to the spot where her mother had left her. Cora realised her daughter had not yet done as she had promised and screamed at her.

'Run! Go now Aurora!' she begged.

Aurora finally found the strength to move and sprinted as fast as she could, dodging the chaos her mother had begun before her, to protect her. With the last ounce of energy that she had left, she reached the stone. She felt something grab her leg and heard a deafening scream. Looking around she briefly saw her mother hanging in the air in the distance, her lifeless body crumpling as the monster threw her across the room. Closing her eyes, she felt darkness envelop her mind and everything went black.

'May I enter?' requested Aurora. Stepping forward, the shadow became solid. The girl was probably around nine or ten years of age, with tanned skin and violet eyes. Her dark hair hung above her shoulders in little twists of curls. Her leafy green dress dropped at the waist, with pastel feathers as its skirt. She stood barefoot, with a Cheshire grin directed at Aurora.

'Password?' requested the girl.

Aurora took a moment and looked at her. Then she turned her head in the direction of the other little voices inside. She could see two others holding hands, spinning in circles in front of the hearth, curiously made out of the body of a tree. Fire burned inside it, lighting up the room with a pleasant orange hue. Aurora knew the password would be the little girl's name, she was too vain not to use it. The Elementals liked to play games, especially with her. She just had to figure out which one she was. The problem was, they looked different from whence she had seen them last. They enjoyed taking on different appearances whenever she would meet with them. It was part of their little game. Aurora went along with it. The more you struggle with an Elemental, the more they avoided answering your questions. It was very painstaking for Aurora, but it had to be done, for she could not see the future, only the past. They always went by their Greek names, this made it easier for Aurora to figure out. She could see their spinning machine next to the fire, with a straw basket full of thread beside it. They also enjoyed being literal to the human myth. As irritating as these three girls could be, she still enjoyed playing their games.

*

The girl watched Aurora in the doorway. Their guest's eyes darted towards her sisters as they were dancing merrily in the sitting room by the fire. She noticed Aurora grin slightly. *Damn*, she thought.

'So? What is your answer?' she asked Aurora, who looked back towards her.

'Well, at first I thought it might have been a misdirect, but in observing your sisters more closely, I resolved that it wasn't. Your sister, Atropos, whether it be by mistake, or she has just grown so used to having them, had forgotten to hide her scissors, which lie delicately in her front pocket. I know how attached she is to them, being that she is the one who cuts the thread, with her great responsibility of deciding an individual's end, she wouldn't leave them anywhere except on her own person. Therefore, to pass her off as anyone other than herself, is an automatic failure. That leaves Clotho and Lachesis. You all seem to have some kind of fixation with feathers this time around, but there is only one of you wearing a feather in your hair. Now, at first, I didn't think it was pertinent, but then I realised what it actually was. Not a feather, but a small measuring rod disguised as a feather. It was too straight to be the latter. Since she measures the thread, she is clearly Lachesis. That just leaves you, the only one without a trinket, because your trinket is too large to carry and is sitting all on its lonesome by the fire. So, my little spinner, I would take it to understand that the password is, Clotho?' she asked, staring at her with bated breath.

Clotho waited a moment but dared not make Aurora wait too long. The Elementals were older than she was, but they knew her strength, no matter their charm, if they got on her *other* side, they knew she would figure out a way to stop them from having their small kind of freedom in the mortal realm.

'Please, come in and take a seat, won't you?' Clotho asked, directing her hand at a tattered leather lounge chair.

'No, I'll stand thank you. Do you have what I have come for?' inquired Aurora.

Clotho skipped over to the tattered chair and leapt into its rugged cushion. She wanted to test the waters before giving the Angel what she wanted.

'Perhaps we do. But why would we give it to you?' she rhymed.

Aurora walked over to the spinning wheel and touched the thread still in the eye of the needle.

'This contraption is important to you, is it not?' she asked. Clotho stiffened as she watched Aurora circle her most prized possession.

'You know it is mistress,' she returned.

'Then why would you continue to play games with me? You know why I'm here, now give me the thread,' she said in a delicate tone.

'We play with you because you allow us to. *They* don't let us, which is why we secretly follow you. You allow us to be who we are. We are sorry we offend you mistress,' said Clotho as she sprung out of the tattered chair and walked towards Aurora with her hand outstretched. Aurora held out her hand and Clotho dropped a tiny thread into it.

'You and your prophecy burn bright. You have the time bead, use it wisely. Once time is up, it becomes dust.' Said Clotho eyeing Aurora's pocket where she held her mother's lone rosary bead. 'You will soon have your seven and in finding them, you will find your innocent. Then the final sacrifice will lead you to the key and the lock will be yours. However, you already know the innocent, don't you mistress? Maybe it should be you who writes their destiny and not we,' she said with a smile.

'Indeed. He will not yet be gone from this world, which is why he can be brought back into it. You were the one that showed me, do you not remember?' prompted Aurora.

'True, true, I am pleased you remembered,' said Clotho.

'Remind me, how many times I can use the bead?' she asked.

'Once, twice, thrice, and two more me thinks. More than that, me thinks not. You can only go so far into the past, as far as your life itself, too far and you'll be lost,' said Atropos smiling.

'We'll see. This is the correct Tyrant I hold in my hand?' she asked watching the fey's eyes.

'It is. He who stole you for them. He who took you under *their* order to kill. It is he.' She said, her eyes not lying.

'Good. Do you have anything else for me?' she asked the Elementals.

'The Angel mourns you once more, not sure he can mourn you anymore,' said Atropos, now playing with her scissors on the floor. 'Broken is his heart, his mind not far behind. Only one more try or he will be left far, far behind,' she teased.

'Have you seen this? Or is it one of your *assumptions*?' asked Aurora, hiding her anxiety at the foretelling.

'It is in his thread, but it is not yet clear. Your decision will direct him on his path. Make sure you decide which direction will not end in wrath,' finished Lachesis who was staring at the flames within the hearth.

*

Leaving the fey behind her, she took out her lone rosary bead and rolled it between her index finger and thumb. She didn't want to be reminded of Tristan, especially after what he had done for her as a child but he was unfortunately a key player within her plan. The seers did not speak of him in the present but of the future, a very dim one for him indeed. Taking one last glance at the now decrepit cottage, she thought of the child. I need to go there first, she thought. Summoning Balthazar, she waited for his arrival.

'You called My lady,' he said silkily.

'I am using the bead, remember to meet me at the church in Brooklyn. Ensure you remind my future self to stay away, perhaps meditation? Once that is complete, I'll head to positions two and three thereafter. Do not forget Balthazar,' she politely ordered.

'I would never! I will see you again shortly My lady,' he smiled, kissing the top of her hand. Hitting him with the same hand on the shoulder, she used the other to turn the bead twice, disappearing in the blink of a mortal eye.

Chapter Nine

The Redeemer

Brooklyn

'It is a man's own mind, not his enemy or foe, that lures him to evil ways.'

Buddha

The city was cold on Aurora's fair skin. The hairs on her uncovered neck stood on end as she

watched the clouds in the night sky move gently northward. It was strange to be in such a

different time from her own. Strange contraptions lined the street, almost like carriages but

smaller and with no horses to move them. The ground itself was hard and black, not cobbled

or muddied. After placing the bead back into her pocket, she raised her right hand vertically

and closed her fingers gently into her palm, except one. She pointed her index finger towards

a bedlam of brick and stained glass and waited as the breath of night began to sway, Balthazar

appeared next to her. Following her gaze, he stopped on a rundown old church.

'Is this it?' she asked.

'Yes, My lady, it is good to see you finally. Be assured, your current self will stay away while

you're in our timeline. Now, before you is The Redeemer. Below the ground in the subway, an underground railway, a mosaic is crafted within the wall with its name is proof enough. It seems that we are not too late,' he responded.

Aurora breathed in the cold air. 'There is death in the air,' she said, still looking at the decrepit church, held up with scaffold.

The night was dark, but Aurora could clearly see the towering outline of the bluestone church before them. According to Balthazar, it was a relic in an unforgiving city, being torn down, brick by brick, for some new development. They stood on the north-west corner of Pacific and Fourth Avenues, listening to the voices that echoed inside the newly hollowed-out building.

'It seems they are gutting it and selling its sacred pieces to the public.' He went on, 'I understand that they will soon be finished with its destruction.'

'Is nothing sacred anymore?' asked Aurora sarcastically, not expecting an answer. 'Well, once I'm finished with tonight's activities, there will be nothing left for them to tear down, except for its outer shell,' she said with a callous smirk. 'Shall we enter? I believe our guests have been waiting long enough.' Aurora stepped through the wrought iron gate, pushed open the large ornate red doors and entered the condemned church.

*

Balthazar looked across both aisles, watching the faces of their quarry transform from apathy to alarm in an instant. Aurora stood at the top of the church's nave slowly tapping a finger on the wooden altar so that the echo of her fingernail could be heard throughout the church. Balthazar loved her form of intimidation, how she quietly moved about, gentle underfoot, looking directly into your eyes in a way that would make you feel as helpless as a cockroach stuck on its back. She was perfect in every way. Even though this was not *his* Aurora, from his direct time, but she was still the girl who he had helped raise from a child to what she was now, and she was nothing like him, not at all. She was nothing like her father either, with exception to his flawless looks of course. She had adopted her mother's personality, without ever knowing her. Balthazar was relieved when Aurora hadn't taken after her father. If she had, they would never have gotten this far. The small gathering of local patrons ceased what they were doing and stared at the intruders, glancing back at each other in curiosity with questions on their lips. Aurora had chosen this place not because of the destruction it was about to endure, but because of these specific mortals, a small group of fancy looking *parishioners*. In truth, they were connected to a gang from this particular area, not a religious flock at all. They were exactly what Aurora required. To complete her mission, she had to perform a number of tasks in order to reach her final goal. She needed the blood of a Tyrant, a traitor, an innocent, and lastly, seven tainted souls. Aurora made her way to the altar and stood there looking over the interested faces of the soon to be victims of the Gods. They stood, huddled together encircling, or hiding, an object in the middle of their group. This particular object was crying hysterically, curled up on the floor. It was a woman. Probably in her mid-twenties, holding, protecting what looked like a doll wrapped up in her arms. Balthazar looked at Aurora. Her eyes went dark. It wasn't a doll.

*

The woman was lying on her side with her knees curled up towards her chest, where she held the infant tight. She was covered in her own blood, probably from the blows she had received from the congregation that surrounded her. What Aurora noticed next was what she heard. The crying wasn't coming from the infant, but from the woman. From what she could sense, the child didn't make a sound and the woman's sobs were not from the pain she physically felt, but by what she desperately didn't want to accept. Aurora could smell death in air and fury rose within her.

'It is mortals such as yourselves that prove to me that the concept of humanity is broken. I look around me and I see the influence of the Gods engulfing the hearts and minds of your kind like a virus. It spreads like the plague, rotting everything within its path. Look at you. Your minds are putrid. You are terrorising an innocent woman, who is desperately trying to hold onto her child. What is wrong with you?' she bellowed. 'No, scratch that. My real question is, why do you not have guards keeping watch, to ensure intruders like my brother and myself here do not interrupt you? The only thing I can think of is that this part of the world is so corrupt that you believe you can do anything that free will can give to you, without fearing any consequences. Well Balthazar, aren't we lucky to find ourselves such a worthy group to help us with our cause?' Aurora continued, looking at the terrified woman on the floor.

'Yes, we are indeed. Lucky indeed, My lady,' responded Balthazar.

'Do none of you have anything to say? To justify your actions here this evening? No? Well, of course you don't, as I am not allowing you to speak. Your vile words will not wreak havoc on my senses. Now, move away from the girl and take a seat while I see what it is you have done to them,' ordered Aurora as she moved towards the bloodied woman on the floor.

Leaning down next to the woman, Aurora touched her shoulder to calm her.

'Can you stand?' she asked without emotion. The woman was silent, out of fear and most probably, out of pain. Aurora presented her hand to the woman and after a small moment or two, she took it hesitantly and lifted herself and the infant off the ground. When the woman took her hand, Aurora could see her memories, it was one of her many gifts that the Gods had *not* granted her. The woman had been walking to the subway entrance just outside the church when the congregation of gang members came across her. They were entering the church when they saw her and grabbed her before she could run away. She had seen them. That was all the motive they required. It didn't matter that she was a mother carrying her child. The beating they gave to her was to ultimately scare her, but as usual, things got out of hand.

'Can you show me the child?' she asked delicately.

The woman shook her head as tears began to roll down her face.

'I won't harm him. It's Charlie, isn't it? It suits him, you named him well Mary,' she said attempting to gain her trust.

The woman's mind was ablaze with thoughts and questions. Taking a deep breath, she finally spoke. 'Who, who are you?' she stammered.

'Just, someone. May I see the child?' she asked again, trying not to push too hard. After more hesitation, which was acceptable to Aurora, Mary unwrapped the muslin from the infant's face. He was tragically beautiful and without breath. Aurora put out her arms as a gesture of taking him. Mary again hesitated not knowing what to do.

'You don't have to trust me, you don't know me. But understand that if you hand him to me, I give you my word, I will return him to you,' she swore.

Mary slowly handed the little soul over to her. Aurora could feel Mary's intense pulse as she grazed her fingers in taking little Charlie off her weakened hands. Staring at the child for a moment, Aurora then whispered something into his little ear and gave him a small kiss on his tiny forehead. After what seemed like an eternity, his cold skin was restored with a rush of red to his cheeks. A small cough and slight splutter, and little Charlie opened his bright blue eyes to the world again.

With a smile and tap on his tiny nose, Aurora handed him back to his sobbing
mother.

'How did you? What? I can't even speak. Thank you so much. I don't know how to
repay you. My heart was ripped in two, but you, you fixed it. My little boy,' she
said, crying.

'It wasn't his time,' replied Aurora.

'What you did for me, I owe you everything,' she said, kissing Charlie.

'You owe me nothing, he has already paid the price. You must leave this place
though, now,' said Aurora sternly.

'Okay, but can, can I ask you one thing please, before I go?' she stuttered, still
trying to catch her breath.

'Yes,' she already knew the question.

'Are you going to kill them?' Mary asked, motioning her head towards the cruel
scum behind them.

Aurora turned to look at them and with a smirk, she simply said, 'Yes. I am.'

Mary smiled, tears blazing in her eyes. She thanked Aurora one last time and as
quickly as her broken body could take her, she left the decaying building.

Aurora motioned to Balthazar to move to her side. 'When we're finished here,
make sure they get home. *He* belongs to me now.' He nodded his head in response.

Aurora turned her thoughts towards the group of brainwashed mortals that awaited
their penance. She could feel the evil seep out of them like a flowing tap. All eight

of them reeked of malevolence. They were the God's perfect little conquests, creators of chaos, ultimately food for the Gods. They would make for the perfect sacrifice. One by one, Aurora looked into their minds to ensure she was correct in her findings. She was. The unfortunate thing was that two of them were only nineteen and they already owned a place within the Pit. That was unfortunate. None of them could speak, as she had willed their mouths shut. She didn't want the whole neighbourhood hearing their screams. Though she could easily block the noise out to the rest of the city, in doing so, it would send a signal of her presence to the Valkyrie and she was not yet ready for them to meet her. Aurora looked around the church and had Balthazar ensure every door and window could not be used for an escape, as it was a fun little game for *her*. She released them from their incarceration on the pew and watched them run around like headless chickens, trying to find an exit.

'The name of this particular church is quite ironic, don't you think?' she asked, as most of them began to give up and stood, defeated, trying to think of something to do to save themselves.

'The Redeemer. It has a nice ring to it. I could've been your redeemer if you hadn't have pulled that horrible stunt tonight on Mary and Charlie. Well, the night is still young, but I have somewhere else to be, I think it is time to up the ante, *incendio deleri*,' she exclaimed and with the flick of her wrist, flames engulfed every last one of them.

*

Balthazar watched as Aurora lit up the floor with murderous fire. The mortals desperately gasped for air, their faces straining with agony. They threw out their hands towards him, reaching for help, help that would never be given. It brought a smile to his face. A woman dressed in black and hot pink sweats, wreaths of gold jewellery hanging from her wrists crawled towards him, desperately clawing at the ground beneath her to get to him. She was not yet overwhelmed in the fire as the others were. Her breathing was wild, as she attempted to gasp for clean air. Her raspy voice struggled between quick uneven breaths. Aurora allowed her to speak. 'Why? Why are you doing this?' she begged, grabbing at his feet.

Balthazar looked down at her and contemplated his answer.

'This is only a small part of what lies ahead, but it is pertinent to what is coming next. The Gods will soon understand their fate and what part we all play within it. You, my child, are merely a sacrifice that is needed to begin my commander's destiny. Your suffering will not go unnoticed. You will be rewarded in the next life,' he said, with a devious grin on his attractive face. 'Well, that last bit was a bit of a white lie but it brought a smile to your face, did it not? No? Well, it is time you cease your incessant breathing and remove your cruel and dirty hands from my Cheaneys,' kicking the woman's hands, he stepped over her and walked towards the altar to open a portal.

*

Once the portal had been opened, a large black raven burst through it. This particular raven was none other than the great Corvis. Once a great Seraph Warrior who had served under Lucifer. He darted across the high arched roof and perched on Aurora's shoulder. Glancing sideways at her, he blinked a number of times, instructing her that they were about to be interrupted. Corvis had not always been a bird. He had an immortal body once. He was a sergeant within the High Guard and one of Lucifer's best swordsmen. However, after the Fall, he chose to stay loyal to Lucifer, the losing side, and was cursed to spend the rest of his days with wings as arms instead of on his back, and feathers instead of flesh. After he helped Tristan escape from the Pit with infant Aurora, he sacrificed himself and was captured by the Sentinels, bringing him back to be trialled by the Gods. He knew as long as he stayed loyal to Lucifer he would eventually be freed. He assumed he would be released upon the rescue of Lucifer, at least that's what Xerxes believes, that they are linked somehow. He looked back into the burning chaos that his mistress had initiated. The Brooklyn church was perfect food for the flames, even with its outward stone body. The intensity of the heat would have suffocated his mistress and her followers if they were mortal. The flickering of flames sent a warmth through their veins, like whiskey on a cold winter's day. As a member of the Fallen, fire was not new to Corvis. He had seen the Pit. It used to be part of his role to place souls there for eternity. He had felt its smouldering heat. His best friend and brother in arms was within it at this very moment. When the Gods sent Lucifer and his beloved to their tragic fate, he stood frozen in place. He was not brave enough to save them, or Styx his own beloved. He, like many others who loved Lucifer and Pandora chose to Fall, but maybe, someday their loyalty to their loved ones would redeem them somehow.

'I have the boy's blood, now I just need their souls. Then we leave,' she told Corvis the raven. As she had brought life back to the boy, she pricked the bottom of his foot, taking a few droplets of his innocent blood in a tiny silver vial. Another task was complete.

*

The building began to bow, pillars started to crack and beams began to fall to their fiery fate. As the fire ate through the walls, it tore down the only support beams it had left. All Aurora could hear was the crackling of flames feasting on everything that surrounded her. The charred remains of her sacrifices laid curled up like tortured souls on the stone floor of the church. Clutching another small vial, a glass one this time, she flicked open its brass lid and eight intense beams of light from all around her flooded inside. Eight corrupted souls. Closing the lid, Aurora moved towards Balthazar who had just opened a portal. Before stepping through, she turned back to look at her sacrificial lambs that had been justly slaughtered. She could vindicate these deaths, *condemn the few, to save the many* she thought to herself. It had to be done, if not them, it would have been someone else. Looking at the small vial, she only required seven souls, but she couldn't let any of these particular ones live, not after what she had just witnessed. Stepping through the portal, she placed the vial into her coat pocket, leaving the flames to do her bidding.

Chapter Ten

The Sands of Time

The smell was something that Aurora would never forget. It was a mixture of rotting

flesh, smelly feet and human faeces. All of which, she had smelt in her lifetime but for the

first time, right here, when she was only five years old. She was now in her mid-twenties,

give or take a number of centuries. She stopped ageing at the height of her maturity,

which, lucky for her, was in her youth. After this place, when she was rescued by

Balthazar and learnt who she truly was, she was worried that she would age and die like a

mortal. Therefore, they worked hard in her youth, to get to a point where someone could

take her place if the need arose. It never did, and now she had returned. The Demon's lair

hadn't changed much; it was just dingier than before. It had more decay and more bones

lying around. Small bones, she grimaced. It was more fuel for her anger, which she didn't

require, not to face this Demon anyway. He would be easy to cut down, all she needed to

do was drain him of his blood before he died. That would be the difficult part.

Subconsciously, she placed the bead back into her pocket, she didn't need it this time, but

it gave her a small kind of comfort knowing it was there. Her memory took over as she

walked on. Each step forward took her deeper into the lair and closer to where her mind

was urging her. She stopped in front of a torn up rusty cage. It was small, but so was she

when she was kept within it. She traced the outline of the ancient padlock with her
fingers.

'Are you remembering it all?' asked Balthazar, following closely behind.

'Mm hm,' was all she managed in response, still in a daze.

*

Balthazar left it at that. He was only there as backup if she required it. Which, he knew
she wouldn't. He had already checked on the child and his mother Mary and returned to
aid his commander. He would probably just have to hold the Demon down while she
drained the life out of him, but anything else, she was too stubborn for. She would do
most of the dirty work herself. She had witnessed many leaders throughout history work
on the back of their subordinates and win all of the glory for themselves. Something she
swore she would never do. Those weren't leaders, they were filthy cowards in her eyes.
She was just like her father in that regard he believed. However, Lucifer's pride got him
in the end. Which is why, he, Balthazar stays with her, to ensure she has the best advisory
team she could possibly have. To him though, she is still the little girl he had rescued
centuries ago.

'I remember waking up, as if from a bad dream, safe within my bed. Only, it was so dark, I couldn't see anything. I remember rubbing my eyes to see if that would make it brighter,' she laughed. 'Obviously, that didn't work. It was never that dark in my room. You see, Mama would always light the fire in the small hearth in the corner of my tiny room. She never failed to do it. Realising there was no fire made me think of the cold and it hit me as if needles pricking my skin. I knew I wasn't in my bed. I went to grab at the linens anyway but all I grabbed were my skirts,' she stopped a moment and then continued on, still tracing the outline of the lock.

'I could feel the cold steel of the cage underneath me. I didn't want to believe it, because if I did, then what I had just dreamt wouldn't have been a dream at all. It would've been real and if it was real, then I was alone. A child, alone in a cage. I could feel the tears fall down my cheeks. I was lost. All I could do was close my eyes and curl up into a little cocoon and try to go back to sleep. Believing that when I woke up next, none of it would be real; that I *was* dreaming and I would see my parents again.' Aurora slowly walked around the cage.

'But, as you already know, when I next woke, I was still in that rusty old cage. Being a child, I was in shock. I began to drown in my own tears, not making a sound. No, I wouldn't make a sound. The tears weren't because I was afraid for myself. They were for Cora. I had realised that it was real and I remembered her screams before everything went dark. My mother was gone and so was my father. I asked myself, how can I live when everyone I know and love has died?' she said, resting her hand on the top of the cage. 'And then you arrived.'

Aurora looked up at Balthazar and smiled at him. It nearly broke his heart to see that tragic smile again. He could remember these cages as clearly as he could see her standing in front of him right at this very moment. He himself, was placed within one opposite her, though, he never went through the same ordeal as she did. He had only gotten himself caught, to gain Aurora's trust, a trust he needed to be able to save her with. He knew that if he had just appeared and taken her, she would not have trusted him at all, especially after what had just happened to her. He believed it was better to transform into the form of a mortal child and try to relate to her. He realised later on that she could see through his glamour, but she trusted him anyway. She needed a friend and it was simpler just to be a child with her. None of it mattered to Aurora. She enjoyed his intelligence. He didn't have the mind of a child, it was uncanny to her, which made her laugh. When he knew she held no fear for him, he transformed into a creature so small he could fit through the rusty gaps of the cage. Once free of his prison, he turned back into the little boy and broke the lock of Aurora's cage for her grand escape. In the end, he decided to stay like her and only transform and grow as she did. He could remember her sunken face. *What an ordeal she had just gone through*, he had thought. The smell smacked him in the face once he began to look around.

'Not quite the same smell as before, but close to it,' he coughed.

'I was thinking the same thing. It's a bit mustier now but I guess that'll happen when you leave your rubbish lying around,' said Aurora, looking disgustedly at the rotting corpses of animals and mortals.

'I am a Demon and there is no need whatsoever to live like this,' he said, with revulsion.

'If you call this *living,* and you're an Angel my dear friend, just a Fallen one,' noted Aurora, as she walked away from her old cage, lingering before the entrance to where she knew the Demon slept.

*

The veil of darkness broke as the five-year-old Aurora awoke from her unknown slumber. Sitting up, she rubbed her eyes to try to clear away the night. It was still dark where she sat and a slight realisation flooded her mind. She went to pull her sheet up over her head, but all she could find were her skirts from yesterday's dress. *Yesterday*, she thought anxiously. She could feel the cold steel underneath her where she sat. Reaching out, she felt the steel continue upward and above her, and then all around. She could just see the outline of her hands before her, they were still human. For a moment, she thought she was a tiny little bird, trapped within a cage. But no, not a bird, but yes, trapped within a cage. Finally, a rotten odour struck her in the face and then, like falling ivory dominoes, a chill crept down her spine and she was enveloped in an icy wind. Tears began to roll down her little face, her young mind swarming with memory after memory of the night before, *or was it the night before that? Or was it the same one?* she asked herself. She heard a slight murmur in the distance, the sound of someone breathing a sigh. 'Mama?' she whispered to the darkness. Nothing. Just a black empty mass surrounding her. She didn't want to panic, there would be no use in that, and she had to stop herself crying, another useless action. She closed her eyes and slowly breathed in, something she had seen both her parents do on occasion. The smell was growing stronger now. She couldn't explain it. In her mind, it reminded her of a time when she found the lifeless body of a lamb, it had died inside the womb before its futile birth. The farmer didn't know it was there. Its mother standing close by, watching over her dead child. Aurora was filled with sorrow. The smell definitely reminded her of that dreadful morning stroll in the moors. She opened her eyes and used all her strength to move to what she believed to be the front of the cage. She grasped at it, feeling it crumble slightly beneath her fingers, she brought them up to her nose, *rust.* She brushed her fingers across all four sides. It was covered in it. The cage must've been quite old for it to be completely rusty or she was somewhere where the air would eat away at cold steel, perhaps somewhere with salt in the air. All she knew for sure was that her head was throbbing and her eyes were beginning to droop. Sleep was sneaking up on her so she decided to wrap herself up within her billowing skirts and sleep for a little bit. Then she would try to escape.

Waking suddenly, she nearly screamed out for her mother but quickly remembered where she was. She had dreamed her mother was embracing her but everything had gone dark and she was suddenly ripped away from her grasp. Her heart ached at the memory of running away from her mother but so was the rest of her. Her stomach growled in its emptiness and she licked her dry lips. She didn't know how long she had been here and she hadn't seen the monster since it had taken her. She wondered to herself if she would ever see light again. It had been so long since she had. Her eyes started to adjust to the darkness that encircled her. She could see the outline of the cage that trapped her. There was something round hanging on the front of it. She maneuvered onto her hands and knees and moved towards the front of the small cage. She couldn't stand but she could lay flat and stretch out her legs. She tried rocking it, but it seemed to be held to the ground by something in each of the corners. She was so uncomfortable, hunger attacked her body and she had used the front corner to relieve herself a few times already. She was ashamed of it but there was nothing else she could do. Reaching out, she grabbed the round thing and realised it was a lock. She tried wrenching it, but there was no give. She moved back to the other end of the cage, feeling for weak spots along the way.

'There's no point,' said a male voice.

'Who's there?' asked Aurora, shocked at how small her voice sounded. His was the first voice she had heard in a while.

'It doesn't matter who I am. I can see you trying to find a way out and it won't work. He has some kind of sorcery he's using on the cages,' continued the voice, which sounded as if it were coming from an area to her right.

'Okay, but, I would still like to know who you are. My name is Aurora,' she whispered.

'I'm Will and my little sister Emily is with me also. There are a bunch of us here,' said Will.

'How can you see me?' she asked.

'You get used to the dark. He never brings light in here so I think we've just adjusted to it,' he answered.

'Can I ask how old you are?' she prompted, slightly embarrassed.

'You ask a lot of questions, but yeah, you can. You don't need to be shy about it. I'm twelve, Em' is seven. How old are you?' asked Will, curious.

'I'm five,' said Aurora.

'Wow, you sound a lot older than that,' responded Will.

'You know, you don't sound like someone who has been locked in a cage in the cold and surrounded by horrible smells,' said Aurora, sniffling as she quickly wiped her nose.

'What does someone locked in a cage sound like then?' asked Will.

'I guess, they should sound afraid. Or sad. And why doesn't Emily speak, or the others?' She answered.

'She's asleep and I guess the others would rather listen. We've been here a while, hoping to be rescued, even though it's pointless to hope,' he said, quieting his voice.

'You're lying,' accused Aurora.

'Why would you say that?' asked Will.

'You smell. And I can just tell that you're lying to me,' stated Aurora, plainly.

'Well I feel slightly offended that you would say that,' said Will, indignantly.

'Which part? That you smell? Or that you're lying?' asked Aurora.

'Both!' he answered.

'I've read about you, in my papa's book. You're big and ugly, with tentacles. But right now, you are trying to trick me into believing that you're human. I know you're not. So, stop please,' she asked.

'Well. You're no fun, no wonder they want you dead. Thought I'd plump you up first before I did away with you,' said the Demon, who was no longer playing. He walked towards her cage, gliding his fingers over its rusty grooves.

'Didn't anyone ever tell you not to play with your food?' she asked.

'No,' was all he said in response, looking into her cage with delight.

'You know that you have to feed me, in order to actually *plump* me up, right?' she scoffed, feeling bold. 'And who are *they* exactly?' she added.

'Excuse me?' said the Demon, now taking on his true form.

'You said, "No wonder they want you dead." Who are *they*?' she asked again, gripping the bottom of the cage with both her hands.

'Oh, you'll learn soon enough. Now, I have another guest joining you this evening. I'm off to fetch him now. Here, eat this,' he said, shoving what looked like a snake through the small gap in the cage.

'What is it?' she frowned.

'Eel. Very tasty,' he answered and then left her.

Alone yet again, she stared down at the dead creature inside her cage. She could just make out its outline. It made her feel queasy but she was desperately hungry. Grabbing at it with both hands, she nearly dropped it. The slime on its skin stuck to her hands. She closed her eyes and bit down. Unsurprisingly, it didn't taste good whatsoever, but she consumed the slimy creature as best she could. He would not beat her.

*

After wiping the cage clean of any traces of Aurora's memories for the enemy to find, Balthazar stepped up beside Aurora, who had been standing in the same position for more than fifteen minutes. 'Did I tell you he tried to trick me into believing he was a mortal?' she asked him, not changing her gaze.

'No, you did not. Enlighten me?' requested Balthazar.

'He transformed into a young boy also, like you, but slightly older. He tried telling me that his sister was with him and that there were others in this very room with us. Of course, I didn't believe him from the moment he opened his mouth. His glamour was poorly done. I didn't know how I could tell, I just could. I couldn't hear anyone else, just

the echo of his and my voice. I couldn't hear their breathing, just his and my own. He

wasn't a very good liar. He wasn't even acting afraid. Such a fool,' she laughed.

'Too much pride mixed with stupidity. Makes a mockery of our kind really. If only he

knew who you were when he took you. Idiot,' sighed Balthazar, shaking his head.

'I don't know why you insist on saying that he is the same as you. He is a Tyrant,

disgusting failures that should've been banished from this realm and all others the

moment they were created. Instead, its creators use them behind the backs of their golden

children. How blind they all are. You are nothing like it, you are merely what mortals

have made you out to be. Just because you call yourself a Demon does not make it so,'

she said smiling at him. Balthazar smiled back and as usual, gave in to her flattery.

'Well, we have reached the inner lair I assume, just as dismal as I had expected it to be,'

he said, facing her.

'It is time,' said Aurora, looking forward.

'Lady's first?' grinned Balthazar, holding out his hand and allowing her to step into the

chasm before them. She hesitated only slightly, and then walked on. Walking deeper into

the makeshift cave, Aurora and Balthazar could see it was created by the very individual

they were hunting. The Tyrant by the name of Cetus, in contradiction to what mortals

believed, was no father of Gorgons or of Gods. He was, however, a monster of the ocean.

Hence the cave and the salty breeze that wafted past every now and then. He had been released from the Pit by the Gods to do their bidding. As they moved forward through the cave, the damp air was almost unbreathable, even for Balthazar.

'I still don't understand why you don't just bring him to us,' said Balthazar, disgusted with his surroundings.

'I think I would rather have the element of surprise, by waking him up myself. I also want to remember everything that happened here. Retracing my steps has done that,' she answered.

Finally, they reached an opening to an even deeper part of the cave, where light shone through a slight crack in the earthen roof above.

'We must be beneath the boulders now. I find it interesting that he would prefer to live at the rear of a cave, where, at the slightest quake, the whole thing could tumble down on him. Very curious indeed,' whispered Balthazar, looking cautiously above.

'Especially since he is a Water Demon,' said Aurora finishing his thoughts. 'Wait,' she said suddenly. 'Can you hear that?' she asked Balthazar.

They both went silent, tilting their heads to get a better angle on the sound.

'Is that, snoring?' she asked Balthazar incredulously.

'I do believe it is. He must really believe that he is untouchable. This is way too easy,' said Balthazar, shaking his head.

'What a shock it will be then,' said Aurora grinning. She moved faster then, towards the sound and found their prey, laying on a wooden bed, in the form of a mortal. Aurora unclasped her scythes and linked them to her arm guards in preparation. They were for secondary force, she only required them to bleed him dry.

'Balthazar, make sure I don't kill him before we have what we came here for,' she requested.

'Of course, that's why I'm here,' he agreed.

Aurora moved around to the head of the bed and placed her hands on each side of Cetus's temples.

'Wake up,' she ordered the Demon.

Cetus's eyes flew open, confusion smothered him for a moment but then he saw Balthazar.

'Brother! What are you doing here? And who is this?' he asked, glaring at Aurora's hands, which were mentally holding him down. Balthazar didn't speak, he wasn't there to speak, merely to observe and help when required.

'Why do you ignore me brother? And what is this witch doing? I can't move!' he started to yell.

'Do it,' instructed Aurora to Balthazar.

Balthazar nodded in acknowledgement, took out a small ancient bone and encircled Cetus, by drawing on the cave floor beneath him, trapping him within his bed.

'You won't hold me in an Angel trap,' he laughed.

'It's not an Angel trap, it's a Demon bone you fool. Oh, and I am not you're *brother*,' spat Balthazar. Once he had completed the circle, Aurora let go of their prisoner and maneuvered herself into his vision.

'Traitor!' bellowed Cetus.

Aurora smiled at him, she would enjoy this very much. 'Do you not remember me?' she asked him.

'And why should I *remember you*?' he said angrily.

'Because you murdered my Nephilim parents in cold blood in another century, brought me here and kept me caged in my own filth for weeks,' she said blatantly.

'You *have* seen the bones, haven't you? I've done that a number of times, well, a lot actually, since I myself need to eat,' he responded.

'I'm the one that got away,' she smiled.

'So? It just means I get a second chance now to do what is needed,' he said, as a matter of fact.

'You do remember me then. Good. I have always assumed that you didn't know who I was. Was my assumption correct?' she asked him.

'Yeah, I guess. I was just told to kill you and then I would be freed,' said Cetus, ignorantly.

'But you didn't kill me and yet you are still free,' she said, raising an eyebrow.

'So, what? I lied. It's not my fault they believed me,' he said, shrugging his shoulders.

'Well, since I am not exactly lying low, I suppose they will send members of the Valkyrie to locate you and most likely dispose of you. Perhaps they knew I would return for you someday, which is why you're still alive. In that case we better make this quick, I require something from you, whether you give it to me willingly or not,' informed Aurora.

'Like a deal?' he asked.

'Not at all. I don't do deals with Tyrants I wish to destroy. I would however like you to transform into your true self, if you do not I'll hang you.' she requested.

'Not going to happen,' he scoffed at her.

Aurora used her gifts and raised Cetus from his laying position and placed him upside down, piercing his thigh with a large butcher's hook she had found on the floor of the cave. Balthazar attached the hook to a railing above Cetus's bed. Cetus screamed in agony, as the pain tore through his flesh.

'I told you, if you didn't transform, I would hang you up. You really need to believe me the first time Cetus,' she said non-apologetically. The next thing that came out of his mouth was very impolite. Aurora didn't appreciate being spoken to in that manner, so she moved the hook slightly, prompting her prisoner to scream again.

'Change! Now! And you won't have to suffer,' she ordered.

'You see, that wasn't so hard, was it? All you needed to do from the start was to follow my instructions and you would've been a lot more comfortable,' she remarked finally giving into her. Seeing his true form sent a rage of fire throughout her body but she needed to keep calm to complete the procedure accurately.

'Your method is unlike any I have ever witnessed Aurora but perhaps we should stop dilly-dallying and finish the job?' said Balthazar respectfully, looking at his watch.

'You're completely right. My apologies. It was my fault he didn't transform straight away,' she said, glaring at him. She took her scythes from her wrist guards and like an artist, made a number of small cuts on different parts of the Demon's body. First, they had to drain his venom, and then his blood. If they did this the other way around, Cetus would be dead within minutes and they would not be able to retrieve the venom. Both were required for her elixir to work, well, Xerxe's elixir. A mixture that would help her to transform into something that she could use, to gain a certain Guardian Angel's trust. Slowly, they drained Cetus of his life, as he had done to so many little mortals throughout history.

'There you go, we're nearly finished,' she cooed. Aurora wasn't about to let him have an easy death. He was now calm, which she would put an end to, as soon as she had retrieved every little bit she needed. Just before the final drop of blood, Aurora removed the tubing from the flasks they had placed beneath the Demon to gather the venom and the blood separately. Placing the caps on, she handed them to Balthazar.

'That should be sufficient,' she said. Cetus was now bleeding out normally from the wounds Aurora had inflicted on his sea urchin body. What she did next was questionable, but in her mind, he well deserved it. She disappeared for a moment and when she returned, she was carrying a bucket.

'What have you got there?' asked Balthazar curiously, as this part of the plan was not to his knowledge.

'A treat for our friend here. Something that should remind him of me,' she answered smiling. 'Cetus, do you remember when you doused me in seawater? You said I was a filthy little rodent that needed a bath.' The Demon was in and out of consciousness at this stage and couldn't really see what Aurora was getting at.

'Well, I think you need some re-hydration. You look a little dry,' she said and drenched him in salt water. His screams pierced their ears, shaking the stalactites above. Once the last of the water had dissipated, Cetus's breathing slowed, until it was no more.

'Was that necessary?' asked Balthazar, pointedly.

Aurora looked him in the eyes. 'Yes, it was. He deserved more than what I gave him. I was being lenient,' she said sincerely.

'That was lenient?' he asked.

Ignoring his concern, Aurora left the cave for the last time. Not looking back at the devastation that had been left behind, she waited for Balthazar who followed her.

'Where to next My Lady?' he asked her.

'Melbourne, you remember the year?' she tested him.

'1921,' he answered confidently.

'Good. I'll return to my own time once the task is complete,' she said, taking the bag from him and removing the bead from her pocket. With a wink, she disappeared. Looking at his pocket watch, Balthazar smiled.

'Time for a cup of tea,' he said, kicking the sand with his fancy leather shoes and disappearing over the horizon.

Chapter Eleven

Required Sacrifice

Melbourne – 1921

Aurora glanced over her evening copy of the Herald Sun, eyeing a particular story that she had been following since its appearance on the front page that morning. Placing the paper down on the mahogany coffee table, she looked outside the window of her parlour room at the Hotel Windsor towards Parliament House. The steps, normally empty, stood overrun by a mob of frightened women, presumably mothers who were also following the story on the front page. The street below was bustling with the evening traffic of workers knocking off for the day. She saw many children wandering the street, lifting valuables invisibly from their adult counterparts' pockets. Valuables that would see these particular children into the next day when they would go out once again, revisiting their tragic cycle of subcelestial life over and over. The small sodden faces were trapped in a world of harsh elements and a society of citizens who didn't even know they existed. Until their lifeless little faces were scattered all over the morning paper that is. Their tiny little bodies were covered in tattered clothes that Aurora thought were not even worthy enough to be used as cleaning rags. Her heart dropped for the poor little souls. She was not here for them though, she was here for something else. Something half mortal and half Angel, a child of the Fallen. She had been here, in this time, for over a week now, using this era's versions of Balthazar and Xerxes. Again, most things were different, less advanced than in Brooklyn, but more advanced than in her own time. It was very intriguing for her to see the rapid change in the mortal realm. It was rather exciting for her too. A knock at the door removed her from her deep thought.

'Come in,' she called out. Sinking back into her green velvet armchair she glanced up at her guests.

'We found him!' beamed Balthazar. 'His vile scent led us straight to him.'

Aurora smiled at Balthazar and Xerxes and stood. 'Good. Now we can start to put the final pieces together,' she said as she made her way over to the buffet table on the other side of the room.

'Coffee?' she offered her guests. They both nodded, took a pewter cup each and sat down at the table opposite her. Aurora noticed Xerxes looking a little anxious as he sipped his coffee.

'What is it Xe?' she asked.

'Well, My lady, it's just, what about Ross?' she knew what he was asking her but she wanted him to say it.

'What about him?' she countered.

'Well, we know him to be innocent, so why are we still using him? We have found the true murderer. Why not release that new information to the mortals investigating?' he asked.

Grinning, Aurora answered. 'Because my dear friend. Unfortunately, he is our decoy. You know he is not truly an innocent. Yes, he is innocent of this particular crime, but not of the others he has gathered in his lifetime. Especially his most recent one of assault against that woman, whatever her name was. We cannot afford to have the true perpetrator, our required sacrifice to be strewn all over the papers, so we need another to take his place before the courts. For this purpose, Mr Ross is unfortunately our intended. There are times when we will have to go against our moral compass if we are to be victorious in our mission Xe, this is one of those moments. In time, people will learn the truth that he was just found in the wrong place at the wrong time, and due to public pressure was falsely accused by the courts. But for now, we need no magnifying glass placed on any of our own tributes to the cause. I don't want the Valkyrie on our tails just yet. Is that understood?' she asked sternly. Both Balthazar and Xerxes agreed with their commander and went on to finish their bitter coffee.

*

Night had fallen on the city of Melbourne, and what a beautiful summer night it was walking down Bourke Street. Aurora and her companions made their way to an area unknown to mortals called the Underground. They stepped off Bourke Street and onto Little Collins, then finally to their awaited destination down Gun Alley. The easement off of the alleyway hid them from unwanted attention, which was perfect for the entryway of an immortal clubhouse. However, they were not the only ones there that evening. The area was cordoned off by police tape and a number of constables stood watch over the crime scene, as this was the very spot where their target left behind his latest victim.

'Why do you think he chose the access area into our world to commit his misconduct?' asked Balthazar. Aurora looked at the white cross that marked the spot where the victim was found. The grungy narrow alley was no place for a little girl, he had brought her body here for a reason.

'The real question is, why would a Nephilim attack and then murder a mortal child and place her body here. What is his message? Does he have a message? Or is it another waste of innocent life orchestrated by the Gods?' asked Aurora out loud.

'Remind me, is the Nephil Demon or Angel spawn?' she asked Balthazar.

Looking directly into his commander's eyes, he begrudgingly answered. 'Demon.'

'Orchestrated by the Gods it is then,' she said in response, as they moved invisibly towards the door to the Underground.

The alley was dingy and smelled like sour liquor and rotten fruit. The police officers on guard chatted among themselves as Aurora, Xerxes and Balthazar slid passed them, unseen and unheard. When they reached the door, Balthazar pricked a finger and let two tiny droplets of blood fall onto an area of the brickwork below, which absorbed it in seconds. Only those with celestial blood could enter this place, but unless there was a guard on the other side of the door, which is next to never, you only needed the blood of a celestial, not the celestial itself to get in. There are always loopholes. Aurora wasn't a fan of these types of places. She was never one to revel in society, unless it was required to complete part of her mission. Such as this particular situation. She had to be there, to see him face to face. If there was one thing that Aurora despised, it was a child killer. Not even she would stoop that low. The door opened and the three of them delicately descended the narrow stairs. As they reached the bottom of the stairwell, Balthazar looked around and spotted one of his men. Signalling to Aurora to follow him, they moved towards the corner of the black and gold Art Deco bar. Xerxes took the back of a chair and slid it out from under the table for her to sit in. Taking her seat, the others joined her.

'Where is he?' asked Aurora.

Balthazar's man, Zachariah, stared down at the table.

'Commander, he is in the back with Styx. I'll go fetch them,' he stuttered.

'Zachariah, look me in the eyes when you speak to me. I won't bite,' she teased.

'Apologies Commander. I just, I am so honoured to meet you finally. But I, I also wanted to apologise for what I did, to your mother. I was a coward and did not stand for her when she needed it.' He said modestly.

'It is true, you were a coward. But, so were many other stronger Angels. What you did after, showed us all your true strength, late as it was. You gave up your wings and found your fate with my friend here.' She said, nudging Balthazar in the arm.

'It is I who is honoured. I understand it was you who found him? Well done. However, you have left him with Styx, so he may no longer be with us,' she laughed.

'I'll go get them now Commander,' said Zachariah, nearly tripping over his chair as he moved towards the bar's kitchen doors.

'Quite nervous that one, isn't he?' said Aurora, staring after him.

'Yes, but very reliable. He has never forgiven himself for taking your parents into custody. Especially after the trial. He elected to take his own wings off you know? He's either very mad, or heartbreakingly loyal,' said Balthazar.

'The latter. Definitely the latter. He has a tortured soul. More than my own. Hopefully serving me will help heal it,' said Aurora smiling.

'Oh, it will my liege, it will,' assured Balthazar smiling back.

Zachariah and Styx pushed through the double doors dragging a bloodied body of a man between them.

'He's still alive Commander. She just knocked him out,' said Zachariah through struggled breaths.

'A few times actually. He just keeps coming back,' laughed Styx, throwing the Nephilim to the ground. 'It was almost like, the stupid Neph wanted to be caught. He wouldn't say anything. Not until he could see you of course Commander, like he has laid some kind of trap,' deduced Styx, picking the Neph up by the crook of the neck, forcing him to face their leader, even with his eyes closed.

'It probably is,' said Aurora. 'I find it is easier to trap the spider within its own web. Which is what this one is trying to do. He just hasn't realised how many other spiders I have within my web that can trap him instead. Wake up!' she ordered and the Nephilim opened his eyes. Bewildered, he realised who was sitting in front of him.

'So, I finally get to meet the Great Angel,' he coughed as he choked on his own blood.

Styx thumped him over the back of the head. 'You do not speak, unless spoken to Neph.' Grimacing at the newly formed lump on the back of his head, he closed his mouth.

'What to do with you? You have caused us a major issue within this realm. Allowing mortals to see you, conducting yourself in the most disgusting of manners, murdering innocents and other non-mentionable actions. You disgust me. Are you going to tell me that the Gods made you do it?' asked Aurora in a patronising tone. Looking up at her again he smiled, showing his broken and missing teeth in between the drips of blood.

'Why do I need to tell you what you already know?' he asked, spluttering specks of blood onto the polished concrete floor.

Aurora smiled back at him. 'You don't need to tell me anything. My warriors also know this, I just thought I'd let them have a little fun with you before I took things into my own hands. I think there is nothing worse than when a commander can't get their hands dirty, don't you?' she asked with a wink.

'What is his name?' she asked Zachariah.

'He goes by the name Jeffries.'

'Interesting. Was there anything else?' asked Aurora, curiously.

'Yes Commander. I looked further into his family and it is just as you thought. His whole bloodline is cursed. One of his ancestors was seduced by a Greater Demon, not an Angel. And, he is the last of his name,' answered Zachariah proudly.

'Well done Zachariah. You and Balthazar finish cleaning up this miscreant's mess above. Styx, let us welcome our friend to our very own Tartarus below,' said Aurora standing up and walking towards another door, one that would lead them deep into the sewers below. Styx grabbed Jeffries the Neph by the arm and forced him forward through the door and down the spiral staircase. Aurora followed behind with another Guardian, closing the door behind them.

Chapter Twelve

Judge and Executioner

The morgue and connecting coroner's court loomed down over Tristan and

Kingston like a foreboding tower. Anyone would've thought they were merely

human in the sight of such a godlike structure. Tristan turned his head towards his

friend, 'shall we?' he gestured towards the gate.

'After you,' responded Kingston. Upon entering the stone building, they found

themselves in a hallway. After some careful investigation, they located the door

into the morgue where they discovered the coroner, Dr C. H. Mollison.

'Ahh Doctor, we finally found you in this God forsaken maze you call a building.

Allow me to introduce myself. I am Inspector Morholt of the Sydney Metropolitan

Police and this is my colleague Detective Lee. We are here to inspect the body of

the young girl found last week in Gun Alley.'

The Doctor glanced up from his leather-bound notebook at his unexpected guests.

'Was I expecting you? I don't recall your names. Though my secretary could have

forgotten to inform me of your arrival. That has happened before. My apologies,

but where did you say you were from again?' he asked bewildered.

Kingston glanced sideways at his friend who answered the Doctor's question.

'We're from the Sydney Metro Police.'

Dr Mollison raised an eyebrow. 'And why, may I ask, are you down here investigating this particular murder? It's not really in your jurisdiction.'

'Of course. We have had a similar case back home and wanted to see if the two were comparable or merely coincidental. I have approval from the Melbourne head office to do so,' Tristan reached inside his herringbone suit jacket to grab out the warrant.

'May I see some identification before we move forward?' Tristan and Kingston grabbed their IDs and provided them to the Doctor. 'With pleasure Sir, there you go'.

*

Leaving the coroner's office, both Tristan and Kingston were sure they were onto something.

'It is exactly the same as the child we found in Sydney last week,' said Kingston.

'And, in a similar locality. Right above one of our entrances to the Underground. Should we take a detour and make a visit to the crime scene before we give them our findings?' asked Tristan.

Kingston looked at his pocket watch and agreed. Walking through the almost empty streets of Melbourne, they found their way to the small alley where the crime had reached a violent conclusion. Tristan counted three officers, and a few news reporters from the local paper taking photos for their front page story.

'Time to glamour?' he suggested.

'Yes, I do believe it is,' he assented and they became invisible to the mortal eye. They strode over to the mark on the ground where the little girl was found. Tristan immediately stopped on the spot.

'What's the matter?' asked Kingston.

'Do you not sense her? She was here, not long ago. We must go down,' said Tristan eagerly.

'Why would she be *here*? Isn't she mortal? Asked Kingston as they entered the Underground.

'I don't know,' said Tristan lost in his own mind. 'She was right here,' he said, pointing at a small table in the corner of the bar.

'Are you sure it's not your grief playing games with you again?' asked Kingston, becoming worried about his brother in arms.

'No! It is not.' Taking a moment for clarity of mind, he breathed in slowly and apologised. 'Sorry, I didn't mean to bark at you. You're right, you must be right, it's just my grief. Losing her not too long ago has affected me greatly. She just keeps popping up wherever we go. It's driving me mad,' he said as he sat down at the table. 'Perhaps I am hallucinating it all. It wouldn't be the first time,' said

Tristan.

'Look, let's get back to the reason why we are here. To stop these celestial murders.

It has to be the work of a Demon. We just need to find out which one and why,'

said Kingston, also taking a seat. A Fallen Angel walked up to them from the bar.

'Are you just going to sit there, or are you going to buy a drink?' she asked.

'Get us two gins, straight. I think we're going to need it,' said Kingston handing the

waitress three gold coins as payment. Glaring at them, she took the order and

sauntered back to the bar, where she whispered something discreet to the barkeep.

'We better not stay here too long, the Fallen don't like our kind very much,

especially you,' whispered Kingston.

'Of course. Though, it's not my fault the Gods merely demoted me and didn't strip

me of my wings,' Tristan justified.

'Yeah, but they mostly chose to Fall, whereas you did not. I know you have your

reasons but they don't know them and they'll continue to think of you as a traitor to

their kind,' he said.

'Alright, just one drink to get our thoughts back in order, then we'll leave. You'll

have to ask them some questions first, and then we can move on,' he said. Kingston

nodded his head in agreement.

The spiral staircase into the seven sewers of the Underground ran deep towards the core of the Earth. The Pit itself was a completely different place to where Aurora and her prey were now situated. Only one of the sewer lines led to a back entrance into the Pit but before you would reach this entrance, it was said that you would be met by the hounds of Hecate who guarded it from intruders. Aurora liked dogs, so she wanted to find another way around destroying such loyal creatures. However, she didn't have the time to go looking for another entrance when she knew there would be traps throughout all of the sewer lines and she couldn't afford losing any of her warriors to those traps. For now, she would leave it. She needed everyone who had followed her parents and now, who were loyal to her. After all, the enemy did have a few Archangels on their side, not to mention the Gods. Aurora wasn't sure how powerful the Gods truly were, there had been no witnesses to any of their creations, or destructions throughout their time within the universe. With exception to their sisters, the Fates. Clearly, she wasn't going to get a straight forward answer from them. They loved their riddles. She just needed to witness their power somehow, to ensure she wasn't putting her people on the losing side, but that was another problem she needed figured out by her future self. Right now, she had to deal with a whole different kettle of fish.

They had found the landing, the stench of sewerage filled their senses.

'Why are these places always so disgusting?' asked Aurora, not really looking for an answer. 'Because it's people's shi...ah!' gasped the Neph, taking another hit to his head.

'It was rhetorical, idiot,' said Styx, thumping the Neph on the back of the head again.

'Right, bring him over here. Sit him down right there. Thank you, Styx,' ordered Aurora, pointing to an area already marked. The Neph began to squirm and panic after Aurora placed a hand briefly on the marking, letting it glow for just moment. Their prisoner finally realising what was about to happen to him.

'There is no point in resisting, you cannot escape a Demon trap. Now, hold still while I look into that disturbing mind of yours,' she said, placing both hands on either side of his head. Going into another's mind can be chaotic unless you know exactly what you're looking for. Lucky for her, she did. She pulled at different strings of his memories until she found the one that she wanted. Stepping into it, she found herself standing before the Gods in their great Hall of Divinity. This was not the first time she had seen this place, others, those loyal to her, had shown her before. Isrea, Titus and Chaos were like Titans to a mere human, giants in other terms. They wore white armour to show off their divinity and phoney purity. No one else could wear the shade of the Gods. *Just as well*, thought Aurora, as she didn't look that good in white. The Nephilim, whose mind she was now taking refuge in, was tiny in comparison. He cowered in horror, bowing and tilting his head towards the ground. She could feel his fear.

'Rise,' said Titus. Jeffries rose as ordered, still not looking directly at them.

'As you ask of us, we will agree with your terms and release you from the curse that your filth of an ancestor stowed upon you.' He looked to his sister.

Isrea continued. 'You must cause disorder and give us blood. Lead us to the spawn of our greatest Fallen,' she finished.

Chaos took over. 'If you do this, you will be free. Redemption will be yours.'

'On the honour that my family once knew, I swear to you, I will not fail,' responded Jeffries.

Aurora let go of the memory and returned to the sewer.

'Well, so that's what they promised you? And it was you who decided who lived and who died, not them, they just gave you their permission,' she said gripping his throat with her right hand and raising him up into a standing position.

'What I do not understand is your revolting obsession with murdering little girls. You know what, I don't want to understand. Why is it though, that every soul I take for my own is a destroyer of children? What has happened to you pitiful creatures?' she asked through gritted teeth.

'Never mind. What I am about to do to you now will destroy *your* soul. You cannot be risen. You will not move onto another realm because you will be gone. Poof! Just like that. Not what you wanted to hear right? Oh, I'm sorry. Am I squeezing too tight?' she said, disdainfully. The skin beneath her touch started to turn amber and then it began to glow white.

'Goodbye Mr Jeffries and goodbye to your bloodline. Your existence on this plain is no more,' said Aurora letting go of the Neph who fell to his knees and slowly crumbled away like burning paper. Leaning down over his remains, she took another one of her many vials from a pocket and scooped up some of Mr Jeffries ash and placed it back within her coat.

Aurora walked over to Styx who was gleaming. Though she would've liked to have killed him herself, she understood why it had to be her commander's doing. Both of them turned their heads towards the surface.

'Tristan,' said Aurora. 'What is he doing here?' she asked Styx, who shrugged her shoulders in response. 'I knew Celeste would be here soon enough, but not him.'

'I guess that's our queue to leave then,' said Styx.

'Please pass on my appreciation to, well, myself,' requested Aurora. Taking the rosary bead from her pocket, she returned to her own time. She now had everything she required to infiltrate her enemy and finally meet Tristan for the first time since she was a child. Now they were equal in physical age, she would use Xerxes elixir against him to get what she required. As demeaning as it was, it was the only way to gain his trust. After leaving her future, she smiled at her present as she greeted the Balthazar from her own time.

'Finally, you have returned to us. I assume everything went to plan?' he asked.

'Yes, everything, so far has gone to plan. Now, we need some soldiers to fill the mortal ranks. I'm assuming we're in Culloden?' she asked him.

'Yes, My lady, the battle has finished. I have identified the ones we want.' He said taking her arm.

'Well then brother, let us finally begin.' She said, grinning ear to ear as they walked the bloodied field, fading into the mist.

Chapter Thirteen

The Oath

Angus MacGregor would never forget his final battle against the dreaded eighteenth

century English. It was the sixteenth day of April in the year 1746. A damp day on

the Scottish moors of Culloden. The number of wounded Jacobite's rounded up in

the marshy field did not outnumber the one thousand that were already lying lifeless

in the mud. The fog still clung to the air but it did not shroud them from their

enemy's unwelcome gaze. MacGregor's men, like the surviving members of some

other clans, did not run away before the fight's end but instead stood motionless at

the mercy of the Redcoat's muskets. They had to surrender, if not for the young

lads who still had breath left in this life, but for their families back home. Most of

the stronger clans fought to the death, but the smart ones deserted and the rest

surrendered. MacGregor wanted his kin to survive but still be left standing among

their brothers with pride. He knew they would be named cowards. He also knew he

had only temporarily prolonged their lives. They merely awaited their deaths at the

hands of the red coated bastards. It was only hours ago that they sat merrily by the

fire singing songs and laughing about youthful reminiscences. Today they had

created a new ballad, about the strength and courage of the highlander men and the cowardly English who took everything from them. History would remember this day, the day they stood up against an oppressive and illegitimate rule. Even if they couldn't be a part of their family's world any longer, they knew they too would be remembered, if not by history, at least by their kin. As the redcoats closed upon them, Angus ordered his men to drop their weapons, dirks and all. They had to try to survive. Mud and blood stung the wounds on his head as he himself dropped his own weapon into the marshy ground beneath him. An ugly gap toothed redcoat moved towards him. The Englishman lifted his bloodstained sword to Angus's face. 'Do you submit Scot?' he said in his raspy voice.

'What do ye think?' scoffed Angus looking down at his own sword that was laying on the ground.

As expected, the Englishman struck him across the face with a closed fist.

'You see here boys, these cowards think they will get away with this treason. No, no, no, you will not. You should've lifted your swords to us and perished in battle, it would have been a kinder death.' The Englishman laughed. Angus felt a change in the wind around them and the marshy mist behind the redcoats parted slightly as a woman in a blue dress emerged from it. She was angelic in her features but her appearance was strong, like armour. The redcoat dropped his sword when he felt her touch his shoulder, he turned to face her and sick with fear, his face turned a greenish hue. The woman looked upon the English and spoke.

'Kneel,' she said in an Irish tone. To Angus's surprise, they all took a knee. Then, the woman turned to face him. 'I believe you are Angus MacGregor, leader of the MacGregor clan,' she stated.

'Aye, I am. May I ask who ye are?' said Angus, attempting to be polite and trying to shake away any rattle in his voice.

'You may, however I may not answer. Though, I will tell you that I have an opportunity for you and your kin. You might believe that if you were to escape here and run to your families that you will all be safe. Or, like the others before you, running into the hills and hiding you will also be safe. This will not be the case, I assure you. The English will turn every rock and burn every house, to hunt every last one of you down. Their King wants retribution and they, being his servants, will do whatever it takes to appease him; all traitors must die. Would you like to know why that is?' she asked him.

'Aye? Go on,' he prompted.

'Because we told them to. It is the way of *my* kin,' she answered.

'And who are your kin?' asked Angus, bemused.

'What you call Angels and Demons. To us it is more specific, but to narrow us all down to one of two groups if you will, that is what we are. I, on the other hand am both in a way, but that just depends on your interpretation of my parentage. Before we go too far into the explanations and such, as there is no time for it at present, I need to explain to you what my opportunity is. The look on your face tells me that you believe me but your mind is twisting in confusion. Don't overthink this, calm

your mind,' said Aurora. Taking in a breath, Angus shifted his weight.

'Good. Now where was I? Oh, yes; you have two choices. Now, remember that my

people, well *my* very own enemy whisper into the minds of men to do their bidding

and their bidding is for chaos and the destruction of your people so that they can

exist. So, your first choice is to forget this ever occurred and go back to your certain

death at the hands of these disgusting excuses for mortals. In choosing that path, it

will also lead to the destruction of your homes, your families and your culture. It

will be the end for the Scots.'

'Your second choice, is to join me. In doing so, you and your kin will be safe. You

will live full lives and the survival of your culture will lie with you. I only ask for

two things in return,' she said, looking away for a moment.

'And what are they?' asked Angus as calmly as one can in the middle of a

battlefield full of fallen Scots, talking to an Angel.

'First, you will serve me as a commander of your people and other mortals who join

us. You and your warriors will live as you do now but will not perish until my

mission has been complete. I warn you, this may take many years, not ten or

twenty, perhaps a hundred or more. Your family will grow and thus my army will

grow. But, I will grant those who are not from the original chosen the chance to live

and die normal lives, if they so choose it. However, there must always be one member from a generation to serve in my army. The ranks need to be maintained as time goes on, you understand?' said Aurora.

Angus had to think about this, it was not just his life he was gambling with. However, this was not the kind of situation where he could take a day or two to decide either. He had to think quickly.

'What is the second request, if I were to choose this option?' he asked.

'*They*, must die,' she said motioning towards the seven red soldiers.

'Can I speak to me men about it?' asked Angus.

She paused for a moment and looked him in the eyes. 'No, you may not. You are their leader, you will make this decision on their behalf. This is not a negotiation of terms. You have two choices, live or die. Surely you do not want to die or else you would not have surrendered to the English. Am I wrong?' she asked.

'No, but that is hardly fair on them not giving them the choice to choose their own path, and how do we know ye is not telling lies?' he debated.

'Angels cannot lie. We can skirt around truth, but we cannot lie. You must decide whether you believe or not. Not that it truly matters because once a life is taken by your hand, once you spill blood of another mortal, you belong to my kind. Your soul is mine. However, I am giving you a choice to work with me and survive. I could just as easily kill you myself before you take your next breath, or allow these creatures to go on with what they were about to do to appease the Gods. Is that not

fair to you? I can be reasonable but in this I, choose not to be. Make your decision,'
she ordered civilly.

Angus Lachlan MacGregor, Laird to the MacGregor clan, understood what decision
was to be made. Survive or vanish from the face of the Earth.

He wanted his people to survive.

Chapter Fourteen

Blood and Bread

Paris – 1789

'To know your enemy, you must become your enemy.'

Sun Tzu

The perfumed aroma of rose water and orange blossom drifted passed Aurora's

nose. Slowly, she opened her eyes and found herself lying in a bed that was not her

own. She was covered in silken sheets and a feather stuffed duvet and almost

suffocating by one hundred or so pillows. Rubbing her face with her hands, she

heard a soft bang as a door closed. Just as she was about to pull herself from the

massive four poster bed, a servant girl promptly opened the curtains and a rush of

sunlight blinded her.

'Good God! What are you doing?' she gasped, her accent altered. It was no longer

her Irish tone, but that of a Londoner. She placed a hand on her mouth, not expecting it to sound like that at all. She'll have to speak with Xerxes about that later.

'Pardon mademoiselle. Je suis vraiment desole,' she pleaded and quickly ran from the room.

'Excuse me?' said Aurora, too late.

Throwing the collection of pillows onto the floor, Aurora was able to push herself up and out of the bed. Looking down at herself, she found she was wearing nothing, but a plain white shift.

'What is going on?' she asked herself aloud.

'Ahh My lady, you're awake! Finally,' said a familiar voice.

Aurora turned to see its owner and found the friendly face. 'Balthazar,' she said with a smile.

'Now, tell me what you remember once I get your lady's maid to dress you. Elise, she's ready for you. I'll wait outside,' he said with a slight bow of the head. Aurora, about to ask him what was happening, closed her mouth and awaited the servant.

'Good morning My lady, you look wonderful! It's good to see you up and about. What do you feel like wearing today? The blue or green?' she asked walking over to a cupboard.

'Um, you decide,' she smiled awkwardly.

'I think the blue. It goes with your eyes more.' she said holding the blue dress up.

Close to an hour later, Balthazar re-entered her room and took a seat at a table in the corner. Sending the servants away, he poured coffee for two and beckoned Aurora over to take a seat next to him.

'Here, drink some coffee. Now, what do you remember?' he asked her.

'We were discussing our plans for Paris, then I remember drinking something, but that's about it. Oh and my voice has changed,' answered Aurora.

'Yes, that is new. It never happened in the test subjects but I think it is a minor variation. Your memory will return within the day but to give you a head start allow me to explain.

We went through the final testing of the transformation elixir and it was a success. So, naturally, you decided it was time for you to take it yourself,' he stopped to take a mouthful of coffee.

'When did this occur?' she broke in.

'Two weeks ago. You have been unconscious for most of that time. We made you comfortable. Xerxes may have gone overboard with the pillows but he was, well, you know how he is. We are currently residing just outside of the city; Paris. Xerxes was able to create the complete non-hypothetical concoction which enabled you to turn into this,' he said pointing his full hands at her body. 'Obviously, he tested it on other Angels but as usual you were impatient and took it yourself and here we are! You are Lady Elora Whinter; niece to the Baron, Lord Henry Whinter. You are his brother's only child and his heir. Both your parents are deceased, so your uncle is your guardian. He has no children of his own. He is back in London sorting out residency for your arrival in October, it is now May third and everything the sisters predicted has happened thus far. There are talks of a revolt. The people are as we expected them to be; angry and hungry. The Angels are definitely playing their part,' he said with a devious grin. Aurora smiled back but then quite an important question came to mind.

'Is he here? In Paris?' she asked, expecting the worst.

'Yes, I spotted him at the barracks two days ago. Now that you are awake, I, I mean, *you*, will send the garrison an invitation to tea in their honour,' he said with a wink. 'And we can finally find that key.'

'It sounds like everything is going as planned. Good. All I need to do is persuade a Guardian Angel to show me where he has hidden the key that can liberate my father. Shouldn't be too difficult.' Both Aurora and Balthazar laughed. 'I just have to live as a mortal for long enough to convince him he loves me,' she said with an uncertain sigh.

'How are you feeling? It may take a few days to get used to being, mortal,' he said with slight abhorrence.

'I feel, weaker. Fragile I think is the word I'm looking for. Everything is a lot duller, colours and sounds are not the same, neither are smells. Taste, is very different. This coffee actually tastes good!' she said in astonishment.

'Okay, well, when something off-kilter happens, please tell me straight away.
Especially since this is your first transformation. Oh, before I forget, Xerxes placed
mortal memories within your mind, just in case he does get close to you. He won't
see these particular ones, he's no longer strong enough to fight my glamours,' he
said pompously.
'Good. And of course, I will let you know as soon as anything happens,' she
promised. 'Let us invite these gentlemen to tea, shall we?' she said with a grin.

*

The French military was in a bit of a shambles upon Tristan and Kingston's arrival
to Paris. Men were either leaving to help with the American war of independence,
or they were returning after months of fighting on different battle fronts. One man
in particular, that Tristan was required to meet, was a great leader for the mortals,
the Marquis de Lafayette. A great man of the ages, according to Kingston who was
in awe of the young man. However, Tristan wasn't there to be in awe of Lafayette.
He was there in an official capacity, as his Guardian Angel. The problem was,
Tristan wasn't provided the appropriate rank to be able to guard over him. Lafayette
had been one of the men who had recently returned from the Americas and who,

incidentally, had been promoted to Lieutenant General while he was there. This is where they had all met and General Washington had ordered the pair to escort the Frenchman back to Paris and also be an envoy for their cause. It had all fallen in place, with the exception of Tristan's lowly position, as he only held the rank of Captain, not near enough to discreetly influence Lafayette. Tristan and Kingston had been discussing the miscalculated error when they heard a knock at their door. 'Enter,' yelled Kingston. A boy of about sixteen years opened the door and informed them, in broken English, that the commander wished to speak with them, now. The pair looked ominously at each other for a moment, then collected their blue short coats. A grandfather clock in the middle of the room made cuckoo sounds as they left.

*

Walking up the stone steps to Lafayette's office, Tristan and Kingston both wondered what it is they have been summoned for.
'Do you think he's sending us elsewhere? I guess it wouldn't matter, we'd just change his mind if that were the case,' asked Kingston, curiously.

'No, I have no idea what it could be for but we're about to find out,' he said as he knocked on their dragoon commander's door.

'Entrez,' yelled Lafayette and Tristan opened the door. Both men walked inside and Lafayette motioned for them to sit.

'Ahh gentlemen, thank you for joining me. I'll get straight to it. The regiment has received an invitation to dine at Whinter Chateau. According to this finely penned letter from Lady Elora Whinter, it is in our honour, for returning from war unscathed. She adds, "it is not just a simple gathering of Ladies and Gentlemen joining together to celebrate our military men but also to highlight awareness into your regiment's barracks, which I understand are in disrepair!" My understanding of her meaning is to raise funds to help repair our barracks, which we greatly need. I have already put a substantial number of livres into this place myself, to my wife's discontent, but it still requires a lot more. So, I think this little event will be good for us. The reason I have asked you here is because I wish for you to join us,' said Lafayette, taking a sip from his canteen.

'Of course Sir. We would be glad to join you. With your permission, we may be able to gather more support ourselves for our own cause back home,' he said looking directly at Lafayette.

'My thoughts also. So, we are in agreement. We will eat, drink, talk to English aristocracy and take their money,' he said with a scheming smile. Tristan and Kingston looked at one another after their commander's strange remark.

'Sir, forgive me for asking, but, did you just say English?' asked Tristan.

'Yes, I did indeed,' he answered.

'How will we, Americans, get money from the English for a war against their kin?' he asked.

'This host is not your everyday Englishwoman. I have heard that her family might be connected to the Scottish Jacobite rebellion of 45'. Which means, they should have empathy for your cause,' said Lafayette.

'Okay, that does sound promising,' said Kingston, joining in.

Lafayette handed them a piece of paper. 'Here are the details, please pass them onto the men. Everyone is to be correctly dressed and ready for an inspection in an hour. We leave at noon,' he concluded.

'Sir,' said Tristan. Both men stood and left their commander's office to ready the men.

*

The chateau was bustling with excitement as the servants hurried around sorting out flower arrangements, the table layout and ensuring the silverware had been polished. Aurora, supervising everything, stood watch over the setup of the dining hall, making sure no stone was left unturned.

'They will be here in two hours, please hurry,' she implored. The servants murmured 'Oui mademoiselle' as they quickly went about their business. Obviously, Balthazar had already arranged everything in regards to this small event, it was what he did. He enjoyed planning and he was very good at it. The layout of the dining hall was immaculate. Golden fleur de lice flowed up the pale blue walls and reached the ceiling, which was painted with a mural of adorable chubby little cherubs and handsome Angels floating on fluffy white clouds. The long royal blue velvet curtains hung from the ceiling and touched the marble floor below. It was a magnificent sight to behold and Aurora absorbed every nook and cranny, familiarising herself with her surroundings, mainly so that if asked a question about her home, she would be able to answer truthfully. That is to say, as truthfully as an imposter could. The long mahogany dining table had been covered in white silk, silver double candelabras with fine china and newly polished silverware. Vases of roses in a variety of colours filled the gaps. Balthazar had outdone himself yet again. He had also instructed that the white napkins be rolled up, laid on the top of the entrée bowls and tied with ribbon in the French colours, red and blue, the white being the napkin. She understood that the red and blue were the Parisian colours and the white, which separated them all, belonged to the house of Bourbon, their King. A smile formed on her face, *very smart indeed Balthazar*, she thought to herself.

The carriage that held Lafayette, his Second in Command, General Jean Moreau, and Kingston and Tristan came to stop just outside a large stone staircase. The rest of the men had left the barracks before them. Lafayette believed there was no need for a ceremonial façade. He wanted his men to feel relaxed and enjoy the afternoon that was ahead of them, they deserved it. Stepping out of the carriage, they were greeted by two ladies. One, the obvious guardian of the other, her age betraying her, wore the Parisian fashions. She stepped forward and held out her hand to Lafayette who took it into his own and kissed the top. 'Lady Grey, you are just as becoming as when we last met. What was it? A few years ago?' he asked.

'Why yes General, I believe it has gone just three years since we all had tea with my late husband. Time does indeed disappear on you, does it not?' she flirted back.

'Yes, it does indeed,' he grinned.

'Allow me to introduce my cousin's niece, Lady Elora Whinter,' she said, signalling for the girl behind her to step forward. Tristan noticed that she was not actually a girl but a woman. Probably, not yet five-and-twenty, with beautiful flowing golden curls, that brushed her face. Her dress, a pale pink with accents of gold, allowed her green eyes to glimmer like emeralds. He was taken with her beauty almost instantly and didn't hear Lafayette introduce him to their hosts.

'Captain, is everything alright?' Lafayette asked Tristan, after saying his name at least twice.

'Yes, of course, my apologies. My mind was taken aback by the beauty of your home, Lady Whinter,' believing his southern charm had saved him, he took her hand gently into his, and kissed the top just as Lafayette and the other gentlemen had done previously.

'Why thank you Sir, it is quite the beauty, I believe an ancestor of mine built it in the late fourteenth century. It is very remarkable. Now please, do come in and join the rest of your men and our other guests. Please, follow me,' said Aurora, leading them all into the chateau. Tristan watched her from his position beside his commander. Her golden curls bounced on her delicate neck sending a flurry of unfamiliar emotion throughout his body. He blushed and Kingston noticed.

'Are you sure everything is alright brother?' whispered Kingston, who was walking on his left.

'Yes, I'm fine. No need to worry,' embarrassed, Tristan shook whatever he was feeling away and focused on the building instead of Lady Elora Whinter.

Lady Grey and Aurora led the party up the stone steps and through the large ornate double doors into the entryway where they were again greeted, this time by servants to take their coats. The men kept theirs, being military issue, but passed them their leather hats for safe keeping. Once complete, they followed their hosts into the ballroom where music was being played in one corner. In another, were small tables of soldiers playing cards. Gentlemen, soldiers and ladies gossiped to their hearts content throughout the grand room.

'As you can see gentlemen, there is more than just dancing, eating and drinking at today's event. I have also had the servants set up *cavagnole* and some other card games if you were to venture into these. I would have it in my mind to join you, if you so wished,' said Aurora with a sweet smile.

'Lady Whinter, could you please explain what exactly *cavagnole* is?' asked Tristan.

'Why, of course. I'm not sure if you have this game in the colonies, but I'll explain the rules. Please, take a seat and we can all play a game or two before luncheon.' Taking a seat at a round mahogany gaming table, Aurora began explaining the rules.

'Each player is given a card by the dealer, which are divided into five sections. These are randomly numbered, from one through to one hundred and sixty. We, the players, speculate on one numbered section of our cards. Then the dealer places *these* little creatures into this bag, gives it a little shake, and takes one out, revealing the number it hides. The person with that numbered card wins that round and it goes on and on till we are either out of livres or wine,' she laughed, holding a green velvet bag and placing a bunch of oblong shaped ivory beads that held a roll of parchment inside each of them, back into the bag.

'Well, that doesn't sound too difficult to play,' said Kingston.

'No, not at all,' agreed Tristan.

'But gentlemen, you must be civil. The French even have lessons on etiquette in regards to these things. You must not insult them. Do you agree Lieutenant General?' asked Aurora in a flirtatious tone.

'Please call me Joseph and yes, it is our custom to not act like dogs who have been awarded treats whenever we win or to show resentment or fury if we lose. Shall we begin?' he asked, mainly of his American comrades. Aurora fetched one of the servants to be the dealer and then sat down next to Tristan, who shuffled slightly in his chair. Once they had gone through at least three rounds, the tension between her and Tristan began to subside, so she decided to give conversation a chance.

'Captain, you do know that it is common courtesy to make conversation with the person next to you, do you not?' she whispered. Tristan didn't move his eyes off of the card before he responded to her chide.

'Is that also a French thing to do Lady Whinter?' he asked sarcastically.

'Please, don't call me that. My name is Elora. And no, it's just common decency. May I call you by your Christian name? Or do you prefer Captain?' she asked him.

'Ahh, I guess Tristan is fine. I'm not much for decorum anyway,' he said, finally looking at her. She knew why he had refused to look at her directly since their first meeting that afternoon. He was an Angel and one that followed the rules. He had never thought he would fall in love like Lucifer had and Aurora could tell, just by looking into his eyes that he felt something for her. She was going to use that against him.

*

The next day, Balthazar and Aurora stood in the dining hall with wide grins on their faces. 'So, was it a success?' he asked her.

'I do believe it was. He put up a wall after we had first greeted each other, but throughout the afternoon, I broke it down, brick by brick. He even asked me to dance. It was the perfect idea, having the luncheon. Oh, and I have an invitation to tea and a tour of the regiment next month. They are conducting a ceremonial parade for the King, if he's still the King by then that is. Lafayette believes the man, Robespierre, will be there. He wants to introduce us, because we have similar ideals I believe. Should make for an interesting conversation at least,' she laughed.

'Another chance for you to sweep Tristan off of his toes My lady. Did they get what they came for?' he asked Aurora.

'The men were able to get a number of investors to help with the American war, so I believe all were happy. It was another star of the plan to bring them here. Our acquaintance has been created and soon, it will bloom into something more,' she hoped, for her father's sake.

'Since you'll be on show to the people, we will have to sort out your wardrobe. We must do away with the spring pastels and come up with something more, rebellious I think. Yes, rebellious,' he said, enjoying his creative thoughts.

'I'll leave that to you. I need to start planning the next phase,' as she spoke she felt something fall from her nose. Looking down, she saw tiny dark droplets fall to the marble floor. She quickly put her hand up to her nose to block it and looked at Balthazar, who had suddenly gone pale. She realised she was running out of time.

'It's so soon, I thought we had more time! This is a sign of the body decaying is it not?' she gasped in shock.

'Yes, a bloody nose is the first sign My lady. This changes everything. I'll speak to Xerxes, he'll want to know. Now we need to push everything forward. You need to see Tristan before the ceremony,' he said, desperately thinking of ideas.

'How long do we have?' she asked, pulling her skirts to her nose to cull the bleeding.

Balthazar stopped pacing and looked at his mistress. 'Maybe a month, possibly two at most,' he said with a grim look.

'Damn it! Damn it all,' storming off, she climbed the staircase to her rooms and ripped off the bloodstained dress.

Ringing the service bell, she screamed 'Elise!' and awaited her lady's maid to dress her.

'Apologies My lady. Is there anything in particular that you would like to wear?' she asked while grabbing the dirtied pile of clothing from the floor.

'The navy one, with the red collar. It's time we got a move on. I need a modest hair style, with the straw hat,' she answered, cleaning her face. The blood had finally dried up. Elise was another mortal bound in service to Aurora. She had chosen to stay when her brother, Scott, had chosen to leave. She missed him terribly but her mistress treated her well enough, and she never wanted for anything. Anything she desired, Aurora gave to her. The only thing she had to give in return was her unequivocal loyalty, something she gave freely.

'Is everything okay My lady?' she asked Aurora.

'No Elise, the decay has commenced. We are running out of time and we have barely even begun!' she cried in desperation, throwing her hands up to her face.

'My lady, you have more vials, maybe this time around it is just a test and the next time will be the one? I don't pretend to know or understand what it is that you are doing but what I do know is that Xerxes will not fail you,' she said with a smile on her young face.

'You have the face of a youngling but the mind of wise old woman Elise. This is why I keep you close to me. The mind of a mortal like yourself is difficult to find, you are a jewel within my crown. Now, enough of this chatter. I need to get dressed and send Tristan a note to meet me at the Duke of Bedford's salon at noon.

Balthazar, make it sound important,' she ordered, sensing Balthazar entering her

room.

Answering with a nod, he walked over to the small table in the corner and conjured

paper, ink and writing implements and began to scribe.

*

The letter reached Tristan just before he was about to go out for his evening ride.

Upon reading it, he wondered if she had known he was given a day's leave and

wanted to tempt him into spending it with her. The letter had a tone of urgency to it

so he didn't want to cause her any dismay if it were an emergency. He just

wondered why she had asked for him and not his commander, Lafayette, or one of

the other French officers she had known a lot longer. Looking at his horse, he was

already ready to go as it was, he pulled himself up onto his grey gelding and turned

towards the city. He would indulge her this once.

Riding into Paris, his horse's shoes clinked on the cobblestones beneath. To him,

Paris was such an unwelcoming looking city, with its bleak buildings and miserable

peasants roaming the streets, searching for food. He wished he could do something about it, maybe whisper into the King's own ear to give his people bread, instead of pain and hunger. But, he could not. His powers had been restricted since he was demoted during the fall. He did not regret his decision to help Lucifer and his daughter. He knew it was the right thing to do. Even though, as an Angel, he was not privy to make those kinds of decisions, he just couldn't let the child perish within the Pit.

Arriving at the Duke's apartments, he left his horse around the side with the others that were awaiting their owners return. Tidying himself, he knocked on the main door, which opened immediately. He was escorted upstairs and found himself entering a grand ballroom. Something he had not at all expected from an apartment.

'Captain!' exclaimed a familiar voice. 'You have arrived. Please come join me,' Aurora, as beautiful as the day they had met, guided him to a table with two blue velvet chaises. Sitting down in one, he did the same in the opposite chaise.

'Is everything okay? Your letter sounded urgent,' he asked.

Her cheeks flushed with pink at the question. 'Yes. I must admit Captain, I made it sound more important than it truly was. You see, I am not in Paris for much longer and I wanted to get to know you better before I left. Silly, I know and I should not have lied to you. I hope that you can find it in your heart to forgive me?' she urged with bright eyes.

Tristan looked away. Her eyes had pierced his soul. He would not allow it to happen again.

'What about your guardian? I do not see her present. How did you get permission to come here and so last minute?' he questioned.

Her face lit with a smile. 'How old do you believe I am, to require a guardian at all times? She is not my sitter Captain. She is my friend and companion, when I need one. Having her reside with me was the only way I could stay here for as long as I have without my uncle's presence. I am almost five-and-twenty, so you can see, I do not need a guardian anymore,' she said, a slight fury in her tone. Tristan smiled at her briefly, then looked away again. It was so easy to look at her, especially her green eyes. But it was torture all the same.

*

The month of June disappeared from view and Aurora's illness grew worse. She was able to hide it from most but she knew it would not be much longer till she was too weak to do too much, let alone keep it hidden. She had met with Tristan on a number of occasions. Their fleeting moments forced his desire for her to grow stronger. A lot was happening in France also, specifically Paris. Aurora started giving out her estate's produce to those from the most impoverished regions close to home, those lower-class mortals from what the French called the Third Estate.

She even began housing children who had lost their parents to the food shortage and bloody violence. In doing this, she was able to have a tight hold on the poorer community. It wasn't out of the goodness of her heart, even though that is how she played it, it was merely what needed to be done to get the attention of her own class. She had made many enemies among her fellow bourgeoisie, enough to use them as her scape goat. As her body died, her connection to Tristan grew stronger by the day, but it was not strong enough for him to completely trust her, nor let her in. All she needed was to connect to his mind, so that she could locate the key to her father's imprisonment. Upon Tristan's own fall from grace, he was ordered to protect the one thing that kept Lucifer locked away, a feather from his wings. What would seem very insignificant to any human, was the most powerful object any Angel could hold over another. This one little feather was the key to his freedom, to which, Aurora would do anything to retrieve, even give her own life. Over the past few months, she herself had fallen deeper into Tristan's emotional pull, but her feelings for him would not stop her from completing her task. Her mother had given her life so that she could live, and it was within her own power, if required, to do the same for her father. She just needed to connect to Tristan's mind, and it needed to be given willingly on his side, something she had failed to do thus far. The reason as to why he was so different to the others she had mind leeched was due to the Gods. Upon giving him this order, he was also burdened with the freedom to give the information to anyone he so wished. Sounds normal yes, but it would be an act of treachery, of which he was already on trial for in saving the child in the first place. If he gave the information willingly, then that would give the Gods grounds to strip his wings. During his trial, they gave him a second chance and he would not destroy it easily. This was a challenge for Aurora, who had welcomed it, knowing that it would not be without its problems.

Staring into her looking glass, her reflection was grim.

'It is time,' she said unwillingly to Balthazar, who in response, looked down at the ground for a brief second.

Aurora donned her red blouse and royal blue, with white trimmings gown. Wearing the colours of Paris, she left the house.

'Balthazar, make sure they receive the letter at the proper moment. I wouldn't want them to get there too early,' she said, as she stepped up into her open carriage.

Balthazar, standing just on the precipice of the doorway, acknowledged her request and looked down at the letter he was holding in his hand.

'I'll see you again soon My lady,' he whispered and walked back inside, closing the door behind him.

Chapter Fifteen

N'ayez pas d'espoir

'Only in the darkness can you see the stars.'

Martin Luther King Jr

Tristan was waiting by the gate for the arrival of Elora, and the King of course, but

his personal priority was her. It was the ceremonial parade day where Lafayette's

men, and the Kings men, would show off their prestige. Tristan's men were also

taking part, they were to form their own troop on the right side of the French

regiment. The Irish and Swiss guards would also join them. A large number of the

King's musketeers were also taking part and his regiment was in full bloom after

the return of the grenadiers from the American colonies. A large quantity of the

Swiss guards, and what was left of the musketeers, were away guarding the royal

family until their arrival. The commoners had birthed a militia, which were close to

threatening what little peace was left in Paris. Tristan had been waiting a while at

the gate, almost thirty minutes for her arrival but she had still not appeared. She was

always on time, if not early. He had an unnatural feeling of intense unease wash over him. He sprinted back towards headquarters to speak with Lafayette. Knocking on the door, harder than he had meant to, he was granted entry.

'What is it Captain Morholt?' Lafayette asked, slightly alarmed.

'I know this won't matter to you Sir but she's late. She's never late. There must be something amiss,' he babbled.

'Do you mean the Lady Whinter? Well, not only is she late, but the King is also. You were sent out there to greet his men remember? Or was your mind too clouded by the woman's face?' he asked pointedly, placing down the letter he was reading before being rudely interrupted. Tristan thought a moment as to why the King would be late to his own parade. Yes, he was a pompous arse but he was always on time to events, especially military ones.

'There's something wrong, I know it Sir,' he begged.

Lafayette looked him dead in the eyes for a moment, his steel blue eyes cold as stone. Tristan's influence on the General working as he could feel his commander soften slightly.

Lafayette stood up and grabbed his hat and gloves. 'Well, what are you doing just standing there Captain? Gather the men, let us go and see what the fuss is all about,' he said, walking out the door.

'You think I am right Sir?' asked Tristan.

'Yes, I do believe you are. When you first entered my office, I was in the middle of reading a note from the King's guards. The man would've rode straight past you and you didn't even know it! Your head is clearly not in the right place of mind,' he said.

'My apologies Sir. You are completely right, she has clouded my judgement. May I ask what the note said?' he pondered, trailing behind his commander.

'It said they were under attack by the Godless militia, so we must leave to protect the King,' he said, walking towards the stables.

'Does it say why they're attacking?' he asked following Lafayette.

'There seems to be some kind of uproar over the dismissal of the finance minister and...' He stopped. 'It looks like they are also angry over the arrest of a certain Lady, of British descent,' he finished.

Tristan's face turned from unease to horror. 'Elora?' he asked, hoping he was wrong.

'I cannot be sure, but who else do we know with ties to the people's cause, that is a lady of high esteem and is English? I'm sorry Tristan. When was the last you spoke with her?'

'Near a fortnight ago we met at the salon, as we have done for the past month. I wrote her only a few days ago and she replied saying she was *both intrigued and excited about witnessing her first military gala of the Great National Guard*,' he said, trying to recall any other pertinent pieces of information.

'So, she could've been arrested sometime in the last few days. If she was, they kept it well hidden. What does she mean by, the *Great National Guard* though?' he pondered.

'I have no idea, perhaps it's what the people are calling the army? I don't know. Does it say on what charge?' he asked.

'Treason,' he said with a heavy heart.

Tristan's eyes lit up in horror. 'Treason?' he gasped. 'She'll be hanged! That means she'll be in the Bastille. I'll gather the men now Sir,' said Tristan hurriedly.

'Wait a moment Captain. First tell me, are we going there to save the King? Or your love?' Lafayette asked patiently.

'I guess that depends on how loyal you are to the King, *or* the people Sir,' he said with a touch of defiance. Knowing his commander, his ward, was sympathetic to the masses. He had even become their delegate at the Estates General, a general meeting of all three classes; the clergy, nobility and the poor.

Lafayette glowered at him for a moment and then grinned. 'Go ring the bell.' He ordered and Tristan ran to the other side of the compound and rang the alarm.

*

The streets of Paris were overwhelmed with thousands of wrathful peasants clawing at their farmhand weapons, thirsty for blood. Tristan even thought they were possessed by Demons, as he witnessed a woman gnashing her teeth, incensed with an inhuman behaviour as she helped drag a thrashing body down the cobbled road.

'What in God's name is going on?' yelled Lafayette. 'Is that the Governor, de Launey?' he asked no one in particular. Tristan and Kingston both looked at the man that was being dragged through the streets by the insane mob.

'Didn't we send Swiss grenadiers to help support him last week? Where are they?' asked Tristan, searching for the soldiers. 'Are those the King's own Guard running *with* the horde?' he roared.

'It looks like it. There is not much we can do here, we are outnumbered. Let us find Lady Whinter and return to the garrison,' Lafayette suggested.

Tristan looked towards the Bastille, smoke bellowed from a number of levels.

'We must hurry,' he said, riding off towards the towering prison.

The remnants of militia, still hovering around the Bastille, put their guard up upon the arrival of Lafayette and his men. Aiming their weapons at them, the leader, a scrawny excuse for a man, spoke up.

'Arrêtez,' he shouted at them to stop. Lafayette gracefully, without intimidation, jumped down off his horse and handed the reins to Tristan. Somehow, he got into the ear of the scrawny man, who ordered his men to lower their muskets and move out of the way.

'Sir, what did you say to him?' asked Kingston.

'Merely that we are not here to stop them, we only seek one of our own who had been imprisoned here a few days ago. I asked him if she was here and his answer was *yes*. He told me where to locate her, but,' he stopped, thinking about what to say next.

'But what Sir?' asked Tristan, desperation in his voice.

'His words were, "n'ayez pas d'espoir," meaning,' again, he stopped, not wanting to translate but the look on Tristan's face moved him. 'Do not have hope,' he finished with a grim expression in his eyes.

Tristan understood the man clearly. He knew every language there was to know in the realm of mortals. It was embedded within his mind from the day of their creation.

'With respect Sir, either take me to her now or tell me where she is.'

Lafayette turned towards the Bastille, and headed for the door closest to them. They moved up a wide stone spiral staircase and down a long and darkened hallway, with nothing but fiery torches lighting their way. They had passed at least four locked doors on both sides of the hall before they reached one that was open, a couple of militia guarding it. Lafayette put his hand out to stop Tristan from rushing the room.

'Tristan, wait. Let me tell the guards to leave first,' he said, with empathy in his voice. Tristan nodded and stepped behind him. Lafayette moved forward to the men wearing the colours of Paris and after a moment of stern discussion back and forth, the guards, and a woman from within the room, left. He looked to Tristan and then back into the prison cell where Lady Elora Whinter laid on the ground, unmoving. As soon as Tristan saw her, he rushed to Aurora and fell to the ground beside her. Taking her head, he pushed away the rags she was resting on and cradled her head in his arms.

'Elora, please wake up. It's me, Tristan. Can, can you hear me?' he whispered desperately. Slowly her eyes opened to his voice, somehow, beneath the dried-up blood that was smeared across her face, was a smile. She opened her mouth to say something but all he heard was silence. Taking a breath, she began to cough, nearly choking on her own blood.

'What, what do I do?' said Tristan looking up at Kingston and Lafayette, completely distraught. 'Is there anything we can do?' he shouted looking to Kingston who sombrely shook his head. The two men couldn't speak. After a moment, Lafayette whispered something into Kingston's ear and left the room. Upon his return, he had a jug of water and some rags.

He leant down beside Aurora and Tristan and gently said, 'All we can do now is make her comfortable.' Soaking the ragged cloth in the water, he handed it to Tristan, who tenderly wiped Aurora's brow. Looking back up at Tristan, she again opened her mouth to speak.

'Tris...Tristan,' she spluttered. Tristan hushed her, trying to stop her from wasting her energy. It was just the two of them left in the small dimly lit cell now.

'No, let me. I, I need you to thank the two, the two men outside. Please,' she begged, trying to raise her arm in the direction of the door. Tristan thought for a moment, trying to comprehend what she was trying to say.

'Do you mean the two militia men that were on guard outside the door?' he asked.

'Yes, yes. They gave me their coats. It's all they have and they gave them to me! Why? Why would they do that?' she began to cry and cough at the same time. Tristan realised then that the rags he had thrown, that were positioned under her head were not rags at all. It was one of the men's coat. The other was still draped over her torso. They had literally given her the clothing off their backs to comfort her. Tears welled up in his eyes then, sometimes mortals surprised him and this was one of those times.

'You have my word Elora, I will let them know. But, who, who did this to you and how long have you been here?' he stuttered. After wiping away the blood and dirt from her face, he revealed bruising and cuts. Under the coat, he saw she was only wearing a shift, torn and bloodied from the wounds that had been inflicted upon her. Touching her face, he tried to see her memories, but they were too broken to comprehend.

'The King's guards. They, they said I was a traitor to the, to the crown. I, I can't remember when.' She coughed, now struggling to breath. Tristan rocked her gently back and forth, trying to silence her pain with his warmth.

'I'm so sorry, I didn't know they had taken you. If I had of known, I, I would have come directly. I would have been here. I didn't know! I didn't know,' he repeated, tears flowing freely now.

'Shhhh, it's okay. Tris-tan, it's okay. You're here now, you're holding me. Don't stop holding me,' she forced herself deeper into his warm embrace. Tristan held her tighter, never wanting to let her go. His heart was beating as fast as a cheetah could run, he could almost feel it in his throat. The blood had rushed to his hands, away from his face, making him feel ill. He knew what was coming next, he just couldn't bring himself to think about it. All he wanted was for her to be okay and retribution for what they had done.

'No, you can't,' she said, reading his thoughts. 'The girl, before you, told me...she said, they took the guards and hung them up outside. Tristan, it hurts, it hurts so much. Please, please make it stop. Tristan!' she cried, coughing up blood. She reached up and grasped his hand with her own, squeezing it tight.

'Elora, I, I,' he couldn't finish the sentence. Her grasp had loosened, and what used to be her bright green eyes, had become dull. Her final breath escaped into the pungent air around them, suffocating him. She was gone. Tristan held her still, rocking her body back and forth, his mind lost to blank thoughts.

Now he understood the pain. He understood what Lucifer had felt, what *he* had lost and he never wanted to feel it ever again.

Chapter Sixteen

The Forbidden Fruit

John Milton

The red apple sat on the granite benchtop, emanating a poisonous air. The room was empty besides Aurora, Xerxes and Balthazar, all of whom were staring intently at the lone apple.

'Is this meant to be a joke Xerxes?' asked Aurora, not looking away from the apple.

'Well, I did think it would be slightly ironic Commander. As it is the new mixture, I thought it was the right thing to do to make the moment, less, serious,' he said with an awkward laugh. Xerxes, unlike his fallen kin was not a warrior. Before the Fall, he was just a simple Lower Angel that followed the rules and stayed hidden within the shadows of those with greater purpose than he. One of those shadows belonged to Lucifer. Like her father, Aurora understood Xerxes and found him to be one of the greatest intellects of her kind. He was a loner, but he realised that it was better to be free and a part of something greater than oneself even for a brief moment in time, than to be forced into servitude for eternity.

Balthazar grinned and slapped Xerxes on the back. 'Will it work better this time around?' he asked.

'Yes. I am quite confident. Whereas, the last time I was only seventy-eight per cent confident,' he answered.

Balthazar rolled his eyes. 'What is the percentage this time?' he asked, sarcasm flashed in his regal tone.

'I would say, at least ninety-one per cent. My test subjects held on until the eleventh-month mark, so our commander, being an Archangel, should reach to the twelfth or thirteenth. I don't need to worry you with the exact calculations, as your mind could not handle them,' he smiled, knowing Balthazar was mocking him.

'There's my boy,' said Balthazar, sending a brotherly punch into Xerxes's shoulder.

'Why must you always hit me!' demanded Xerxes, rubbing his arm.

'Gentlemen. That's enough. Balthazar, have you informed our connection within the house of my pending arrival?' asked Aurora, still looking at the apple.

'Yes Commander, she knows exactly where to locate you. You have prepared her well, she will be an asset.' Turning towards her with a look of concern he continued. 'Aurora, are you sure you're ready for this? It won't be like the last time, or the time before that. Witnessing him see you die more than once, I can see has changed him greatly. He won't be as easily seduced, especially if he believes you to be some kind of demonic entity, which I think he will this time,' he added, attempting to get her attention. Aurora blinked, turning her eyes away from the apple to focus on Balthazar.

'I'm ready. This is it. Our last chance to get the key. We have only one elixir left after this, but that must be used at a later date. If I can't get it myself, plan B it will have to be. Either way, we will succeed. My last two attempts were failures but he will see who I truly am this time,' she swore, turning her gaze back to the apple.

'Maybe this technological world was what we were waiting for. France and Germany were not the right times,' said Xerxes.

'They were our stepping stones to this very moment. We needed them to see how the elixir worked with my body. I needed them, to introduce myself to him. Manipulating him through our own means. In a way, through truth,' she sighed.

'So, you do love him then?' asked Balthazar.

'Perhaps. It is something I will have to put aside however. My priority is father,' she said without emotion. Balthazar and Xerxes glanced quickly at each other.

'On another note, here are your new credentials Commander,' said Balthazar, handing over a manila folder to Aurora. Opening it up, she took out an A4 sheet of paper with details about her identity, a London driver's licence, an Australian study visa, a British passport, credit cards and a mobile phone.

'My name is El Smith? You couldn't have come up with something more plausible?' she grumbled. 'I'm assuming you hope that my accent will be English again?' she added.

'Well the last two times it has been that way, so I think it is an accurate assumption. Or, you could just fake it,' said Xerxes, matter of factly.

'And I'm an archaeology student in Australia? Why would I be studying archaeology in Australia if I'm from England for goodness sake?' she questioned, slightly flustered.

'Well, it would seem you are interested in their Aboriginal culture. Your specialty is mythology. You've studied all of the classics and now you want to do something out of your comfort zone. So, Australia it is!' said Balthazar with a beaming grin of excitement.

'Indeed. What about the girl?' she asked.

'Elizabet? Yes, I have been watching her of late and discreetly formed new memories within her mind. She will think you to be her best friend, even though you have never actually met. Having a new aged descendant of MacGregor will be useful here,' he answered. Seeing her face become slightly flustered he added, 'Aurora, calm down. Our plan will work this time. It has to,' he said, putting a comforting hand on her shoulder. Aurora sighed in defeat and placed everything back into the folder. After gripping his hand with her own in response, she moved around to the other side of the bench.

'Fine. Let us play this game for the last time then, shall we,' she said, picking up the apple and walking over to an armchair. Taking a seat, she made herself comfortable.

'Remember to only tell me what is required before we move to the next stage. We don't need any mistakes. Oh, and Balthazar. Please take on a more realistic human form this time, I don't think your last one was really convincing especially since I was merely just a nurse,' she implored.

'What was wrong with Churchill? I didn't think it was that unconvincing,' he laughed. Walking over to her, he kissed her on the forehead.

'For Lucifer,' he said in remembrance.

Aurora looked up at him and said in return, 'And Pandora.' Taking a bite from the apple, she immediately felt a change in her body. The gut wrenching pain took over, closing her eyes she willed herself to drift off into unconsciousness, the transformation into a mortal taking effect. It was amazing what a Fallen Angel with some mystical ingredients and a recipe could do to change one's fate. Balthazar picked up her limp body and took her to her bedroom, where he laid her down in her bed.

'How long will it take this time?' he asked laying a woollen blanket over her.

'I couldn't say. You know the elixir is not fully tested. Without another Archangel it will always be inconsistent for her. We just don't have enough of it left. All I can do is analyse her whilst she has taken the draft we have in play. So I would be guessing and I do not like to guess,' Xerxes responded.

'Let us hope that this one goes well.'

'It has to, it's our last chance. If what the Fates said about Tristan comes to pass, anymore attempts will cause him great harm, and not to mention we would need another Tyrant. You know how hard it is to find them unless they have been released from the Pit. In a way, we were lucky they let this one go to destroy Aurora. If they had not we would be stuck, no plan for the return of her father,' said Xerxes.

'You forget brother, I am aware of all of this. Enough, let's leave her until she wakes. We need to inform the others; the plan is now in motion,' finished Balthazar, leaving the room and Aurora behind.

Chapter Seventeen

The Watchers

Melbourne, Australia

Sometime in the Present

The training room was silent. No word was uttered, nor could the sound of a single breath be heard. The senior Nephilim stood in a straight line, facing their leader, waiting for his next command. They hadn't moved for at least thirty-five minutes and would not, for another thirty-five more if Kingston had anything to do with it.

'Everyone, relax,' spoke Tristan quietly as he looked out at his Nephilim warriors. 'Now, do you see how difficult it is to not be heard for longer than it takes for this tiny insignificant candle to melt?' he asked.

'I'm annoyed that the packaging clearly states that it is a one hour candle, I want my money back,' demanded James, in a not so serious tone. The others sent him a sideways glare, hoping to the Gods that Tristan didn't make them do that again.

'Indeed,' said Tristan. 'Perhaps we should move onto stage two then?' he incited with a grin. 'Kingston, you're up. I'll be in my office if you need me,' he yelled behind him as he left the training hall. All of the Nephilim turned their heads to James, sending imaginary daggers his way.

'Come on guys, why does no Angel have a sense of humour?' he asked with an awkward smile.

'After ten years of being our ward James, you have clearly not learnt anything about our "sense of humour". Everyone, on my command, make your way to the pool. Our next phase is to practice what we have just completed, within the water,' commanded Kingston. Everyone turned white with disbelief.

'He's kidding, right?' asked Liam hopefully.

'No. I don't believe he is. His face suggests otherwise,' answered Cyrus.

'Move!' ordered Kingston. The Nephilim moved swiftly to the edge of the pool, where the next command was given to dive into the deep end.

'Now that we know what time we need to beat, commence silent manoeuvre,' he ordered, and everyone, begrudgingly, dove into the water.

After a full day of training, Tristan's sterilised office was the solitude he had desired. It was a symbol of his oath to never fall in love again, with anyone, or anything. Keeping everything clean and crisp, or, *dull and emotionless,* as Sienna always said, was what helped him to forget his pain. Since he had met Elora, the first time in France and then as Lora in Germany during the Second World War, he had never forgiven himself for letting her take his guard down. Both times, in the wake of her death, or deaths, he had been a complete wreck. He believed himself to be cursed by the Gods, cursed to love her and then see her die again and again, as if he were stuck within some tragic soap opera or teen movie. He was just waiting for it to happen again. Whenever he stepped out onto the street, he was always searching for her in the crowd. He didn't understand how she could come back, he knew of people being resurrected but she needed someone close to her to do that. Someone who cared for her enough to gather what was required for such a dangerous procedure. Both times he had met her, there was no one else; he knew this, as he would secretly look into her mind. He wasn't completely sure yet of what was required for a resurrection as it was a power given to those way above his current rank status, but he had his best warrior on the case. Training the Watchers kept him busy, and secretly investigating his lost love's fate was something he was keeping on the side, away from prying eyes like the Valkyrie. His brightest Nephilim warrior, a Watcher of mortals, was helping him to do so. So far, Estelle had figured out that a number of sacrificial blood acts were needed, but she had yet to decipher of what or who. They had realised together that there may be a connection to all of the blood killings they had been investigating, as a celestial force conducted them all. They knew this because there was a sign of celestial interference left behind at all of the sites where the victim's bodies were located. They just needed to narrow down the *who*. This was difficult though, as they weren't actually permitted to investigate any celestial crime. They were only

Guardians. Kingston and Tristan were the protectors of the Nephilim Watchers that they had charge of. They were required to train them and guide them, because *they* were the protectors of mortals against the demonic celestial forces. It was only on rare occasions that either of them would join the Nephilim on a hunt, but since the rise in mortal deaths at celestial hands across the century, they have joined them every now and again.

Tristan sat down at his computer and scrolled through his emails. He had subscribed to a number of different mortal investigative news reporters, following them on Twitter and Instagram to see if any of their reports unknowingly picked up on any celestial activity. One amateur student journalist he followed was obsessed with linking every story to the supernatural. At first he dismissed her for one of those ridiculous Melbourne hipster types, but then he noticed something in the background of one of her posts that had randomly popped up in his feed one day. She had posted an old photo of a Melbourne alleyway that showed a taped off area and some police officers. What had caught his attention was that *he* was also in the picture. He was standing behind one of the officers with a shadow of another man beside him, Kingston. Intrigued but slightly unnerved that he had been caught by the photographer, he clicked *subscribe* on the girl's blog, *Paper Truth*. Nothing out of the ordinary had happened over the last couple of weeks for Tristan to justify sending the Watchers out for a hunt. They were growing bored, and with boredom comes disorder. He needed to get them outside before they became too idle. His eyes lit up when he saw a new post from *Paper Truth*. She wrote, "I have heard rumours of a demon hideout in the Melbourne Underground". He was interested to see if these rumours were true. As usual, the amateur sleuth was hiding her sources, but so far her findings, unbeknown to her, had actually been quite accurate. She was becoming very close to receiving a visit from the Valkyrie as she was very near to breaking the surface to their secret world. He hadn't been to the Underground in nearly a century. It was too much of a coincidence for him not to join in on the hunt this time around. He reached for his phone and dialled Kingston's number.

'We have a hunt. Get them ready, we leave at dusk,' he ordered, ending the conversation with the touch of his finger.

*

The sky began to darken and the Nephilim gathered in their library, dressed to impress. Kai, Estelle's twin brother and a loner, was already halfway through *Little Dorrit* when he was interrupted by Tristan's voice.

'Guys, move in. Tonight is a simple one. There are rumours of a demonic hideaway within the Underground. Now, the best way for us to get in, is most likely through the tunnels, as the members will not let us in through the main entrance. We all know how friendly the Fallen are especially to those who police them. So we will have to do this the dirty way. If you look to the board, here is where I mean,' said Tristan, pointing with a bronze dagger at a photograph of the underground train tracks.

'Is that Flinders Street?' asked James, taking notes on his commslink, a lovely little piece of advanced gadgetry created by Liam, their engineer-in-training.

'Yes. There is a door to the Underground through the upper tunnel. We will need a glamour, to hide away from prying eyes but other than that, it should be easy enough to get in with a blood key. The Nephilim blood-link to the Celestial world is not as strong as ours, so Kingston and I will take care of that. Once we are inside, we need to split up into three groups. So, Liam, Cyrus and James, you're together. Sienna, Caleb and Kingston another. Finally, Kai and Estelle, you're with me. We can stay in contact as usual by our commslink. Estelle, step forward,' taking a step to the side, Tristan allowed Estelle to explain the rest, as it was her plan in the first place. Slightly nervous, as she was not expecting this, she moved to the front of her peers.

'What we're looking for are signs of a demonic presence. There have been numerous sightings in this area by members of the Fallen, but nothing concrete as of yet. And no one reliable enough is speaking, so we are going off of old news and hearsay. It is mostly rumours at this stage, as you would all know, the Fallen don't like to tittle-tattle on their brethren. There is however, evidence of a large quantity of missing people around this particular area over the last century. They range between the ages eleven and twenty-eight and they are all female,' she stopped for a moment to let it all sink in. 'Before I go on, are there any questions so far?' she asked the others.

'How many have disappeared? And do we have exact dates of their disappearances?' asked Kai.

'The exact number of missing persons is ninety-nine. The dates of their disappearances obviously differ from each other, but they begin in 1921, with one for each year until now. The only complete body that has been found was the very first little girl that went missing in 1921. Her details are in my report,' said Estelle.

'So, if this has been occurring over a ninety-nine-year period, we are nearly at some kind of one-hundred-year anniversary then.' stated Liam.

'Yes, you are correct.'

'So why are we only doing something about it now?' he continued.

'Because, it is something that has not really had a light shined upon it until now. The deaths were not important enough to the Valkyrie. There was not enough celestial evidence left behind for mortals to comprehend and use to prove our existence with. Kingston and I investigated the first celestial murder of the young girl but after that, we were forbidden to investigate further.' Tristan answered.

'What about Valkyrie now? Have they finally come to their senses?' asked Kai.

'Celeste is embarrassed by this outcome, so we will not receive any support from her. I have been given the opportunity to prove myself and in doing so, so have you. We must figure this out, and soon, before the next disappearance in the New Year. Oh, I'll also add, that the man responsible for the murder of the first missing child was apprehended,' said Tristan.

'And?' asked Sienna excitedly.

'And, it wasn't by us. It was by whomever it is causing the multiple deaths and sacrifices around the globe. This is something Estelle and I are still working on, so I'll not worry you with the details yet. This Angel killed the murderer; we know it is an Angel because of what was left behind by the perpetrator; the remains of the murderer. It was obvious that Angel Light had killed him. Also, the murderer was not human either. He was Nephilim, possessed by his own demons,' said Tristan, returning to the back of the room. The Nephilim warriors began to whisper in excitement to one another. Estelle took charge again.

'Okay, quiet please. Back to why we are here. What we need to look for is sulphuric powder residue, burns or slime. As you all know, when a Demon manifests from a human form into their original form, he or she leaves behind one of these three things. We need to take samples and if there is a definite trail left behind, we need to investigate further to see if we can locate some of these girls and hunt some Demons,' she finished, blending back into the group. One by one, each member of the hunt asked a question or two, ensuring they understood the plan. Huddling closer as a group, with one hand on another's shoulder, Tristan took out a portal-stone and surged them to the Flinders Street tunnels in the blink of an eye, appearing out of thin air beneath the station's main entry point.

'I'll never get used to that,' whispered Liam into Sienna's ear, who responded with a slight giggle. Night trains passed them by, the passengers unable to see the group of Nephilim Watchers and Guardian Angels as they stared numbly out their windows.

'Guys, this is it,' said Tristan in a low voice, feeling around for the concealed door. Both Tristan and Kingston brought a blade to the palms of their hands, slicing them gently and wiping the blood onto the surface of a graffiti smothered wall.

'Remember, once we're inside, spread out and be on your guard. Once we're on the other side of the entrance within the club, be sure to change your attire to suit the locale. Be bold, be brave and never forget those who stand beside you,' said Tristan, hitting the left side of his chest with his right hand, tightly curled into a fist. In perfect unison, his warriors followed suit, their right hands, curled into fists and landing on the left side of their chests. Tristan turned and walked through the opening in the wall, the others following their leader.

Chapter Eighteen

Through the Veil

A cool breeze brushed past the warriors as they pushed through the pitch black of the hollowed-out wall. Every now and then, the smell of rotten eggs would smother them, making them almost gag. Sienna, the youngest in the group, had wrapped a black scarf around her face before reaching the door, in preparation for the horrid stench. This wasn't because she was the brightest bulb within the batch, merely because Estelle, who was the most intelligent of this particular Nephilim troop, told her to bring it, just in case. When she asked why, Estelle had answered, 'Because sulphur doesn't really smell bad at all. It's sulphur dioxide or hydrogen sulphide that has the 'delightfully tangy' or rotten-eggs stench. They can occur in most heated underground areas, or bacteria-infested waters, and because we mostly locate demonic entities within these particular areas, they have a certain smell about them, as well as leaving a residue behind. Fascinating, isn't it?' Sienna rolled her eyes and apologised for asking. At the same time, she secretly shoved a small scarf in the pocket of her jacket anyway. They had finally reached the Underground, a *celestial only* nightclub, where mostly the Fallen and other Angels hung out.

Splitting off into their groups, and trying to look normal, they began to investigate discreetly.

Thirty minutes into being inside the Underground, Sienna and her team pretended to be interested in a Fallen Angel's story about finally getting a tattoo. At first, they believed she had known something but it turned out to be just a story about her tattoo. It wasn't very interesting to any of them but they had to look inconspicuous to everyone else around them. Sienna had a limited amount of patience so she faded away from the conversation without the tattooed Angel ever realising. The other two watched her disappear into the crowd with a slight look of panic on their faces. Sienna was the type of girl who loved to gossip and be the centre of attention, not this time though. She really wanted to find something significant to get the investigation rolling. Obviously, she wanted to be the first one to locate evidence, but that meant blending in. This was something she was not quite used to doing. She pressed up against the back wall of the nightclub and looked around the room. After a few moments, when the music eased, she thought she heard a thump. Attempting to debunk the noise, she glanced sideways at the Angels closing in on the wall, about a metre to her right but no, it wasn't them. They were barely leaning against the wall to make a sound like she had just heard. *Thump!* She heard it again but this time she felt it too, directly behind her. *Thump! Thump!* Again and again she heard it. Looking left and right, she saw that the left side of the wall curved inwards. Following it, a tacky silk curtain rudely interrupted her. Believing it was covering up a hidden door, she moved it slightly but only found a solid brick wall behind. Underwhelmed, she drooped her shoulders slightly but almost immediately was shaken, literally, by two unknown hands grabbing her shoulders. Slightly freaked out, she grabbed the hand on her right shoulder and flipped the owner over her body and into the solid brick wall before her.

'Argh, Sienna! What was that for?' complained Liam.

'Liam! I'm so sorry. You scared the crap out of me. Why in Hades would you sneak up on me like that?' she protested.

'So, it's my fault, is it?' he asked, rubbing the back of his head.

'Well, what are you doing over here with me? You're meant to be with your own team!' she snapped at him.

'I just saw you over here looking like you had found something, so I thought I'd come and see what. But, I guess, looking at the wall that you smashed me into, you haven't found a thing,' he said, with a sly grin on his face. His sun-kissed skin and brown eyes made up for everything he had just done. Sienna helped him up and kissed him on the back of the head, then on his cheek.

'Is that all you got?' he asked with a puppy-dog look. Liam and Sienna had been together seven years and that look still worked.

Grinning back, she slapped him on the bum and said 'Good boy.'

Before he could retaliate, another *thump* was heard, this time by both of them.

'You heard that, didn't you?' she asked Liam, who nodded in reply.

Feeling around the brick, Liam turned back to Sienna and gave her a kiss on the lips. Before she could scold him for the public display of affection, the grinding of gears stopped her and the brick wall in front of them slowly moved out of view.

*

There was a sharp pain digging into Aurora's arm, she reached over slowly with her other hand to brush whatever it was away, but found it was actually tightly imbedded into her skin. Shooting her eyes open, she angled her head towards her arm to see a plastic tube, crudely taped down, with some kind of grey liquid either going into her body, or coming out, she couldn't be sure. Her whole body was aching, she tried to get up and pull the tube out of her arm but realised she was tied down to something. Once her eyes had focused properly, she could clearly see that she was tied with some kind of cording to a concrete slab and she wasn't the only one. Tilting her head from one direction to the other, she could see maybe two more slabs with others also tied down. Closing her eyes, she tried to remember anything that had happened prior to this very moment. She couldn't. The only exception being, her name, El Smith and that she was a student but couldn't remember what she studied exactly or where. She stretched her body to see how loose the cord was and she was able to pull her right arm out from underneath. Whoever it was that had taken her did not go to Scouts that was a definite. She pulled herself loose from the rest of the terribly knotted cording and, counting to three, she pulled the plastic tubing out of her arm. Dropping it to the floor, the grey liquid oozed out. *It was going in*, she realised. Slightly disgusted at the thought of an ooze that was being pumped inside her body. She moved to the wall that detained her and the other two girls. After looking around for an exit, she realised that she should probably check on the other prisoners. Checking the younger of the two first, she looked to be in her mid-teens, her pulse was weak but it was there. Aurora moved onto the other, who looked like she was maybe in her thirties, unfortunately, she couldn't find a pulse. Placing the back of her hand to the woman's face, Aurora assumed that she had been gone a little while, the icy touch of her skin sent a shiver down her spine. She shuffled back to the younger girl and tried to wake her up but she seemed to be unconscious. She untied her and removed the tube from her arm. Aurora was very weak at this point and barely able to hold herself up. She leaned on the girl's concrete slab. She had no idea how to get out of this place. There were no windows and no doors. The only thing she could see letting the slightest bit of air in was a grate in the ceiling. There were two lights and four slabs, what you might find in an old surgery. Panic rose up within her now and all she could think to do was bang on the walls to see if there was anyone who could hear her, which she would continue to do till her heart let out.

*

Tristan noticed Liam separate from his team, following him with his eyes, he saw Sienna disappear into a different part of the club. He decided to inform the others to also break away from the dance floor and lounge area that they were all hovering around, intermittently, to see what Sienna had found. When Tristan came upon the two Nephilim, he witnessed Liam find an entry point on a brick wall behind them, which opened up.

'Well done guys. How did you find this?' he asked them.

'*I* found it, just by my brilliant analysis of the scene. I noticed that the wall curved inwards, and thought it was strange, so I followed it around and there it was, a random brick wall,' answered Sienna, pompously.

'Well, you didn't know if there was anything different about it till I figured it out Si,' said Liam.

'Whatever. I still found it. Anyway, are we going in? Where are the others?' asked Sienna, looking around nonchalantly.

'Yes, just waiting on them to get here. Here they come. No one is saying a thing, so I don't think we're going to get many answers to our questions from this lot. This little hide away however, is very interesting,' said Tristan, glancing behind him as the others started filing into the small hall-like space.

'What is with the design of this joint? It doesn't make sense at all. You have barely any doors, which I get, because everyone is mostly Angels, who don't need doors. But, what about these random arse shaped walls? I mean, why does it curve like this? And then lead up to nothing but a curtained brick wall?' complained Caleb.

'That's because this isn't just a wall Caleb. It leads somewhere and look! Sulphur residue!' said Estelle, pointing at the ground beyond the wall.

'The slimy kind,' said Cyrus, finally speaking.

'Wow, he speaks!' said Sienna laughing, greatly amused with herself. Cyrus merely kept his eye on the dimly lit cavern before them, ignoring her childish comment.

'Are we going to enter Tristan?' he enquired.

'Yes, I believe we are. Spread out, it looks like it'll become quite narrow the further we go. Is there anything else we should know Sienna?' asked Tristan.

'Oh! Yes! I heard thumping on the wall, like someone was punching it from the other side.' She answered.

'That could be the missing girls. Strange that Nephilim can hear the noise, but not the Angels. Do you think they know what lies behind the wall and don't really care?' mused Estelle aloud.

'Possibly, most miscreants that come here are of the Fallen and are not widely known for their compassion towards mortals. If it doesn't affect them, it doesn't matter. Let's go, if it is them, they could be trapped. I can't seem to sense anything off anything though so I guess the walls must be spelled. Estelle, take a sample, we'll test it back at the lab. Move out,' ordered Tristan.

He stayed in the front, with Kingston holding the rear. Moving forward, they came across a number of animal carcasses, namely rats, leaving a horrid decaying smell behind them. The yellow lights on the walls high above, glimmered intermittently. *Why had he never known this area was here?* He asked himself. He understood there was an area below, where the remains of the little girl's murderer back in 1921 was located but not this part. Unless it was newly placed here not long after. The sample would answer his question. Each member of the team held out their own version of an Angel blade as they moved further down the narrow space. Once a Nephilim graduated from their initial training, they were handed a piece of Angel steel from the Gods. The member would then craft their own weapon, being a set of throwing daggers, a bow and arrow or even a long sword. Whatever it was, it needed to be practical for its owner to yield in battle. Only the highest members of Seraph Warriors, such as the Valkyrie and High Guard yielded weapons made from Featherstone, gifted usually from their own wings, making them truly belong to those who held them. Everyone else, yielded the Angel steel, which was forged in the Incendium, making it flawless and untouchable to any type of mortal weapon.

Prior to entering the hallway, the hunting party removed their club attire, revealing their hunter's dress. A uniform, that only qualified members of the Nephilim Watchers were approved to wear. It had the ability to shrink close to the skin, so it could be hidden beneath normal mortal clothing. Finally, they had reached a precipice, some kind of celestial threshold. Behind it, they could hear movement, more thumping on walls, and even a voice.

'Did anyone else hear that? 'It sounded like a female voice,' asked Sienna, closing her ear to the wall. Upon touching it, it glimmered slightly and revealed the other side.

'It's a glamour. I can see three people, two alive one possibly deceased,' said Kai. Tristan focused his eyes on a young woman moving slowly around the room. She was the one making the noise, attempting to get someone's attention, not caring whose. For a moment, he thought she looked familiar but he couldn't see her face clear enough to figure out why or who she was. Before moving through the veil, Tristan sent Caleb and Cyrus back to stand guard at the entrance. This was now a scene of celestial misconduct and possible murder. Once they had deemed the area safe from demonic activity they would bring in the big guns and close down the Underground.

'Everyone ready?' asked Kingston. Everyone nodded their heads in acknowledgment and, with Tristan leading the way, they walked through the glamour and entered the enclosed room beyond it.

Chapter Nineteen

Stone Cold

"Bitterness is like cancer. It eats upon the host. But anger is like fire. It burns it all clean."

Maya Angelou

Aurora's hands began to bleed from the continuous blows that she forced onto the walls

that surrounded them. Stopping for breath, she moved back to where the younger girl was,

to see if there was any change, nothing. She felt as she should just give up, just lay down

and die but she couldn't. *What if there is someone out there who loves me*, she thought.

She couldn't do that to them, that was selfish. She just couldn't remember if there was

anyone, which made her heart sink. Out of the corner of her eye, she saw something

shine. Turning her head towards the rear of the room, she stood up straight and stared at

the wall for a moment to see if it was just her mind playing tricks on her. She saw it

clearly now, as if a curtain had been hung from the ceiling above, shivering slightly in a

non-existent breeze, glittering in the grey room. She wasn't sure what to do. She could

feel her blood rise, sending anxiety throughout her body. Thinking quickly, she moved

behind the concrete slab in front of her and ducked down, attempting to hide. Hearing

voices, she stole a look from around the corner of the slab and saw a number of people dressed in strange clothing move in through the shimmering wall. Her mind was a maze of questions as some of them, were moving towards *her*.

'Step out from behind the bench, slowly,' said a commanding voice, a voice she thought she recognised.

'We will not harm you, we're here to help,' said another, more compassionate voice, *female* she thought.

Slowly standing up, she manoeuvred herself so she could lean against the slab or bench as they had called it. Her tattered clothing clung to her clammy skin, torn by, what she could only assume was the attack that brought her here. She stared back at her onlookers. They looked human but she couldn't be sure, with them walking through a wall and all. She scanned their faces for the one who belonged to the voice she thought she might know, one face came into view, *his face*, she thought, *I know his face.* He began to walk towards her, a stone-cold expression on his face. He spoke no words as he approached her. When he reached her, he placed his hands on either side of her head. The pain Aurora felt was incredibly intense, enough for her to release an audible scream. Her sight disappeared and all she saw was a bright white light and nothing else. She could feel her knees about to give way, her body started to shake under his excruciating touch. She heard a mix of different voices, yelling out and shouting at him to let her go. When he did let go, she stumbled backwards, out of fear and exhaustion. The ache she had felt previously had electrified tenfold and all she wanted to do now was fall, and fall she did, with everything that was grey turning black.

Chapter Twenty

Resurrection

Tristan's office felt brighter than usual as he paced the white room, slowly beginning to wear out the carpet. *It was her*, he thought. *It had to be her, but how?* He asked himself, over and over again. Kingston sat, watching him quietly move backwards and forwards repeatedly. Tristan was at a loss for words, or comprehension. He knew the God's punishment for his small betrayal would never end but he never thought they would go this far.

'Do I have to go to them and beg them to stop? Is that what they want? Me, to go down onto my knees, and beg?' he asked in disbelief.

'No, you know my view on this, I still do not believe this is their doing. If you go to them, you'll be admitting your feelings for a mortal, and dig this pit of yours even further to Hades,' said Kingston. Standing up, he walked over to his brother in arms.

'Brother, we'll figure this out. If she is who she says she is, we'll know. If she is a resurrection of Elora and Lora, then, well, we'll deal with it. We just have to figure out, why she dies the way she does so we can maybe counteract it. We know the signs now, let me help you figure this out,' pleaded Kingston.

Tristan continued to pace. 'Was I too harsh? Lashing out like that? Sienna hasn't spoken to me in days because of it. Cyrus is more standoffish than normal and Liam doesn't know where to stand, with his girlfriend or with me. I told him he didn't have to take sides. He thinks that he does though,' he rambled.

'Tristan, stop! Just stop. Sit down now, you're giving me a migraine,' said Kingston grabbing Tristan's shoulder and directing him to the seat he had just vacated.

'Yes, you did overreact but as I know what you have gone through, I understand your reaction. However, it may take us more time to get her to open up to us now. After that little misunderstanding, she will not trust you. At this stage, there is no need not to trust her. From what you saw within her mind, there was little incriminating against her. She's just a normal mortal, serving her time within this life,' said Kingston, sitting on the edge of the desk.

'A sick part of me wanted her to be a Demon, to justify the pain she has put me through. I, I don't know If I can go through that again but seeing her face, it, it brought back so many memories and emotions that I swore I would never bring myself to feel again. I think I need to leave, for a short while, to get my head wrapped around this. Can you take over for me brother, until I return?' he asked Kingston, looking at the ground.

'Of course. Do what you need to do. I can take care of this lot.'

Tristan stood, placed his right hand on Kingston's left shoulder and bowed his head, a sign of unspoken respect and gratitude. He walked to the door but stopped just before exiting.

'Tell them I've been tasked but I'll return soon.' Kingston nodded and Tristan closed the door behind him.

*

Once again, Aurora was placed in a vulnerable situation and, as usual, this particular situation found her waking up in an unfamiliar bed, in an unfamiliar room, having no idea where she was. Hearing voices outside the door, she laid her head back down, pretending to be asleep. The door slowly crept open and she heard a number of footsteps, as they entered the room. A hand gently touched her forehead and was gone in a moment.

'Her fever has broken. Hopefully she wakes up soon,' said a female voice.

'I can't believe he did that! What was he thinking?' spoke another.

'I don't know, but Tristan would have his reasons. There is always a purpose behind what he does, whether we agree with it or not. Perhaps he knows her,' said the first voice.

'What a way to react to someone you know! She would have to be pure evil for him to torture her mind like that! Have you ever seen him do that before?' the second voice asked.

'No, never. Maybe, he thought he knew her? In the past? But was mistaken? I don't know Sienna. All we can do now is wait for his return and wait for her to wake up. Then we can make the next move. Come on, let's go grab something to eat, you're on the first shift remember,' said the first voice, leaving the room.

Sienna, waited a moment, then followed her friend, closing the door behind her. Aurora heard an audible click. *They locked the door. I guess it's to be expected, I am a stranger after all*, she thought to herself. Lifting her head from the pillows, she tried to get her body to follow but fell back down into the bed in agony. Her body felt like it had been stabbed continuously all over. Her left arm was bandaged and so was her right leg. She couldn't remember a wound on her leg but she did remember limping slightly. Suddenly, like a flash, she remembered the name the first girl had spoken, *Tristan*. She knew that name. It must belong to the one who burnt her mind when he seized her head in his hands. Her head started to ache from the thought. It did however trigger a new memory for her, reminding her of the real reason for being here. It was for him. *But why? Why can I not remember?* she thought. She also thought she should keep it to herself. They would be back and, at some point, they will want to question her. Since she couldn't move, she decided to go back to sleep. There was no point in making herself feel worse than she already did, especially if Tristan was not present in the building. They said he had left. She hoped he would return soon so she could get her own questions answered.

*

'Who do you think she is?' Asked Liam, while crunching on an apple. Cyrus and Caleb sat at the dining table with him. Cyrus was reading the Herald Sun, while Caleb was playing on his phone, oblivious to Liam's question.

"Oi! Guys!' he yelled. Both of them lifted their heads slightly.

'I don't know. None of us do. Damn it, you made me miss a candy!' said Caleb, now looking back at his phone. Cyrus rolled his eyes, and went back to his paper.

'Good conversation,' said Liam, slightly deflated. The common room door opened, and Estelle and Sienna entered the room.

'Good, finally someone to talk to,' said Liam, sighing with relief. Sienna gave him a kiss on the cheek and sat down next to him, her only sign of affection towards him in days. Estelle walked over to the fridge to see what there was to eat then slammed it shut.

'Why isn't there ever anything to eat? Caleb! Isn't it your turn to get groceries? Why haven't you done it yet?' she asked.

'There hasn't been any time,' he protested.

'Oh! So, you answer *her* straight away!' complained Liam.

'Stop it, all of you,' said Kingston, as he appeared out of nowhere and stood behind the couch.

'Ahh, I hate it when you do that! Could you at least give prior warning, or appear outside the door and then enter!' cried Sienna, nearly jumping out of her skin.

Kingston moved around the couch and took a seat at the long dining table. Crossing his legs, he made himself comfortable.

'How is everyone? Where's James and Kai?' he asked them, curiously.

'How do you think?' countered Estelle. 'We have been abandoned by our lead Guardian and left in the dark about this mysterious woman upstairs. You know his reaction was way over the top and unjustified, right?' asked Estelle, picking up an orange.

'Yes, it was and he knows it too. Which is why he has left. Not abandoned you, only giving everyone some space so he can understand what he will do next,' he said, diplomatically.

'But why? Why does he need to? Does he know her?' asked Sienna.

'Yes. Well, a version of her anyway. It seems she may be some kind of resurrection of a soul we once knew. This is our third encounter with her and the previous two were quite a strain on his, wellbeing. So, you can see why he reacted the way that he did. It is up to Tristan to tell you more, as it is not my story to tell. Let us just agree that he needs some time away to figure things out.' He said, raising himself from his chair and walking over to the espresso machine.

'Now, how does this contraption work? And where is James and Kai?' he asked.

'I'll show you, they're probably training,' said Estelle, getting up to help him.

'So, that's it then? We just have to wait now, till he returns so we can deal with the elephant in the room upstairs?' asked Sienna.

'Yes. We wait,' said Kingston. 'Today, however, between your shifts looking after said elephant, you will go on with your language studies. Latin and Greek are on the schedule for today. Aramaic and Coptic tomorrow. Thank you, Estelle, I will see you all in the study,' he finished his espresso, and faded from sight.

'Bloody Angels, I'll never understand them,' said Sienna, stealing Liam's apple and taking a bite from it. 'Okay, guess I'm up. Time to see if she's awake yet. See you guys later,' said Sienna, chucking the apple back to Liam as she left the room and made her way upstairs.

The room was dimly lit as Sienna opened the door and entered the bedroom. The mysterious woman, probably in her early or late twenties, had not moved since they were last in the bedroom. She was pretty battered up, bruising covered her body and one of her legs had been sliced open and crudely sewn shut, which Estelle, being the house first aider, had diligently corrected. Sienna removed her phone from her shirt pocket and slumped down on the window seat beside the bed. Glancing at the girl every now and again, she decided the girl was fine and went on checking out

the fashion from the latest episode of *Project Runway*.

Chapter Twenty-One

Acceptance

Dawn began to shine through the tiny gaps where the blinds brushed the surface of the windows. Estelle put her empty teacup into the dishwasher and let out an exhausted yawn. 'Well that's me, I guess. I'll see you guys in a few hours,' she said about to leave the room. Kingston appeared, yet again out of nowhere.

'Really Kingston? It's way too early for you to just pop in like that,' said James from the couch.

'You do not need to go upstairs Estelle, not yet anyway,' said Kingston, sitting down in his favourite dining chair.

'Why is that?' she asked, placing her elbows down onto the kitchen bench and cupping her face with her hands.

'Because Tristan is with the girl,' he said plainly. Both James and Estelle gave each other a look of surprise.

'And we want to leave him alone with her. Really?' she asked confused.

'She is fine. I feel he no longer holds any anger towards her. He is there to say something, once she wakes up,' he answered. Sienna burst through the door and jumped onto the couch.

'Well, I'm pooped,' she said, yawning loudly.

'Well?' asked Estelle.

'Well, what?' asked Sienna back. James steered clear of the conversation.

'Tristan!' said Estelle, probably too loud.

'Oh, yeah. He actually knocked on the door, unlike someone else I know,' she said glaring at Kingston. 'And yeah, he just wanted to apologise to her when she wakes up. I wouldn't have left him in there alone with her if I didn't think he was being sincere Stell! Who do you think I am?' disputed Sienna.

Estelle just shook her head. 'So what's he doing now then? He's just sitting in her room?' she asked.

'Yeah, I guess,' answered Sienna.

'You mean to say, he is sitting in her room, alone and in the dark, I presume. What, like a creeper?' Estelle was getting frustrated.

'OMG's Stell! Yeah, he's being a creep. Let him be the creep for once,' argued Sienna, flabbergasted.

'Okay, whatever. I'll just sit here and wait then, shall I?' she said, sitting down on the chocolate leather recliner in the corner, clearly dispirited by the short argument.

*

After seeing Sienna out of the girl's room, Tristan sat down in the window seat that was off to the side and watched the sun peak through the clouds as it rose towards the horizon. It was a typical stormy day in Melbourne, his favourite kind of day. The girl, or woman, he wasn't so sure of her exact age by looking at her, or even by seeing into her thoughts, appeared to be sleeping. He hadn't found anything to help him in her mind. Not because she was unintelligent, but because her memories had gone. This was curious indeed, something else for Tristan to figure out. Though, when you're being pumped full of demon blood you're bound to forget who you are. He continued to think everything over in his head, from the moment he saw her face in the grey concreate room, right up to now. He had called on the Valkyrie to finish the investigation and once again, they found nothing. They had even pursued past questioning techniques to try to get answers from the Fallen who ventured into the Underground often, but to no avail. Estelle's own findings were inconclusive, finding no specific demonic bloodlines to narrow down who could've taken the girls.

He turned and looked at her. Her face was calm, her heartbeat was not.

'I know you're awake and I know that you are scared. I regret my actions towards you earlier and hope, if not now but soon, you can forgive me. I am deeply sorry, there is no excuse for what I did to you,' he said. Taking a breath, he waited but there was no reply.

'My name is Tristan. You don't have to say anything if you don't want to. I just wanted you to know that you shouldn't feel afraid of us here. We want to help you.'

'Why?' she whispered.

Tristan knew exactly what she was asking. It had nothing to do with what he was saying, but what he had done to her. He just didn't know how to answer her. Looking away from her battered face towards the glistening light outside he responded with the only thing he did know. 'I can't say why just yet. That is to say, I'm not sure you're ready to hear why.' He said softly.

'Please, leave,' said the girl weakly.

'As you wish,' said Tristan disheartened and he promptly left the room. Appearing in the lounge, Estelle, James and Sienna were in deep conversation about sea urchins and how their venom can counteract demon blood infections.

'So, that is what I used on her. I created a kind of anti-venom from the little creature. They are such magnificent little guys. I don't know why mortals don't use them for their own medicine. Tristan! You scared me,' cried Estelle, grabbing her chest.

'Can we just put a bell on the two of you? So, we can hear you coming?' asked Sienna, slightly annoyed.

'Welcome back to the fray,' said James.

'Estelle, you can go to her now. She needs you,' he said, nodding at James.

'What did you do?' asked Estelle, getting up off the couch.

'Nothing, but she is still upset, which is understandable,' he answered, taking a seat next to Kingston.

Sienna yawned again. 'Well, I'm off to bed. Don't talk about too much interesting stuff while I'm away,' she said with a wink and left the room. Tristan and Kingston sat silently at the table, while James sat awkwardly on the couch.

'Well, I guess I'm off too. Catch ya's later,' he said, briskly walking out the door.

'Did my leaving upset them that much that they don't want to talk to me?' Tristan asked.

'Give them some time. They felt abandoned by it. They may need a couple of days to shake off their own anger. You look exhausted brother, you should go and meditate a while,' he said, patting him on the back with affection.

'You're right, I'll be back in a few hours. If you need me, I'll be on the roof,' said Tristan, disappearing into the air.

Chapter Twenty-Two

A Frozen Mind

Staring into the mirror that hung beside her bed, Aurora traced a healed scar on her forehead down to her brow. She had only just noticed it. *Why haven't I seen you before?* She thought to herself. She had been out of bed for weeks now, getting to know her savours, people who called themselves Nephilim. She had never heard of the term before, so the girl named Estelle took it upon herself to educate Aurora about their history. Surprisingly, the tale of ancient Gods and Fallen Angels was quite interesting, even if it did sound slightly odd. Aurora could feel her body going back to what she could remember being its normal self, it had only taken a month and she was back on her feet, thanks to Estelle's skills as a healer. Her mind was also gradually healing itself. She could remember bits and pieces of her time at university, and the time she spent with her close friend Liz. There was something else nagging at her memories though, a deep longing to be with a certain Angel who seemed to be avoiding her since she told him to leave her room. Feeling guilty at being a burden to her hosts she had re-enrolled for university and was hoping to reconnect with her friend Liz, to ask if she could possibly move in with her. She hadn't yet informed Sienna or Estelle that she was leaving; she wasn't sure how to break it to them. Tristan still hadn't come near her, and neither had the one they call

Kingston. So she didn't see the point of being there, even if she knew she needed to

be there for him. She still could not remember why. Aurora knew that there was

something missing, that being in an unfamiliar place could be muddling her mind,

so she asked if she could meet up with her mortal friend to see if that would make a

difference. Everyone seemed to agree with her, so off she went. Liz sounded really

worried on the phone, not having known where she had gone, she had just

disappeared.

'No text, no call, no Facebook chat, nothing,' said Liz. All Aurora could say to her

was that she had lost her phone and there was an emergency back home, so she had

to get a last-minute flight to London. She called the university and informed them

what had happened but as her phone was gone, so were her contacts, so she

couldn't call or text and she didn't have time to jump onto social media, with a

death in the family and all. Somehow, Aurora felt as if everything she had said was

the truth but in actual truth, it was all a lie. She had been taken by Demons but she

couldn't tell a mortal-budding journo that. When she had re-enrolled, however,

someone had deferred her studies, the signature was her own but alas, she could not

remember doing it. So, the guilt in lying was not as hurtful to her, as a part of it

could just be the truth anyway.

*

They met at a little French café on Lygon Street and ordered lunch. Sitting down, they continued their conversation.

'I did ask the girl in the administration department to inform my tutors but it seems the message didn't get passed on,' she tried to justify.

'Typical! Bloody typical. Again, people can't do their job! What is she being paid for anyway? To just file things away! People like her really annoy me,' she said in her Melbournian accent. 'Sorry, I was just really worried. I even filed a missing person's report with the police, which was put to the back of the pile, literally, I saw them do it! No one cares anymore. We're just photos on pieces of obsolete paper, lying in wait for a hero,' she said with a negative air.

'This isn't you Liz, why are you being so pessimistic?' asked Aurora.

'El, it started when I first looked into that little girl, you know the one who went missing back in 1921? Then, you went missing and again, nothing. I don't think I'm going to finish my report now. There's no point,' she said deflated, staring into her coffee.

'Don't be like that! You've been following this story since, what? 2010? Keep going, you have some strong evidence. Push through this negative barrier and get it done,' said Aurora, feeling proud of herself. 'Someone has to care about this girl and the man who was wrongly accused of her murder. And, if you have evidence that suggests the supernatural, use it! I mean, yes, I was sceptical at first but I am definitely a believer now,' said Aurora.

'El, what would I do without all of your positivity? Thank you for returning to me,' she said with a smile. 'Well, I think we're done here, I can walk you back to Collins Street if you like?' asked Liz.

'Sure. That would be great. Thank you. Here, I'll go wait out the front,' said Aurora, handing over a twenty. As Aurora stepped outside, her mind froze. A slight gasp escaped from her lips, as she grabbed her head. She shuffled over to a hidden enclave next to the café and waited for it to stop. She was blinded for a moment and then everything within the street appeared to her again. As she regained her sight, memories flooded her mind. She remembered who she was. Not a mortal and her name was not El. Yes, she was El, the mortal-archaeology student to her Nephilim saviours and human friend, but to her, beneath the lie, she was still herself, Aurora, an Angel trying to get back what was so brutally taken away from her. She saw her two sides again but they saw just the one. She desperately wanted *him* to be able to see both, but until she had completed her mission he needed to be blinded to the truth for just a little longer. The pain of it all was smothering her soul once again, and she wasn't so sure how much more of her betrayal towards Tristan's trust she could undertake.

'Hey, are you okay El?' asked Liz stepping out from the shop front.

'Yeah, I think I had one of those cold headaches quickly, which is weird. Come on let's get back,' she said and they made their way towards the centre of the city. When they arrived out the front of Kodak House, Aurora waved goodbye and promised to see her again soon. It had been a month since she had arrived here, under the noses of the Angels and their warriors, and she had not even seen Tristan, with the exception of when he attempted to apologise to her. Angry at herself for not accepting his apology, she understood why her mindless-self had brushed him off. It causes quite a lot of pain when you try to force someone to give into you, to force your way into their mind in search of memories. It's like having a drill push itself slowly into your skull, it's not very pleasant and you don't always get what you want, especially if the person you're trying to steal memories from either doesn't have any, or they're unwilling to give them up. This is why Aurora had to lie to Tristan in the first place. He couldn't know who she was, not yet. If he figured it out too soon, she knew he would have no choice but to have her taken by the High Guard. He was bound to the Gods by an invisible tether that could only be released by the destruction of his wings. Aurora didn't want that for him, so she chose to manipulate him instead. She needed his memories willingly or she couldn't find what she was looking for because she knew he would have those memories buried deep within the caverns of his mind. All she required was his trust and in gaining that, she needed his love to open him up to wanting to trust her. Now that her memory had returned, it was time for her to work. Before entering the building, a sudden feeling of being watched flooded over her. There was only one place she knew where this deviant could be lurking.

Deciding to cross the street, she went into a bank and found a door that went back outside, into a small private courtyard.

'Are you wearing it?' she asked the invisible entity.

'My lady, yes, I have the flame, nobody can eavesdrop on our little conversation. You have finally returned to us,' spoke her dearest and most loyal friend, Balthazar. 'It took an unnaturally long time for you to regain your memories this time.'

Aurora smiled at her dapper friend. 'We have wasted so much time because of it. I need to speed things up now. I think I'm going to have to do the obvious actions but in a calculated manner. Sienna has requested that I stay with them for a much longer period, she gave some excuse about me not being completely recovered and that it was their duty of care to ensure I was not a threat to the human race if they released me, you know, with the demon blood being pumped into me. Why did we do that again?' she asked him, having genuinely forgotten their reason.

'Because we know it's harmless to you, even in the form of a mortal. And, it was the only thing besides possession we could use that we knew would make them take you into their headquarters. Possession was plan B but as you know, it's much less pretty and too unpredictable,' he answered, confidently.

'What about the other girl and the dead one? I don't recall signing off of those two,' she said, studying his response.

217

'They were a last-minute suggestion from Styx. She had two souls she was giving to her men and thought it would be less conspicuous if there was more than just yourself in there. They had already been attacked by a stray minor Demon, we didn't think it could hurt,' said Balthazar.

'What about the stray? Was it destroyed?' she asked him.

'Yes, immediately, once it had been located. It was the one that had mutinied in the last year. Her men had been tracking it since it had rebelled and he finally made a mistake. But...' Balthazar hesitated. 'It may have left behind one of its young.'

Aurora glared at him. 'You mean to tell me, it created a changeling, right under our noses?' she asked, angered by the clumsy mistake.

'Yes. It's still quite young though and the transformation is not yet complete. I believe it is still in its birthing tomb, within the city's cemetery,' he said, apologetically.

'Find a wasted soul and leave it for the beast in the next hour and let the Nephilim deal with it. This can be their answer to what has been taking the women. I better get back. Inform Corvis that the garden on the roof, if the chance should arise, is a nice place to gather one's thoughts,' she ordered, opening the door to leave.

Balthazar dipped his head in acknowledgement and disappeared, leaving her alone once more to walk back over to Kodak House, the Watchers of the South's headquarters.

The Nephilim were all situated within the lounge room, waiting for her return.

When Aurora walked through the door, Sienna jumped up to greet her.

'Finally, you're back! Did it work? Do you remember anything?' she asked

enthusiastically, pulling her down onto the oversized leather couch.

'Yeah, actually, it did help. Nothing happened at first. It was when we were leaving

I felt a sudden feeling of deja vu, then it hit me. It hurt like hell but I remembered

going there with Liz before. Then I remembered I did book flights home and when I

returned to Melbourne, I was taken,' she mused.

'Do you remember if you saw who took you?' Asked James.

'It was a man; at least I think it was. He looked like a man. I got out of the taxi to

head into the college accommodation, but he sideswiped me as I got out and took

my purse. I yelled at him, and then stupidly, ran after him. I know, I'm an idiot. I

didn't realise until too late, that he had actually led me to the cemetery. I went to

leave but he hit my head from behind I guess. I don't remember seeing anything in

front of me. Then, I remember waking up in that place, pulling the tube from my

arm and screaming and banging on the walls for help. What happened to the two

other girls?' she asked them.

'They both perished at the scene, I couldn't do anything for the younger girl. She was too far gone. We've only come across a scene like that once before, so we're still trying to figure out an action plan for it. You had just been hooked up to it, so you were lucky you didn't have more of the demon blood inside of you. We returned the girl and older woman to their families' said Estelle sighing. A buzzing sound came from James's commslink and he read the message aloud for everyone to hear.

'Guys, "There has been an attack at the Melbourne Cemetery in Carlton. It is believed to be celestial. Pick a team to investigate. Report to me in 10 minutes for orders." Sweet, we haven't had this much action in years,' said James, happily.

'Great, let's go,' said Sienna. Aurora sat uncomfortably on the lounge as the others filed out of the room.

Sienna stopped just before exiting and turned to Aurora. 'Do you want to join us?' she asked.

'I'm human though? Why would you want me tagging along? I highly doubt Tristan or Kingston would allow it.' She argued gently.

'It's either a yes or a no? Leave the rest to me,' she said with confidence.

'Ok, sure. I'll bite,' she agreed and they left the room together.

*

The library was bleak with the only light coming from a projection on the wall at the back. Tristan was prepping their orders for the counter-attack in the cemetery, as everyone started to pile into the seats in front.

'James, why is everyone here? I told you to pick a team,' said Tristan annoyed.

James smiled awkwardly to the guys around him. 'They all wanted to come. I couldn't say no,' he shrugged.

'Why is the mortal here?' he asked no one in particular.

'Tristan, I asked her to join us. I think she could be some help or find a clue at least,' said Sienna.

'How so?' asked Tristan.

'Well, she just told us that she remembered being taken and it was in the same cemetery! Is it just mere coincidence? I think not!' said Sienna happy with herself.

'No, she's not coming. I would never willingly put the life of a mortal in danger,' he said.

'What if, I volunteered?' asked Aurora quietly.

Tristan turned his eyes to her. 'You would willingly risk your life, why?' he asked her directly.

'No reason, if you guys need help finding whatever did this you can use me as bait. If I'm truly safe with you all, I'm all in. If you'll have me,' she said with a smile. A smile that sent a warmth throughout Tristan's body, muddling his mind with thoughts of the past. Shaking them off, he stood up straight.

'Fine, but Sienna, she's your problem. You take care of her, that's final. Now let's get to these orders. Kai and Estelle, you're sitting this one out. Don't whinge, I need you two in the lab,' his word final.

Sienna looked sideways to Aurora and grinned. 'Told ya I'd get you in,' she whispered.

Once the orders were finished, everyone left to get suited up for the hunt. Aurora stayed sitting in her wooden seat, waiting for the others to return. As Tristan went to leave, she stood up and blocked the walkway.

'You know I can just portal myself out of here?' he said, not fazed at all by her move to block him in.

'But then you wouldn't know what I'm about to say then, would you? Unless, of course you try to read my mind again,' she said with a devious grin.

'I'll never live that down will I? Okay, go ahead. I'm listening,' he said, awkwardly smiling back.

'I wanted to thank you for saving me. Even though, there must've been something awful you saw in me, or thought you recognised when you saw me, to make you react the way that you did. It must have been unforgiving but you still saved me and welcomed me into your home. I'm sorry I put you through that and I now accept your apology,' she said, looking at him timidly, then to the floor. Without thinking, he stepped forward and took her hand in his, which sent a familiar tingling feeling through his fingers and up through his arms. He stood very still when she looked up at him, not knowing how she was going to react. The last time they had touched, he had caused her tremendous amounts of pain and she had blacked out for a number of days. She hadn't come near him since, until now. Mind you, he had given her very little chance to. She gave him a small smile, squeezed his hand back and was about to say something when the others reappeared through the doorway, hastily he took his hand away and she, awkwardly sat back down on the chair. As he moved away from her to leave the room, Tristan wasn't sure if he felt relieved or afraid at her reaction, either way he couldn't let himself get too close this time. If he was indeed cursed he wouldn't survive the same fatal outcome a third time. He was a fool for even taking her hand! But the flush of warmth he had felt in his chest and head when his hand touched hers, it was unimaginable to even think that he could stay away from her any longer than he already had. Her beauty, her voice, even her perfume attracted him. She reminded him of everything he had lost in the past, but yet, he was completely and utterly lost in her, which did not bode well for him at all.

Chapter Twenty-Three

Bloom and Grow

Aurora huddled behind Sienna as they stalked the cemetery for their prey. She was

still buzzing from Tristan's touch that she couldn't even remember leaving their

headquarters. They had just arrived at the Melbourne Cemetery and had located

tracks that led from the site of the attack and ended at a grave. It belonged to a Miss

Emily Pettifleur. According to her headstone she *lived 1860 and died 1886. A loved

one terribly missed.* Aurora wondered if she had a gravestone back in Paris, or

Germany, she had never really thought about it until now. Her men would take her

remains, no matter how long she had been gone from this world, and give her the

antidote to regenerate. Then, after a time, she would wake and be her true self once

more. She never really asked Balthazar what had happened after she had died.

Perhaps, that was a question for Tristan when the right moment arose. The trail that

had led them to this particular grave seemed to stop right on top of the gravesite

itself. Sienna, James and Liam all unsheathed their weapons. They could see

something that she clearly could not, and somehow she had positioned herself

between Sienna and the invisible creature.

'El, move slowly back behind me,' whispered Sienna. Acknowledging, Aurora stepped back behind the Nephilim. Knowing that this could get very messy, she didn't want to get in the way. The creature revealed itself after receiving a blow from James's blade. It was hideous, bipedal, overly large and slimy with a hunched back. Its ribs protruded from its marbled flesh and it had curled up horns sticking out of what must be its head.

'A Minor Demon,' yelled Liam. 'What in Hades is a Minor Demon doing here?' he yelled again, just missing the creature's elongated claw with his blade.

Tristan moved out from the shadows. 'It is a changeling, the young of a Minor Demon,' he said, brandishing his own blade at the creature.

'Whoa, Tristan, where did you come from?' yelled Caleb, as he dodged the creature's spiked tail.

'Apologies, I made my way here as soon as I saw it on your commslink. There was no time to waste. You have not faced a changeling before and they are a lot stronger than their parent during their transformation into adulthood,' said Tristan. Upon noticing Tristan and his angelic qualities, the creature burrowed down into the grave it stood on.

'Don't move, just listen,' whispered Tristan and everyone froze in place. They could hear what sounded like a grumbling noise beneath them. Immediately, Tristan did a reverse vault jump and landed right beside Aurora, who was standing as still as she could. There was a slight vibration in the ground below them and Tristan quickly held out his hand.

'It can smell you. Take my hand, now!' he ordered her. After the slightest hesitation on her part, she looked him square in the eye and took his hand. He brought her into his body swiftly, embracing her tight. Just as he did this, the creature broke free from the ground below, aiming his taloned fangs where Aurora had just stood, only to have Tristan land his Angel blade right into the top of his skull. As his blade pierced the creature's flesh, blood spewed out of the wound, spraying the collar of Aurora's black jacket, burning through to her skin.

'Ah!' gasped Aurora as she went to reach her free hand up to her neck. Tristan stopped her and signalled to Sienna, who quickly threw a small chrome spray can into Tristan's stretched out hand.

'Here, let me. It will clean the area of the acid,' he said, leaning in close to spray her neck.

'Acid?' asked Aurora, pretending to be in shock at the thought of acid on her skin.

'Yes, their veins are wrapped in what is similar to a hydrofluoric acid. It's a kind of defence mechanism. Before you ask, the vein is protected by what we think has a similar substance to plastic, only, its organic matter. It's quite fascinating really. Problem is, as soon as they die, they turn to ash,' just as he finished, the creature deteriorated rapidly before them.

'How does that feel?' he asked her, pulling her collar back to view the affected area. As he gently grazed her skin with his fingers, it sent a shiver down her spine, electrifying all of her nerve endings.

'Ahh, it's okay, I guess. It's numb now at least,' Tristan smiled at her, then stepped away and took up his blade, which was stuck in the ground, covered in the dust of the deceased Demon.

'Liam, take a sample, we need to know if its parent is still alive or if it has also perished. I'll mend the gravesite. The rest of you head home,' he ordered, moving over to Emily's headstone. Liam strolled over to where Aurora stood, took a small test tube looking device from his side guard and used it to scoop up some of the ash.

'How will that tell you if its parent is dead?' asked Aurora, curiously.

'That's a question for Estelle but it has something to do with its cells or whatever. If they're a certain shape, the daddy is dead but I don't really know the specifics,' he answered her. Before they had left headquarters, Kingston gave James a portal device, which apparently would lead them to a portal door, as they were never in the same spot when they had gone through it the first time. They all grouped back together and followed the device's beacon, leading them to a hollowed-out oak tree.

'Here we go,' said James, putting the device away. Only those with celestial bloodlines could go through portals, but if you were touching someone or something within one, it would transport you where that celestial being needed or wanted to go.

'Hey El, you're with me again,' said Sienna, holding out her hand. Aurora went to her and they held hands inside the decaying tree. Next minute they were standing in the library of Kodak House.

'I don't think that'll ever be normal to me,' she said, releasing a deep breath. Sienna gave a laugh and headed for the kitchen for food, signalling her to follow.

Chapter Twenty-Four

Gossip Girls

The smell of pastry filled the air of the common room, heightening the lust for food for all who stayed awake to fill their empty stomachs after the night's hunt. Aurora sat silently on one of the brown leather lounges listening to the whims of her new friends as they went about the kitchen creating the delectable delights. The clamour of utensils and girly chatter ceased, and she heard their footsteps approach her from behind as she stared at the blank wall in front of her. Estelle sat down next to her on the lounge and offered Aurora a plate full of pastries. 'How are you? Really?' Estelle's look of concern was plastered across her face.

'I'm fine, really. It's just so strange that's all.' Sienna leaped onto the other side of couch next to Aurora as she responded to Estelle's question.

'So, what about Tristan though?' she asked as she nudged Aurora in the shoulder with her elbow.

'What about Tristan?' asked Aurora in return. Sienna laughed in disbelief at her mortal friend's response. 'Really? Are you really telling me that you didn't see the look on his face when he took you into his arms?'

'No. I guess my eyesight isn't as good as you half-mortal. All I could see was a beast trying to eat me!' she lied.

'What are you on about Si? Tristan can't be with a mortal, you know it's their law.' Said Estelle through a mouthful of pastry.

'Yeah I know. But that doesn't stop them from falling in love with mortals though does it. Look at us! Case and point. We wouldn't exist if an Angel didn't have relations with a mortal.' She rebutted.

'Yes, but those Angels we call kin are Fallen, and did not follow the rules to begin with. Tristan does. You know that.'

'I still say that he is smitten with you El. I wonder if that has anything to do with his reaction when we found you.' She said to no one in particular. Estelle shoved Sienna in the leg sending a small yet painful blow up her thigh.

'Ouch! What was that for?' she asked rubbing her leg.

'I don't think they want her to know yet.' Estelle answered through gritted teeth.

'Know what exactly?' requested Aurora, staring curiously at the two girls beside her.

Sienna shrugged her shoulders, 'it's nothing really. Just something about your past, or past lives that Tristan knew. We don't really know. He's not an open book, keeps personal stuff to himself. What we do know is that you two are connected somehow. I think it's part of the reason why you're still here with us.' She smiled.

'Okay, I will agree with you there. For once, I think you're right Si. El, you're the first mortal that has ever been brought back to headquarters. It's a wonder that the Valkyrie haven't barged their way in yet to take you away. Perhaps they haven't reported you to the High Council yet?' pondered Estelle.

'I don't know Estelle, don't they have spies everywhere? They would surely know that we brought a mortal here? Wouldn't they?' asked Sienna.

'Yeah, I guess. I don't know what I was thinking.'

'Uum, can I interrupt please?' requested Aurora cutting into the Nephilim's private chat.

'Sure,' grinned Sienna as she took a bite of a miniature croissant.

'So, when I didn't think things could get any weirder, they do. Though, to tell you the truth, since you guys found me, I have felt something between Tristan and I. I can't explain it, even when I had barely any memories I knew I was meant to be here, with him.' She blushed.

'Yes! I knew it! You like him!' beamed Sienna.

'Shh Si! They'll hear you!' said Estelle slapping her on the shoulder. 'You know the hearing of an Angel is clearer than our own.'

'Sorry, it's just, it's about time we had something decent to gossip about in this locked up bunker we call our home.' Answered Sienna, deflated. Aurora felt a wave of sorrow in Sienna's words. 'I'm sorry Si. It must really suck to have had everything laid out for you from birth. No freedom to be who you want to be, or to do what you want to do but train all day and night to look after mortals who don't even know you exist. I'll be happy to let you live your mortal dream through me if it means you get to break away from the structure of Nephilim life for just a moment.' She smiled. Sienna reciprocated and quickly embraced her.

'I wonder though, what's it like to kiss an Angel.' Asked Sienna with a sly grin. A knock on the door silenced the girls immediately. Tristan entered the room and all three girls turned a bright shade of red. 'What was that Sienna?' he asked the youngest of the three.

'Oh, nothing. Just woman talk. You weren't invited.' She responded hastily. Smiling at them, he moved swiftly over to the espresso machine for his night cap and just as quickly as he entered he had left, coffee in hand.

'Who has a double espresso at midnight?' asked Aurora breaking the awkward silence. The other two girls immediately burst out in laughter. Not sure what else to do, Aurora joined in, completely dissolving any embarrassment that had just occurred.

'Angels don't sleep El. Sorry to laugh, but that was the best timing ever. Do you think he heard anything?' giggled Estelle.

'Probably.' Said Sienna.

'Oh! They don't sleep. Ok, that's not strange at all.' Responded Aurora.

'They meditate if they need to relax or unwind or whatever. Wow, we need to do this again ladies. I however am off to bed, we Nephilim being half mortal do need sleep.' Said Estelle.

'We definitely need to do this again Aurora.' Said Sienna as she took her leave, 'goodnight.'

*

Aurora sat back down on the lounge once both girls had left the room, closing the door behind them. She felt she needed to linger there just a moment longer and within only a few minutes she understood why. The door yet again opened revealing Tristan as he passed over its threshold.

'Oh, I believed you to have left. Is everything alright?' he asked her.

'Yes, I'm fine. I just wanted to embrace the quiet for a little bit before heading upstairs.' She responded, sending him a kind smile.

'I'll leave you alone then.' He said, and turned to leave.

'No, it's ok. Please stay. I actually wanted to thank you, for well, saving my life again.' Aurora laughed nervously.

'Well, it's just a part of my role as a Guardian, it was nothing.' He responded, instantly regretting it.

'Oh, okay. Thank you anyway. Uum, I think I'll head to bed now then.' Said Aurora awkwardly standing to leave. Tristan moved to the side to let her pass.

'El. Wait.' He said as she brushed past him. Stopping, she turned back to face him. There were only a few centimetres between them now. She could feel his breath on her skin, causing the fine hairs on her neck to prickle.

'Tomorrow, would you be comfortable if we were to speak privately? Away from prying ears and eyes? I need to tell you something, and it's too much to take in right now.' He said, his eyes waiting anxiously for her answer.

'Yes. You still need to tell me *why*, remember?' she grinned.

'Yes, I do. I'll find you tomorrow then, when I'm free to talk?' he asked her.

'Ok, but now that you have filled me with curiosity, I don't think I'll be able to sleep.' She laughed.

'You could always try and meditate,' he answered slyly.

'Indeed, well goodnight Tristan.' She laughed, knowing exactly what he meant.

'Goodnight El.'

Chapter Twenty-Five

Centuries-Old Kiss

Aurora stood in her ensuite and stared at herself this time in the fogged bathroom

mirror. Much time had passed by and she was still present within the Nephilim's

house. They had refused to let her leave because, when the time finally did come

for her to part ways with them, it would be for good. They had made a normal-ish

friendship with someone outside of their celestial world, which was unheard of in

their society, even frowned upon, but they didn't care. El, as they knew her as, was

their friend and once she was no longer living under their roof, under their

protection, her mind needed to be wiped. Any knowledge of the celestial world was

forbidden to a subcelestial being. She knew it would begin to creep up on them

slowly, her end as a mortal would always come. She really needed Xerxes to fine-

tune it but they had run out of time. If they didn't succeed this time, they would

have to somehow find another Tyrant to bleed out but they were all inside the Pit,

where she wanted to get to in the first place. The problem was, as long as they had

the power to control her father physically, they had the power to control her too, *if*

they knew she was his daughter. She also knew, when she finally revealed herself

to the universe, they would then try to use Lucifer against her, but she would have

235

the key when that time came, so their control over him would be non-existent, they just wouldn't know it until it was too late. Of course, they would place the Pit into lockdown, so even if her father were strong enough to save himself and escape, they would use his siblings to stop him. In truth, Lucifer would be too weak to escape, which is why she had to go to these extremes to liberate him from their crushing hold in the first place. She did not know, on the other hand, how Tristan would react. Once she revealed her true identity to him, after everything they had gone through over the last few centuries, she assumed he would be devastated. There was a part of her soul that wanted him to forgive her but her logical sense told her he would never do that, but as there is with every story, she did have hope. This was something the Greeks had given to her with their story about her mother, Pandora. She would never let that go.

Tristan's attachment to her was true though, and she knew it. She wasn't sure how much longer she could hold up this farce. It was destroying her from within, but she had to hold on for as long as possible. She didn't matter in all of this, her father did and her people. It was all for them. If she failed, her people would continue to suffer under the Old Gods and it was time to renew. Their children would rise up and send them into their own prison of twisted torment and eternal nothingness. At least, that's what she told herself daily as motivation not to fail. She didn't have to torture Tristan this way, it's not as if she enjoyed it. If Tristan had just given her what she needed when they had first met, then it would have all been done and dusted a long time ago. Regrettably, that did not happen. However, she was nearly there now, this time she would succeed. She had to. She only had one vial left, and that was to be used at a later date.

Aurora went upstairs to sit in the September sun. She could feel her time on this plain was going to be cut short again, very soon. As soon as she had entered the small greenhouse on the roof terrace, which overlooked central Melbourne, she could feel Tristan's presence. She went to walk to the other side but he called out to her.

"El, hey. Please sit down. Don't let me stop you from enjoying the view,' he said to her, with a heart-melting smile on his Adonis-like face. 'I'm free to chat if you like?' he asked as she walked over and sat down next to him on the carved wooden bench. There wasn't an awful lot to see really, mostly other towering buildings, as their 20's style brick structure was no longer the tallest one in the area.

'I didn't mean to disturb you,' she said, nerves vibrating her entire body from head to toe. Even just sitting next to him made her nervous all over. She felt like one of those silly little mortal schoolgirls who have a crush on the cute guy in their class, but are too nervous to say or do anything. She had to make some kind of move, without him thinking something was unnatural about it, even though any feeling she had for him was completely natural, forcing anything felt wrong.

'You're not disturbing me.' Tristan shuffled a little closer to her as he spoke. 'As you know, there is something I want to say to you. Something I've wanted to say since I first saw you but never have had the chance to do,' he said anxiously.

Aurora looked slightly afraid, as the moment they had first met, in this life, he

nearly killed her. So, it couldn't be anything good. He must have realised her

thoughts and so moved closer again to her on the bench dismissing her

assumptions.

'No, no, it's nothing untoward at all. Well, at least I don't believe it is. I meant to

say, from the very *first* moment that I met you. We did not first meet in the

Underground. It was elsewhere,' he explained casually. Obviously, Aurora

understood what he meant but she couldn't let him know that.

'Okay, you'll need to be a bit more specific,' she said looking curiously at him.

Tristan began their tale of woe, and Aurora sat quietly until he was done, as she had

done before.

*

Tristan did not think El was going to take his story as well as she had. He was

slightly surprised by her calm serenity at their story of revolutionary adventure,

love and then her untimely death. Then, he told her about the second time they had

met. She was a British nursing officer, serving in Normandy, who had been

captured by the Nazis. He was also a prisoner of war and they were able to rekindle

their love between survival and her skills as a nurse being employed by the

Germans. She wasn't allowed to speak with the British soldiers, only to check them for disease and wound festering but then she met him. He was in complete shock when he saw her sitting at an administration table as they were being brought in to be initially checked. The Germans in this area had lost their medics and they hadn't sent their nurses to the front, so they had decided to use the enemy's own instead. If they were killed, then that was that. After D-Day, the Germans holding them went on a rampage and started using what rounds they had left on all of the prisoners. Only a small number survived. Lora, the name she went by then, was not one of them. Days prior, she began coughing up blood and she believed she had been infected with epidemic typhus, common among the men. At that point, he knew she didn't care if she lived or died.

'When the guards patrolled close to our cells, we overheard their radios and as I was a translator, which the Germans had no idea about, I was able to keep my men apprised of what the German's plans were next. Not long after that is when the Germans began executing the men and even the nurses. I felt them coming for my men, so I stood in between them and the enemy, the reason why I was there in the first place, and as an SS officer aimed his luger at me, Lora, she stepped in front of *me*. She, *you*, gave your life for mine and for the second time in my life, you died in my arms.' Wiping a fallen tear from his blushed cheek, he continued.

'The pain I felt that day cannot be explained. I could not die, but how were you to know that? I was filled with so much guilt, even though I knew you were dying, I didn't want to be the reason why your life was cut down. What I wanted to tell you, every time I saw you, every time I heard you laugh or cry. I wanted to say...'

Tristan tried to finish his sentence but he was cut off by a loud bang of the door as it tore open from the inside. Both he and Aurora flinched and quickly moved apart from one another.

'Oh! Hey guys, sorry for interrupting but I think I've found something! Tristan, can you join me in the lab please? Sorry El,' said Estelle, apologetically.

'No, that's fine,' she said, blushing. Tristan got up and swept past her, *accidently* brushing against her leg, sending a bizarrely nice shiver down her spine and then he was gone, again. Time ticked by while Aurora looked out at the sheer number of buildings that stretched out towards the sky around them. Her mind was abuzz with the mix of emotions fluttering about within her head. *Stupid Estelle*, she thought. He was nearly about to tell her what she had been waiting so long to hear. Once he admitted it, there was no telling what he would do next, perhaps, inadvertently allow her to read his mind showing her the location to her prize. In her daze, she felt an unnatural breeze move past her right ear. Quickly turning her head towards it, she saw a small black bird sitting on a branch of a small tree in the corner of the greenhouse; Corvis. Corvis reminded her of so many things but in this instance, he reminded her of a bat hiding in a dark corner. Even though he was a bird and she a mortal, his mind was still open to her and hers to him. That's how they had always communicated and they didn't know why it still worked when she was human.

Perhaps he was still powerful enough to break through her mortal mind and hear her thoughts. He had come there to be the architect of her new plan of escape. Once she had taken what she needed from Tristan, and Celeste then she would have to go. *'Is it done?'* she asked him.

'Yes, My lady, the signal has been sent. When the time comes, they know what they need to do.'

Aurora smiled as she thought, *'Ensure they do it right this time Corvis. We want the Valkyrie to believe what they're facing is true. We are not strong enough yet to go in head on, we need to be smarter than that, I need that portal, it is the keystone to all of this,'* she finished.

In the blink of an eye, Corvis was gone and just in time too, as the door behind her opened. Tristan walked through, went straight over to her and with great confidence, pulled her up from the bench and pressed his lips against hers. She didn't fight it, she didn't want to fight it. His touch on her mortal flesh melted into her. They were both energised with an electrifying urgency that she had never before felt. One second they were standing out on the roof terrace and the next, they appeared inside what looked like a bedroom.

She stopped for a moment and looked around. 'Is this your room?' she asked him. He nodded his head sheepishly in response. She pushed him up against the white wall and they continued to shower each other in three-century-old caresses. Even at their age, they were both new to this kind of physical emotion. If one believed in soul mates, this is what you would call them, because it wasn't just their bodies

intertwining with each other, their minds had finally connected as well. Their

bodies comfortable with one another, they backed up slowly towards the inviting

bed but once again, there was an extremely ill-timed knock on the door.

'Is it gravely important James?' yelled Tristan. Aurora stood silently, trying not to

laugh.

'Well, no, not "gravely". I'd say it's mildly important news,' he answered through

the door, not noticing his Guardian's tone.

'Well, discuss it with me later, closer to dinner. I'll be in my office,' he shouted.

'Ok,' James answered.

Once they heard his footsteps dissipate down the hall, Aurora placed her hand on

Tristan's cheek, tracing his chiselled jawline down towards his neck. She gently

tilted her head upwards and stood on her toes so she could reach his lips with her

own and kissed him again. He forced himself to stop, for just a moment, so he could

speak.

'I love you,' he breathed. 'I have wanted to say that to you for centuries. I love

you,' he whispered again and they both fell into each other, blocking out anyone

else within the universe.

Chapter Twenty-Six

'Till Death, do us Part

There was a loud banging on the other side of Tristan's bedroom door, which repeated itself like a damaged record. Tristan sprung from the covers of his bed, while Aurora quickly disappeared into his ensuite, making sure she had not left any evidence behind as she hid. As it were, Tristan and Aurora had been lying in bed for hours discussing anything and everything about their entangled past. This also included Tristan's own history and the rules he must follow for it was forbidden for an Angel to be romantically connected to a mortal. Hence, the hiding away.

'Tristan! Tristan you have to come down to the library. The Valkyrie are here,' yelled Sienna through the door. 'And…Celeste is with them.' Tristan threw on the clothing he had previously been wearing that morning and opened the door.

'Okay, stop banging on the door Sienna. I can hear you. Has she said why she's come? This is unexpected,' he said holding the door slightly ajar. Sienna looked at him curiously.

'No, she's just standing in the library not saying a thing till you get down there. She won't even speak to Kingston. What are you doing with the door? Have you got a girl in there that you're hiding?' she asked grinning ear to ear. His heart pounded at the question.

'No, I just like my privacy. Why would you ask that?' he rushed, now panicked.

'I was just joking. You Angels have no sense of humour,' she sighed and walked down the hallway. Tristan closed his door gently, ran over to the bathroom door and knocked. Aurora opened it and with an unforgettable smile, she leaped into his arms.

'I know, I should probably let you leave but I really don't want you to go, not yet. I don't want this to ever end, especially as it does every other time. Not that I can remember any of it. It's just so beautiful to know we actually belong together,' she said giving him a kiss on the cheek, trying to believe what she was saying to him. Tristan smiled back at her and placed her lightly back on the carpet. Cupping her face with both his hands, he stared into her eyes for a couple of seconds.

'I just want to remember you like this, happy and loving me. There is only one reason as to why Celeste is here right now,' he said, letting her go.

'Do you think she knows?' she asked him.

'Yes, one of her spies probably saw us on the roof,' he said, tidying himself up.

'What do we do? I don't think I can go back to not knowing you,' she asked in a panic. He moved closer towards her and took her up into a comforting embrace.

'We do nothing but speak the truth. But, what you can do for me is go to your room and stay there until one of us comes to get you. I don't want them taking you away just because they see you downstairs. I don't want to give them any reason to take you in. Because trust me, she will,' he said, letting her go again.

'What do you think she would do with me? Sienna told me that the Valkyrie are like some kind of police for Celestials. Will she interrogate me? What do I tell her?' she asked him anxiously.

'It's true, but they are more than that. They are also punishers, and they enjoy what they do which makes them a whole lot worse than your typical interrogator. But look at me El, I will do everything I can to stop them if it is a part of her plan to take you away.' He promised.

'Ok, I guess. Once you leave, I'll wait a little bit then head to my own room,' she grasped his hand and pulled him in for a final kiss. Breaking away from each other, he left the room. She did as she said she would and waited a few minutes, then left his room as inconspicuously as she could.

As soon as she entered her own room, there was a knock at the door. Begrudgingly, she opened it, and found Sienna on the other side with her wide annoying grin.

'Can I come in?' she asked. Aurora opened the door wider and allowed her entry.

'What is it Sienna?' she asked, curiously. The Nephilim girl was silent as she closed the door and turned the key in the lock. Leaning down to the parquetry floor she took what looked like a small sharp bone from her pocket and began drawing symbols onto the wood, encircling them within the ancient markings. She stood up straight and faced Aurora, her demeanour quite changed from the silly teenage girl she portrayed to her Nephilim brethren.

'Now that they cannot hear us. I assume you have what you need?' she asked, straightening her stance even more. Aurora looked down at the bone circle Sienna had just traced onto the floor around them, it was amateur at best, but it would stop anyone else from hearing their conversation. They just needed to stay within the ancient spells, and their secrets would be kept well hidden from inquisitive ears. At first she was slightly confused at the question but soon realised what Sienna was actually asking her. The thought hadn't crossed Aurora's mind at all since being with Tristan. She had to think for a moment and then she remembered; she knew where he had the key. Even though she was human, he had given himself completely to her, his mind was no longer a locked door and she was able to see into his soul.

She had never thought about it at the time but now she had what she had been looking for for centuries, since her very beginning. Somehow though, because of Sienna's question, a wave of guilt punched her in the stomach. Her first phase was complete and so she was no longer required to be here but that strong invisible thread that tied her to Tristan was tugging at her mind, and her heart.

'I believe you're right. It's time for me to go. You know what you need to do?' she asked her.

'As soon as you direct me to its location, I'll have it for you the next time we meet,' Sienna answered. Aurora leant out her hand to release the information she had just gathered from Tristan's mind and Sienna took it into her own. As Sienna went to leave the bone circle, she stopped a moment.

'It has been an honour to serve you Commander. I hope that my grandfather's shame will now be forgiven.' She asked eagerly.

Aurora smiled back at her. 'Zachariah has only to forgive himself Sienna. I hold no grudge against your family, you know that. You owe him nothing, nor me child.'

'We owe you everything Commander. Without you, my bloodline would have ceased with grandfather. Your acceptance of him into your forces gave him a hope that he could redeem his past, ultimately giving me life. But I digress, I believe Celeste would like to see you now. So, we shall meet again,' she said.

'And so, we shall.' Aurora finished Sienna's sentence with the Fallen's ode. Sienna stepped out of Aurora's room and closed the door behind her. Staring silently around the room, Aurora didn't want to move. The time had finally come, but her whole body and mind didn't want to complete the final piece of the puzzle, not now, not after she and Tristan had finally connected. She felt like a fool. After a moment's grace, she cleaned herself up, wiped away the inscribed circle and cautiously went downstairs, knowing that this was the last time she would see any of these people ever again, as a mortal.

*

The Nephilim were waiting outside the library when Aurora descended the stairwell. Tristan saw her immediately and stood protectively beside her. He was feeling rather flustered but relieved that Celeste was not here for the reason he had previously thought, only to ask El some questions. Celeste was beautifully pigheaded. Others would call her malicious and cruel. Tristan knew first hand of her cruelty but she was also capable of rationality, sometimes. Her dark chocolate skin glistened in the library's light, throwing off a golden sheen. Tristan had always wondered why she was the opposite of Pandora, in personality and physicality, as they were twins after all. Celeste was dark, whereas Pandora was light, he guessed that was why Lucifer had fallen in love with her. Celeste wore her Valkyrie armour, which gave her an air of authority. Her Angel blades were strapped to her sides and a portal whistle was attached to the side of her bronze belt. Only Commanders and Sentinels held them. It was the easiest way to exit the Pit, entry was only through Hecate's Gate where her hounds stood guard. Tristan thought she must never take it off, which was probably true. He knew there were rumours of other entry points into the Pit, but they all lead to the one Gate. Hecate made sure of that when she designed it. Celeste noticed Tristan eyeing her and turned away from him to look at Aurora.

'Good. Come forward mortal,' ordered Celeste. She placed a hand on Aurora's shoulder and closing her eyes, she stood a moment in silence. 'You seem to be free of the demon blood,' she said, turning her head to Tristan and Kingston. 'Why is she still among you if she is healed?' she demanded.

Kingston stepped forward. 'We were able to use her scent to locate the changeling. Once we had finalised everything, we were going to send her on her way,' he answered.

'You used a mortal as bait?' asked Celeste, raising an eyebrow.

'Yes. It was her idea and we agreed to it as it was the most viable plan we had in destroying the creature,' answered Tristan, confidently.

'Very well. I will be taking her in for questioning. The Gods would like to know why the transfusion did not kill her. It is curious that you found three mortals, but only one lived.' Said Celeste as she studied Aurora. 'I will clear her mind when we are done and send her on her way,' she finished, preparing to leave.

'No way! Don't let her take her, they're questioning is clearly not going to be just with words!' interrupted Estelle.

'Quiet Nephilim! The girl is now under my authority. We are taking her now Tristan. If you have any objection to it, go and express your grievances through your chain of command.'

Tristan looked over to *the girl* as Celeste had put it. Aurora's expression had changed from curiosity into fear and Tristan had no power to help her. Using his mind to converse with her he attempted to calm her heart.

'El, listen to me. You will be okay. I will go quickly and request your return to us. I'll send notice to someone I know who will be present during the questioning, to get them to try to hold Celeste at bay.' Aurora looked him in the eyes and sent him a small smile, acknowledging him.

'Follow me,' ordered Celeste.

After Sienna had handed Aurora her belongings, she said her goodbyes to her Nephilim friends, all of whom would have refused her release to the Valkyrie if they could. Tristan informed Kingston of his plan and left to get the authority for her release, not knowing

that this would be the very last time he would see her in her present state.

*

Leaving the building under the guise of a glamour, Aurora was marched in silence down

Collins Street to the closest portal entry point, down a small alley. The sky had started

growing dark with blackened clouds slowly covering the light from the sun, and Aurora

could hear shuffling in the hidden corners of the alleyway. Bins full of rubbish suffocated

the graffiti protected walls, shielding from view what actually laid in wait behind them.

Celeste abruptly stopped in place, allowing Aurora to accidently bump into her. Celeste

turned her head towards Aurora and glared at her.

'Watch yourself mortal, get over there and don't do anything unwise,' she said quietly.

She then started to bark orders at her warriors who moved out towards the suspicious

sounds that surrounded them. Something had clearly spooked her and Aurora knew what.

She had a bit of a chuckle to herself as she moved back towards the wall behind her. Little

did Celeste know she had custody of her own niece. Since taking that last step off of the

staircase and moving into the charge of the Valkyrie, Aurora did everything in her being

to not lash out at her aunt. It was her fault that she was an orphan after all. Instead, Aurora took what she needed from Celeste, and bracing herself against the wall, she waited for

the fray to begin.

Chapter Twenty-Seven

A Guardian's Woes

"Somewhere, someone is training harder and better than you, and when you meet them face to face in combat, they'll win..."

Buddha

Walking through the Hall of Divinity Tristan greeted Chaos with a bow of the head.

'My Lord, I appreciate you meeting with me at so late a notice,' he said lifting his head.

'What is it that you want to discuss Tristan?' asked the God.

'I need you to release the mortal we have been sheltering these last months. She is still under our care and if you require interrogation, either myself or Kingston are happy to do it,' he said, his tone poised for dispute.

'No. Celeste has it under control. You have become too close to the girl, which is why she has taken her. There is information inside her head that we require. You are not needed Tristan. If Celeste requires your guidance, she will ask,' he said with finality.

'But Sir...' started Tristan.

'QUIET! You have heard what I have to say. There is nothing more.' He ended the conversation by dissipating into the celestial air around them, leaving Tristan to stew in his own despair at his failure.

'My Lord! Where is he?' yelled a female voice. 'Oh, what are you doing here?' enquired Celeste, coming into Tristan's view.

'You have to ask?' he spat, annoyed.

'Have you seen Chaos?' she continued, ignoring his tone.

'He just left. Where is she? Shouldn't she be with you?' he asked, looking for El.

'We were attacked by the Fallen just outside the portal. They knew we were there,' she said.

'What about El?' he asked, fury enveloping him.

'She was taken. It seemed that she is very important to them. So, I guess we're not going to see her again,' she said, giving up on the mortal.

'Are you kidding me? It is our duty to protect them! To protect HER!' he yelled.

'Watch you tone Guardian. If you're so worried about the girl, you rescue her. I'm done with the mortals.' She calmly stated.

'Now something will finally get done then!' he said as he turned to leave the Hall.

'If you find anything be sure to let us know,' she shouted hardheartedly.

*

Tristan stared distantly down the long table in the dining hall, just off the common room. The Nephilim were regrettably finishing off their lunch plates, while Kingston sat beside him at the head of the table, becoming familiar with the afternoon news reports in the paper, circling in red, celestial related events. They had traced every step that El would've taken, looked at every CCTV footage they could, and followed every celestial trail they found in relation to her disappearance, he was at a loss. Shaking himself out of his reverie, he focused on something that was printed on the back page.

'What's that?' Tristan asked Kingston, pointing at the paper.

'What, oh that? Yeah, I circled it inside. Eight people burnt alive within a church called The Redeemer. I thought it seemed fitting to highlight. I believe Celeste was saying something about a church fire in this exact location at our last orders a few weeks ago. She might have been the team that went to investigate,' said Kingston between mouthfuls of tea.

'When are our next orders?' asked Tristan.

'Tomorrow evening. They were brought forward because of the rise in alleged celestial murders, why do you ask?' queried Kingston.

'Are you sure it says eight? Not seven?' he asked grabbing the paper.

'Whoa, okay, take it. No, it clearly states *eight*, right there,' said Kingston pointing at the number.

'Maybe they got it wrong,' he said, searching the paper for more information.

'They do that time and time again,' he said, distracted. After a few minutes, he gave up and placed it down on the table.

'Okay, what is the matter, besides the obvious?' asked Kingston, concern in his voice.

'We have to look into it further. The three sisters said there would be seven, I thought she had skipped it, but it says they were burnt in The Redeemer! It's got to be her! It's also the same week El was taken,' he said, thinking aloud.

'You still don't have me,' he said confused.

'Sorry, you weren't there with us. I keep forgetting. After the Fall, Styx and I went to the Incendium to discuss, well you know what, and Corvis was there. The Elementals appeared to us in the Flame and told us about Lucifer and Pandora's child. Some kind of prophecy. The child *will redeem seven in fire, bleed one, destroy another and drain the last.* "Eight are killed, as The Redeemer is engulfed in flames!" You can't say this is just mere coincidence! It has to be her. The Demon that took her from the place I had her in hiding was found last week by the Valkyrie, drained of his blood. He was either *bled* or *drained*, I haven't decided yet as I haven't found any other connections thus far with reference to those parts of the prophecy. She has already completed the third part, *destroy*,' he said, looking at Kingston.

'How do you know?' he asked, putting down his cup of tea.

'Do you remember when we were investigating the murder of those girls back in the twenties?' he asked Kingston.

'Yeah, sure I do. The murderer was found disintegrated beneath the...oh.' he stopped, seeing the look on Tristan's face. 'You mean to tell me, the Nephilim that killed those girls, is a part of this prophecy thing? Are you going to tell me next that this prophecy will bring upon us the end of the world as we know it?' he said, laughing cynically. 'Oh, and also, why have you kept this from me? We've been partners for centuries and you're only telling me this now? What else have you kept from me?' he asked Tristan, slightly offended.

'I, I don't know why I've kept it from you. I guess maybe I just wanted more evidence before I brought it to you. I mean, you know everything else. You know that I helped save Lucifer's daughter by hiding her, only for her to be taken by a bloody Tyrant, which I believe was orchestrated by Balthazar. Then there's Elora, or Lora or even El, I don't know. I feel as if I'm going mad,' he said, trying to think of anything else.

'And the fact that Styx and Corvis were present?' Kingston added.

'Didn't you know that? I thought you knew? We were trialled together, remember?' he urged, hoping it wasn't something Kingston would hold against him. They were like brothers, they needed to trust one another.

'I wasn't really there, I was training during most of it. They wouldn't allow us *Lower* Angel's entry into the trials. Okay, well I won't hold that against you, if it was public knowledge. I can't believe you kept the other stuff from me though. Did you tell *them* about it all?' he asked, glaring into Tristan's eyes.

'Yes, I had to. The only thing I refused to tell them was the whereabouts of the child. So, they demoted me. I was in shock. I was ready for them to strip me of my wings but they didn't, they made me a deal instead. In making me a Guardian they gave me 'you-know-what' to secure, until they deemed me fit enough to be promoted again and sent me to the mortal realm. Then you introduced yourself to me and the rest is history,' he said.

'Yeah, it seems strange for them to give up on the location so easily. Do you think they got the information from elsewhere?' asked Kingston, intrigued.

'I've never thought of it that way. That could be true. You don't think...no, they wouldn't,' he mumbled to himself in disbelief.

'What?' asked Kingston.

'It was just a small thought but, you don't think that they sent the Tyrant to the Nephilim family where I put the child and not Balthazar?' he asked, his eyes wide open.

'It would make sense, we would just need to find out who, or how they found out. It's a pity she killed the Demon already, we could've gotten answers from him,' said Kingston, slightly defeated.

'Well, there might just be a way to find out,' said Tristan hopefully. 'It may not work though, because we would have to locate the Elementals,' he said, a smile inching its way across his face.

'Well this should be exciting,' responded Kingston.

'When is it never exciting?' asked Tristan, leaping from his chair. He made his way out of the hall. Popping his head back around the corner. 'Are you coming?' he yelled to Kingston, who jumped up and followed him.

The ocean breeze brushed through Tristan's hair like a comb. The sun was rising above the horizon and the sea was aglow from its beaming rays. Tristan looked out at it peacefully as he awaited Celeste's arrival.

'How much longer did she say she would be?' asked Kingston, kicking the sand underfoot.

'Any minute now,' he answered as they waited. They had seen the Elementals and had not received much from them. Which was usually expected. What information they did get was cryptic but they were able to make it out as, *Speak to your adversary,* and so they would.

'Hello boys,' said a familiar voice from behind them.

'About time you showed,' said Tristan walking over to her.

'What do you want?' she asked with a curious look.

'I just wanted to ask you a few questions about what occurred here. Could you show me where exactly you found the remains?' he asked her.

'Why don't you just read my report? Oh, wait. It's because you're just a Guardian Angel now, so why should I give you information about something that doesn't involve you? This is also not the case I handed over,' she said condescendingly.

'Same old Celeste, it's good to see time does not change you at all,' said Kingston looking back at her with a fake grin.

'Ah Kingston, it's good to see you're still hanging with Lower Angels, I guess it's difficult for you to degrade yourself even more than you already have. How is guardianship going for you two? Being a babysitter must be so rewarding,' she smiled back.

'Stop it, both of you. This isn't just about me or you, or him! It's about all of us. I think I know what is happening, but before I explain it to you, I need more evidence, which is why I've asked you here,' said Tristan, starting to raise his voice.

'Really? You're going to be insubordinate to me again?' she asked rhetorically.

'Celeste, you are no longer my superior and the longer we play this game, the longer you will be here in the mortal realm, which I know you very much despise. Besides, the case you gave me the lead on has a connection to this one,' he answered.

'Indeed, let's get this over with,' she said turning to walk into the uninviting cave behind them.

All three of them moved inside, dodging vines and a myriad of spider webs. Both Kingston and Tristan followed Celeste through to the rear of the cave, passing rusty cages, big and small. All three of them covering their faces to guard their noses from the horrible stench clinging to its cold damp walls. The only light flickering from an open torch Celeste held illuminated the whole interior. It wasn't your normal kind of flame, but flame she had brought with her from the Incendium. She kept it on her at all times, just like her whistle. A whistle, which Tristan had just noticed was missing. As they walked, Celeste described the scene as she and her officers had found it. According to her, they had been watching this particular Demon for some time but were not informed as to why.

'I wanted to arrest him and throw him back into the Pit where he came from but apparently, he was too valuable for that. I had to allow him to keep on killing, until finally someone other than myself put a stop to it,' she said as they walked.

They came to an opening at the very back of the cave. The crown of the cave reached high above their heads and looked as if it was beginning to crumble. The stalactites pointing down towards them threatened to fall, daring them to step underneath. Little bits of light shone through cracks all over it.

'Is it just me or is the sky looking like it is about to fall down upon us at any minute?' asked Kingston, eyeing the deadly spikes above.

Ignoring him, Tristan continued to listen as Celeste explained what they had found.

'The Demon had been drained of blood and venom. The creature who did this knew what they were doing. They knew exactly where he hid away,' explained Celeste. 'This is where the body was found,' she pointed to a railing.

'Hanging?' asked Tristan, looking at the large hook in the middle of it.

'Yes, upside down. Not a pretty death I must say,' said Celeste.

'Do you know why they needed his blood *and* venom?' he asked.

'No. Do you have any ideas?' She eyed Tristan.

'Not at present, no. But I think it's linked to El. She was being pumped with demon blood remember? I'll have to go back and do some research before I pass on my theory,' he said.

'And when do you suppose you will let us all know your theory?' she asked sarcastically.

'At the next orders I should have something significant to provide you with,' he challenged, avoiding Kingston's questioning look.

'Forgive me for not having any faith in your abilities but that is tomorrow, you realise?' she asked smiling.

'Of course, I know. I will have something for you, whether you believe me or not.' Looking around him, he changed the subject 'There doesn't seem to be any struggle.'

'None at all. Strange, isn't it? That a Tyrant wouldn't struggle when being attacked. This means it had to have been an Angel of some kind,' she speculated.

'Or another Greater Demon,' suggested Kingston.

'Indeed. We'll know once we question some suspects, but there is nothing solid yet,' she finished. 'Is that all?' she asked Tristan.

'If you were watching him, why didn't you catch the perpetrator?' he asked curiously.

'The Seraph on watch at the time of the killing swear they saw nothing. It seems a very strong glamour was used to cover their entry and exit,' she answered.

'We'll stay here and keep looking around. Oh, my final question. Were there any imprints found?' he asked her finally.

'No, the murderer didn't touch anything from what we could sense. The wounds were clean of any kind of imprint. They were good,' she said. 'I'm leaving now, I'll see you both at the orders. Goodbye,' she waved and was gone.

'I wonder...' whispered Tristan aloud and went back towards the entrance to the cave.

'What?' asked Kington slightly baffled. Following him, he saw Tristan stop at the cages, looking for any kind of imprint left behind by the murderer. The imprint, or touch by someone, usually leaves a memory of them behind. They can be unclear, if someone has attempted to clean them away, but there can be residue, which one can still attempt to decipher.

There were at least twenty or more cages of all shapes and sizes within the entrance of the cave. It took them a number of hours to go over all of them properly.

'Nothing?' asked Tristan.

'Nothing,' responded Kingston.

'Damn it to Hades,' swore Tristan. Ready to give up, he looked around him one last time. Moving back to the largest cage, he stood in front of it. It was one out of four that had animal remains left inside, and what looked like fossilised mortal excrement in one of the corners. It was all old and dried up, but still, he had a thought.

'These four are different from the rest. From the objects left inside, I assume these are the ones he trapped his victims within. Maybe we should try looking inside them for imprints rather than the outside. It's a small chance, but the murderer could've been someone he had captured. This one, in particular, seems to be pulling me towards it. I feel connected to it somehow,' he said, staring inside the cage. Kingston agreed and both set about opening the cage doors to look inside. Straight away, both Tristan and Kingston are pulled away into the memories of the children the Demon had slaughtered. There were too many to count, and none significant enough to be a suspect, until Tristan came upon one child he recognised. Aurora.

'What?!' he shouted as he released himself from her memory.

'What's wrong?' called Kingston, moving towards him.

'One of the children... he was the one that took her. He kept her here,' he mumbled.

'Tristan, stop! Look at me and tell me what you saw?' begged Kingston.

'It was her, Aurora. Lucifer and Pandora's child, her eyes are so familiar. She's the one I saved from the Pit.'

'Did you see what happened to her? Did he kill her?' Kingston entreated.

'She escaped. That means she's still alive! This is the evidence we need. Everything that has occurred has been by her hands! This is part of the prophecy, she is making it come to light!' he gasped. 'We must take this with us,' he said.

'Why? They don't know what she looks like, only you do. Remember, you hid those memories from the Gods so they couldn't find her,' said Kingston, staring at the cage. 'They will just have to take your word on it, or take it from your mind themselves,' he finished.

'And trust them to believe me? I doubt they will. I'm such a fool for leaving her with Nephilim, and for my own idiocy in protecting her memory all of these years. Fine, we'll leave it here. Come on, let's go,' he said, slightly defeated.

Leaving the cave, he felt as if he was leaving a part of himself behind and he couldn't fathom why. The sun was high in the sky as they exited the cave, and they were met with the waves thrashing before them. Breathing in the salt air they both looked back at the cave before disappearing into the air that surrounded them.

Chapter Twenty-Eight

A Pocket full of News

Elizabet stared at the grandfather clock for what seemed like near an hour, but in reality was only fifteen minutes. The room she was in made it seem like time didn't matter at all. It actually reminded her of a period in her childhood when she had to go into hospital to get her tonsils removed. It was nearly the spitting image of her sterilised hospital room, minus every object she had, as this particular room had only the mere basics. As you would see in most waiting rooms, there were no germ-infested magazines, nor were there pictures on the walls or vases full of exotic plastic flowers. There were however, a couple of white, hard-as-steel chairs, an off-white desk with a white phone and of course, the out of place roughly painted white grandfather clock. Behind the desk, surprise! Was another white chair and a door. Liz thought this joint needed to be updated and not just the out of date tech but maybe a pop of colour could be added to spruce it up a bit. Another thought also crossed her mind, *where the hell is the receptionist?*

When she had entered what *used* to be known as Kodak House, an Art Deco building built in the thirties situated towards the heart of the Melbourne central business district, there were plenty of people moving about. After some glancing around a watch and repair shop on the lower level, she was able to find the lift that

would take her to the floor that housed the office of the man she was to interview.

Liz, being a journalism student at Melbourne University, was looking into the tragic

death of a child during the depression era. More so, she was looking into *who* killed

the child than the child herself. Her reason for doing this came from her love of the

supernatural, and her close friend El who had for the second time since meeting her

had disappeared. This was the last place she had left El, dropping her off just across

the street. So now, Liz was investigating two mysterious cases. In her spare time

she was an avid ghost hunter and she had seen a lot of strange things, which helped

to fuel her cause. She believed there was more to both cases than what laid on the

surface, something not quite comprehensible for a normal mind and she wanted to

find out what. She had been understudying a friend on one of his Melbourne City

ghost tours and one story was about the spirit of a little girl that lingered in one of

the alleyways. She took some interest in this particular part of history. When she

went to look for the alley where the body of the little girl was found, it had been

taken over by a new occupant, a massive skyscraper. So, unfortunately, there was

absolutely no evidence to be seen, with the exception of what was locked away in

archives at the coroner's office. After some thorough research, spanning eight long

months, she believed that the rest of the answers lay with one scrupulous individual,

a Mr Tristan Morholt of The Hour Glass. She had found that one of his ancestors

was an inspector of sorts who worked on the case, so she wanted to see if Tristan

Jnr had any information about it lying around. He was a difficult man to get a hold

of but after a few months of calling, emailing and snail mailing, she finally received

an invite to his office for that golden interview she had been craving, for what felt

like over a year. Knowing that he could be linked to both the little girl and now her

closest friend, it also seemed very coincidental that his invite arrived just after El's

disappearance. Now, sitting in the sterile office, she was beginning to feel like it

may have been a mistake.

'Don't leave, just stay put. You've waited for this moment for months now! Don't

screw it up just because they are still making you wait. El needs you!' she said

aloud staring intently at the grandfather clock.

*

The ancient citadel in the centre of Rome was a flurry with the overwhelming buzz

of tourists. The Italian heat made the city shine under the brilliance of its burning

sun, illuminating the ancient sculptures and colossal buildings, almost bringing

them to life. Tristan could never understand why mortals liked decrepit old

buildings such as the Vatican. He assumed it was because it connected them to their

past but this, of all places, was not a good looker, architecturally speaking. He did

remember when it was first created, along with the rest of Rome's treasures. They were beautiful to the eye of a beholder but to him, it proved their mortality. Humans creating giant statues to immortalise themselves and their conquests. The ancients were the worst for it, but at least *most* of them had honour. Now they just go onto social media and have their fifteen seconds' worth of fame for doing something stupid like buying clothes or falling off a trampoline headfirst. On most days, this realm was the bane of his existence but before the creation of the human's monotheist ideology, another manipulation of men's minds by the Angels roaming the Earth, war was humanity's and the true Gods' main substance for prayer. This city's civilisation, back in the day, went about its duty to destroy other cultures. He never understood why the Gods would allow such violation from their creation. The abhorrence of their bloodthirsty culture was always a popular topic within orders, according to Celeste. The Guardians were too low in the chain to listen in on their orders back in the day, until now. They didn't know what had changed, whether it was just time itself, or if it was his link to Aurora. Perhaps it was the curse they put on him to add to his punishment. He believed they felt with just a small demotion in rank they were being too lenient on him, so in place of stripping his wings, they cursed him instead. Fallen Angels, who do have their wings stripped, are free to do whatever they please walking among mortals, but Guardians have restrictions. They still follow the Angel Lore, in other words, *the* law. Tristan has an extra rule; he cannot fornicate, meaning he can never physically love another. After Lucifer and Pandora's fall from grace, he vowed to never to do the same, never fall in love, whether it be with an Angel or a mortal. So, when he met Elora that first time. It changed everything. Then she died, and he understood he was cursed. Though Kingston believed it all to be in Tristan's head, that there was no such curse, there were other forces at play. Tristan was a stubborn Angel, so it didn't matter what he had to say about it really.

Kingston stepped out from behind the colossal statue of Michael and stood beside Tristan, invisible to the human eye. Normally they would both walk among the mortals and use less of their angelic gifts to try and fit in with their Watchers, but they didn't really feel like they could deal with infuriating mortals right now. So, veiling themselves to the humans, they did.

'Well that could've gone better,' he said, frustrated.

'I just don't understand them! They destroyed their favourite son to be rid of this child. Now I have evidence that she's back and creating havoc in the mortal realm, but they don't seem to give a damn about it! Am I missing something?' he asked in desperation.

'I don't know. It does seem strange that they would ignore your request to investigate further, or even to hand your material over to Celeste to use for herself. At least you can say, you warned them,' Kingston said with an awkward smile.

'Why do I even bother? They demoted me, then bloody cursed me, so why should I even care to help them? Why didn't I just take my wings myself like Styx and the others?' said Tristan scratching his head.

'Because, you're a glutton for punishment brother. You feel guilty for Lucifer, but you're also guilty for those feelings. You have put yourself in a no-win situation. You have to choose a side, his or theirs. Until then, you'll be stuck in this artificial limbo you've created for yourself forever,' said Kingston, slapping Tristan on the shoulder.

'Let us go relax and grab an espresso by the river. Is that café still there you think? It has been, what, fifteen years since we visited that place last?' he said as he stepped down off the spiral stone staircase towards the Roman cobblestoned street, with Tristan slowly on his heels.

*

Tristan glanced at his watch and realised he was running late for his next appointment.

'Blast, I have to get back to the office, El's friend that journalism student Liz has been waiting over an hour now.'

'Oh, let her wait. We've made her wait months as it is, another couple of hours won't hurt. She's persistent, she'll stay. What are you going to tell her anyway?' asked Kingston, sipping his espresso.

'Not sure yet. She obviously can't know the truth, I'm just going to have to deny as much as I can. Ultimately, we need her to stop looking on both fronts. The closer she gets to the little girl's killer and El's disappearance the more harm she puts herself in. I doubt the Seraph will treat her kindly if they find out how close she is to the truth.' Tristan finished his latte and stood to leave. 'Are you coming?' he asked Kingston.

'Nah, I'll stay a while. It's not every day you get to be in Rome, basking in this glorious sun. Melbourne is so dull with its weather at the moment, I need a break from the cold,' he answered, taking another sip.

'I don't know what you mean. Melbourne's weather is wonderful. Anyway, I'll see you back there for the debrief at eight?' he urged.

'Sure boss,' smiled Kingston.

Tristan left the glory of Rome behind him and found his way back to his office door in just a short blink of the eye with the use of a portal. Composing himself, he opened it to find the curly red headed girl sitting in the waiting area, her back to him, talking to herself.

'Don't leave, just stay put. You've waited for this moment for months now! Don't screw it up just because they are still making you wait. El needs you,' said the girl, quite distinctly out loud. Tristan had to bite his tongue to stop himself from letting out a laugh.

'Do you normally speak to yourself out loud for all to hear Miss Munro?' Tristan walked over the threshold and closed the door behind him, gesturing for her to take a seat at the desk.

'Ahh no, sorry about that. I didn't hear you come in,' she stuttered awkwardly.

 'My apologies for keeping you waiting, yet again. We are like two ships passing each other in the night, but we have finally caught one another. I am Tristan and you are Liz? Am I correct?' she nodded in response. 'Now please, take a seat. Would you like a drink? Or, something to eat perhaps?' he asked, delaying the questioning.

'No, thank you. I'm good. I had a muesli bar while I waited and I never go anywhere without my trusty thermos,' she grinned, motioning to her bag

'Good, good. Well, how can I help?' said Tristan, wondering anxiously how to avoid every question she would ask of him.

Chapter Twenty-Nine

Seeking Truth

A number of hours flew by when Balthazar finally saw the budding journalist, Elizabet Munro, known to him as MacGregor, leave Kodak House in a huff. Reaching into his jacket pocket, he took out his mobile and dialled his commander's number.

'My lady, she's leaving, would you like me to follow her?' he asked.

'No, take her and bring her to me at *Lebassa*. I'll be in the drawing room,' ordered Aurora.

'Roger, we will see you all soon.' Ending the conversation, he neatly placed the phone back into his jacket pocket, transformed into a four-legged feline and made his way up Collins St to follow his quarry. Not too far up, she crossed the street and headed down Manchester Lane, *this would be the spot to grab her*, he thought to himself. Slowly catching up to her, he became stuck between two cars which had inconveniently stopped in opposite directions, one attempting to get out of an underground carpark, while the other trying to get in via the same entry or exit point. The laneway was narrow and only one car width across, so you could see his conundrum as he did not wish to be crushed beneath those metal beasts. His target was moving swiftly down the lane. Balthazar pounced on to the top of the closest vehicle and dove off landing directly in front of her, knocking her off her guard. 'Holly crap, what the?' she gasped looking down at the grey cat who had just appeared out of nowhere.

'Why hello young lady, allow me to make your acquaintance, I am Balthazar,' he said in his noble-like manner, offering her his paw.

'What? Are you...are you...' she stammered, quickly looking around her to see if anyone else had witnessed the talking cat. 'I must be going mad! You are cute though.' Recklessly taking his paw.

'Off we go,' taking hold of her hand, they disappeared from the laneway and materialised inside the drawing room of his commander's mansion. Liz felt a hard jolt disperse through her body as she landed on the hard ground. The cat she believed to be of supernatural origin, had changed into the form of a man and let go of her hand and walked casually towards a baroque fireplace. As her vision cleared, she could see its beauty. It was decorated with *fleur de lis*, golden roses and little faces of chubby cherubs. Slowly regaining her balance, she snorted.

'Whoa! That was amazing! Really weird but amazing!' Liz sputtered. 'Hey, where are we?' she asked looking at her ornate surroundings. The walls were an off-white, with pale blue panelling. It was magical, no, *majestic* she thought. She felt as if she had been brought into the world of King Louis VII as she looked up and stared at the roof, *is that a trompe l'oeil ceiling?* She wondered. Liz had briefly studied architecture before deciding the world of writing was more her cup of tea.

'Wait. Are we in France? Like, literally France? Is this legit?' she asked. Her captor continued to ignore her, so Liz walked over to him. As she walked over, she glanced at a newspaper on a small side table and nearly hit herself over the head for being an idiot. *Definitely not in France*, she thought. Her captor had his back to her and was quietly in an intimate conversation with a woman that was standing by the fire, who was staring sombrely into the flames. The woman turned around and looked at her then. More like, *examined* her she thought. She was beautiful, just like her surroundings, ornate and decorative like one of Tolkien's elvish princesses, *no, Queen, she was like an elvish Queen* she thought again. This elvish Queen smiled at her. Then Liz thought she looked kind of familiar all of a sudden, like they had already met.

'I've never been called a Queen by a mortal before, let alone an elvish one, though I guess the elves had to be imaged off of something.'

Her voice was like silk, she was definitely not human, that's for sure, thought Liz.

'Hey, what? Did you just read my mind?' she sputtered.

'Perhaps. Normally I prefer not to be in the mind of an Unknown of your age. You are all so flighty with your thoughts. But you Elizabet, you are something different,' said Aurora.

Liz didn't speak for a small moment, trying to take in what she was saying to her, *an Unknown? What the hell was an Unknown? And where had she seen her before?* 'I don't know what you mean. What is an Unknown? I'm just a normal person from Frankston, nothing *unknown* about me. But you and him, you're something *different,* aren't you? And, have we met before? Can you tell me what's going on, coz' I really need to get the tram home, like now?' she babbled, as she tended to do when she was nervous.

'A moment ago, you believed yourself to be in France. What has changed your mind?' said Aurora.

'The Herald sitting on the table over there. I doubt they get those in Paris,' she sniggered, pointing at today's morning newspaper. 'I thought they had stopped printing them,' she assumed aloud.

'They have, but I have my ways. There is nothing better than reading the morning paper while having a cup of tea at breakfast. Please join me, take a seat,' she said, gesturing to an Edwardian white and peach striped chair with golden arms and legs.

'No thank you, I'm fine. I think I should...' stuttered Liz. Before she could finish, Aurora rudely cut her off.

'I insist,' she demanded calmly.

Liz felt then that she wanted to sit in the chair, even though she didn't. It was like a Jedi mind trick. Sitting in the uncomfortable antique chair, against her will, she looked at the woman in surprise.

'No, I am not a Jedi.' Aurora grinned at Liz as she finally sat down.

'No way! How does she do that?' she asked Balthazar who stood quietly behind his mistress. He merely smiled, then asked the woman if he was still needed. She waved him off and he left the room.

'He's really good at ignoring me and not answering my questions. Is he your servant?' she asked the women, now staring intently at her.

'In a way. I've known him since I was a child,' she answered.

'So, what are you then? A Demon or something?' she asked.

'No, well, that depends on what you believe a Demon to be?' Aurora countered.

'Well, something from nightmares really. Big ugly monster type creatures. You don't seem to fit the bill though. Is *he* a Demon? And what is an Unknown?' asked Liz.

'Demon, Fallen Angel, monster, victim, whatever he is, he is my friend and brother. He has taken on the human image for *me* you see. There was a time when I was a child that I needed liberation. He provided that. In doing so, he took on the image of a child about my age so that I could trust him. It was a time in my life where trust was like trying to walk on water, it couldn't be done. He did it so that I could feel comfortable with him and not afraid. I could see right through his disguise, but he did not know that. I could also see that he truly wished to help me, so I trusted him and he saved my life. And an *Unknown,* my dear, is a human or mortal being. An alternative term from subcelestial that we Angels use. The young Nephilim

Watchers started to say it a few centuries back and it has caught on quite brilliantly,' said Aurora.

Liz stared at the women bewildered. 'Why are you telling me all of this?' she asked.

'Because Elizabet MacGregor, I wish you to know everything.'

*

Aurora had thought about this plan of hers over and over. It was just a small piece of the puzzle, but an important one none the less. It was a pity that the girl was not as advanced in the mind as she had hoped her to be. Fortunately for her, Aurora had help for that lack of knowledge and wisdom. You see, Liz was not just a normal human girl from Frankston, as she had believed herself to be, she was more than that. She came from a bloodline of great

warriors, a number of them had and still do follow under Aurora's command. It was her four times great-grandfather who had begun the tradition and it may just be her who will help to complete it. Aurora sat still in her golden chaise thinking about what to say next. Sitting across from her in the large antiquated drawing room, she looked directly at Elizabet.

'What is the matter?' she asked.

'Why did you call me Elizabet MacGregor? My surname is Munro. Are you sure you have the right girl?' she asked.

'What is it that you dream of at night while you are asleep? Can you remember?' Aurora asked, ignoring Liz's question.

'Kind of. Sometimes I guess I can remember my dreams. What does that have to do with you calling me the wrong name? And why don't you people ever give straight answers?' asked Liz, slightly frustrated.

'Our dreams are our way into the different realms of this universe. They are the door to another life that is also our own. Once you grasp that concept, you can use them to your advantage. My dreams constantly remind me of who I am and what I am to do to bring this world out of its inevitable misfortune. There is one constant dream of mine that I cannot seem to understand, however. I am running freely through the autumn woods with my wings burning behind me and there is someone far in the distance before me. I cannot tell who they are. The faster I run towards them, the further they are from me. A part of me believes it is my love, that would make sense to me but then their shape changes and it looks like a woman. That is where I am at a loss you see. Not that that matters to you.' Said Aurora looking back into the fire. 'Who do you really think I am Elizabet?' she asked after a moment's silence.

'I, I don't know. You're talking about alternative realities and what I assume might be the end of the world? I think you could be insane but I'm not totally sure I believe that either. Perhaps you're the Devil himself, or herself,' she said.

Aurora smiled at this, *smart girl* she thought.

'Not the Devil, no, but close. I am his daughter. The one who will set him free and save this world of ours from certain destruction. There is no need to be frightened, I will not harm you. Unless you force my hand that is. You have come very close to finding all of this out on your own, I have only intervened to stop you from doing something that I could not forgive.' Pausing, Aurora delicately picked up her English china teacup and sipped some of her French Earl Grey.

'Tristan, how can I say this, is one of our kind who can easily forgive mortals. I am not. There are things in this world that would destroy the mind with one small glimpse. That is something I would not have happen to you. But, you have come awfully close to revealing to the rest of your kind our secret world and even if the likes of Tristan don't give a damn that is something that *we* cannot allow. Do you understand what I am saying to you?' she asked elegantly.

'I think so. I think you do have the right girl and you want me to hand over my research. What happens if I don't?' she responded.

Aurora knew she would be stubborn, but at least she was not as stupid as she thought she was half an hour ago. 'Would you like to find out?' she smiled, exposing a glimmer in her eyes.

"Umm, nope. I'm good. But, what do I get in return? I mean, you still haven't really told me that much and you said something before about me being different. What did you mean? Oh and there is still the name thing,' she added carefully.

'Please, drink your tea and have something to eat,' Aurora motioned to the assortment of sweet delights that were being laid out before them. The girl picked up her own china teacup and took a sip, then treated herself to a petit four.

'Good. I'll start at the beginning shall I, briefly that is. As I have already said, as a child I was in need of rescuing, however, prior to that, I was living a normal life as one of you. Innocent to who I truly was or who I would become. Have you heard of Nephilim? That confused look on your face tells me no. Well, they are the children of Fallen Angels and men, half-human and half-celestial. They are what we call the Watchers, as they guard the lives of mortals watching out for dangerous Celestials who would like to harm them. As an infant, I was given to a Nephilim couple, who were thought to be able to protect me. However, they could not. So, I was taken, by what you would understand as a Demon, and tortured, nearly losing my life. Until I was freed by Balthazar. He, and others, helped to raise me and educate me on the knowledge of my people. When I came of age, I began the mission to save my father from his prison. Over time, I have gathered objects to help with my cause, as well as warriors and friends. I offer them opportunity,' Aurora took some more tea.

'What kind of opportunity?' asked Liz.

Aurora motioned at the doorway with her hand. The door opened and a stout looking highland man stepped over the threshold. Walking over to them, he formed a slight grin behind his stained ginger beard.

'This is where I leave you for the moment. Before I go, please, permit me to introduce you to Commander Angus MacGregor. He is your... what is it MacGregor, four times or five?' asked Aurora.

'Aye mistress, four I reckon,' said MacGregor.

'Ahh yes, it is. Elizabet, this is your four times great-grandfather. Your name may be Munro, but you are also a MacGregor. Please sit Angus, I will be back momentarily,' said Aurora as she left the room.

'So, ye my kin are ye? C'mon, stand up, let me see ye,' spoke Angus gruffly.

'Ah what? I can't understand a word you're saying. Maybe we should wait for the lady to get back. How are you my great, great or whatever pop anyway? Shouldn't you be like, dead?' asked Liz.

'I nearly was, but the *lady* as ye say, saved me. Sit down, I'll tell ye the tale if ye can bear to listen?' he said as he sat down on another chair close by, his Scottish accent still as strong as ever.

'Go on then, I'll let you know if I can't understand you,' said Liz sitting back down and taking another petit four, as her great-grandfather, times four, took his own sweet treat and began his story.

*

Angus sat, dishevelled in the uncomfortable chair, leaning to one side trying to forget his failings of the past.

'So ye see young lass. There were no other choice for thee to take. It was make a deal with the Devil or vanish from these plains forever, taking my whole clan with me,' said Angus.

'And when you say *whole clan*, you mean?' she asked.

'Aye, the *whole* clan, from my time to ye. It would've been the death of all what I loved if she had not arrived in time. The English were about to, and nearly did, obliterate all that we ever knew after that battle,' said Angus, scratching an old scab on top of his head.

'So, paint me a picture, what *exactly* happened? And in *English* this time,' asked Liz, taking a sip of tea.

'Aye your *Ladyship*, that I'll do,' he said with a grin. 'Like I said already, the men and I were strugglin' to stand in the muddy field, while the vultures in red encircled us. They were going to kill us ye understand. They were just playing with their food as pompous bastards do. One finally slowed down in front of me and lifted his bloody sword to me face. I felt it dig into me cheek, I went to slug him but then I saw *her* appear out of nowhere behind him. We didn't know what to think ye see, was she the Devil in disguise? Or was she an Angel? The English turned and faced her too, they were scared of her. You could smell their fear above the odour of death that surrounded us. She were glorious, we started to think we were already dead when she spoke,' he said.

'What did she say?' asked Liz.

'Never mind that now, all ye needs to know is that she gave us a choice; death or life, we chose life ye ken. The deal was, the blood of our blood belonged to her till she no longer required it. And we, the original clan members stayed living till our debt to her was done, to see she did not falter from the agreement. Till then, we serve her loyally and without waiver, and those of our kin follow in our footsteps if they choose, unless there is no other to replace them. Now you have a choice lass. I'll leave you to make your decision,' said Angus as he stood to leave.

Coughing from a mouthful of cake, Liz gasped aloud. 'What? I have to decide what? If I want to join her? I don't know anything about this world of yours, this is insane!' she said.

'Why do ye think she had ye brought here? Don't be daft lass. You've reached waters that ye cannot think to cross, on yer own anyway. Coz' of your snoopin' you have to be dealt with. As ye is kin, she has shown ye mercy. Take it, ye might learn somethin' from it. I bid ye well daughter of my own and hope to see ye again. Depending on ye choice, ye will get the family ye yearn for. Don't look at me like that, I've been around long enough to know people's looks. Your eyes say it all lass,' he said, and left the room.

*

Liz sat alone by the fire's edge until her tea went cold and her petit fours turned hard like rocks. It wasn't until she felt a hand touch her shoulder that she awoke from her stupor. She faced the shadow and saw that it was Balthazar smiling down at her. The strange man sat down where her great-grandfather was sitting not long ago, telling her that her life had pretty much ended.

'What do I do?' she whispered, not expecting an answer.

'You could sing? I understand you have a lovely voice, classically trained are you not?' he asked with a sly grin on his devilish face.

She sighed. 'Don't mock me, this is serious.'

'Oh, don't misunderstand me Liz, you don't mind if I call you Liz? I know how serious this is. But, you're not going to become her slave if you choose *her* you know. You were just born into a promise, one that your mother could not undertake and did not allow you to have a say of your own. It is unfortunate that you had to learn about it this way, not being able to comprehend the delicacy of it all. I like you Liz, so I will tell you something.' He leaned in close and whispered into her ear. 'She's not the Devil, but she is the Devil's child. No matter the path you

285

choose, you will not be harmed but understand, if you do not choose her, you must forget all that you have come across and leave this place,' he stood and walked towards the door.

'If you do choose her though, there may be no end to whatever it is you could do in this world and what good you can give to it,' leaving the room, Balthazar flicked a piece of paper in her direction. 'Perhaps, you could make something of this? Maybe that ballad Angus told you about,' with a wink, he left the room.

Liz's mum always said she had only creative bones in her body, she could hold a note with her voice, play the violin and, on the odd occasion, would sketch something. She looked at the paper in her hand, it was quite old, probably as old as her grand pop, *just Pop* she thought, she would call him Pop. Looking over the note, its age showing as if stained with tea. Unfolding it to reveal what was hidden within she found blotted ink scribbled over the page. She had to focus her eyes to a perfect twenty-twenty vision to decipher what was written, if you would call it writing.

Angus MacGregor, 1747

Thistle's dance

The wind whistles of courage stained with fear,

And the thistles dance to catch its song.

In the meadows do they spin and weave,

At the soldiers moving through the throng.

The muddy coats of royal red,

Clashing in a sea of woven thread,

Moving to the beat of an internal drum.

Exhaustion chimes with the sound of metal,

Catching on flesh and taking little,

Yet the small taste of freedom they had,

That was worn proudly on their tartan plaid.

Should the woven warriors never give in,

The dance of the red coats will go on,

Until the bitter end of clan and kin.

And the thistles end their dance, as the wind no longer sings their song.

'Wow,' she thought aloud.

'It's lovely, isn't it?' said a voice from behind her. Liz jumped.

'My apologies if I startled you. You looked deep in thought reading Angus's poem. I didn't want to disturb you,' said Aurora as she made herself known and sat down in front of Liz.

'No that's ok. I didn't think he could...' she stopped.

'Write? Let alone write poetry? It's true, he doesn't come across as someone with schooling as you might say. But, he was. He lived in Edinburgh at a boarding school before he came of age and took over the clan from his father. He wanted to be a poet, alas that was not to be, not in that time. Though it did not stop him from writing,' said Aurora.

'I misjudged him I think,' she said blushing. 'It is beautiful, but tragic at the same time. I couldn't imagine living in a world like that,' said Liz looking back down at the paper.

'You may have to Liz. You may not believe it now, but this world is in chaos and soon it will fall as many civilisations before it have. It is only a matter of time, which I am running out of. You have until the next blood moon to decide if you want to continue in this world, unknowingly floating on shards of glass. Or, if you want to help piece the broken shards back together again. You may go if you wish or if you find yourself in another room, let us say the next one over, you may want to stay a while longer.' Aurora smiled at her one last time and disappeared.

Chapter Thirty

Idle Minds

Tristan discreetly watched the door close behind the mortal girl named Liz as she finally left. Besides being El's friend, and an amateur journalist he followed on social media, there was something odd about that *Unknown* girl, but he couldn't put his finger on it. Her name wasn't familiar at all from his past. Other than her blog, he had never heard of her name before that. So why was she so close to finding out about their world? Only those with a connection to the celestial realm could see past the walls that they have put up to hide behind. She walked right through them and into the elevator and right into his very white, mundane office. Not to mention all of those questions about the past that didn't really concern her at all.

Picking up the white phone, he dialled the only number it could dial, *one*.

'Kingston, can you come to my office when you're free?' he asked. 'Cheers,' he said, hanging up the phone.

The rear door opened as Tristan lifted his hand from the white phone.

'You rang?' said Kingston, as he entered the room.

'Yeah. That girl that was just here, can you send someone out to follow her please? I need to know more about her. I should've looked into her when she wrote that piece on the Underground. There is something about her, I just can't figure it out,' he said scratching his head.

'Will do. Did she ask about the girl and El? What's that now? Two people in the space of four years asking the same questions about a girl from the twenties? I get the first guy who came in but the girl looking for evidence to prove Ross's innocence in the girl's murder, but what was her angle?' he asked Tristan.

'Apparently, she's a ghost hunter.' He rolled his eyes. 'She thinks there is something supernatural about the girl's murder. Especially in the location she was found in. I should not have been in that bloody photo,' he sighed.

'I told you it would haunt you,' Kingston grinned. 'And El?' he continued.

'She doesn't have any relevant information on El's disappearance, at least nothing we don't already know. Well, hopefully I subdued her, for now. I would still like to know more about her though. Ask the others about her and send Sienna and Liam to trail her. Tell them, it's a training exercise, just follow unseen. Observe and take notes,' ordered Tristan.

'Roger. I'm sure they'll be thrilled by the task,' he said, still smiling as he left the room.

*

Kingston made his way down to the common room where the young warriors loved to sit and swoon over their most prized possessions. As he entered the room, Estelle was sitting by the dining table drinking tea and reading *Moby Dick*, Sienna was by the kitchenette creating an edible masterpiece as usual, while the three boys were playing war games on the Xbox.

'Sienna and Liam, you have been tasked. Get yourselves into clean skins and wait for orders in the library. Be there by 0900,' ordered Kingston.

'That's in five minutes! I just made my breakfast damn it,' said Sienna irritably, looking at her commslink.

'Well you have approximately four minutes and fifty seconds to eat and get into clean skins. Go! To the rest of you, have you heard of a girl named Liz Munro?' he asked.

'Yeah, that was El's friend, from uni. Why do you ask?' enquired Estelle.

'That's all that I require, thank you. You two, get going,' he ordered once more and turned and left the room. Pausing the game, Kai and the other guys looked at each other, wondering what the task could be.

'Why are you tasked for this?' said James. 'I'm in charge, not you. I should be the one to go,' he argued.

'Go ahead mate, you go and tell Kingston that, or better yet, go and tell Tristan that he's sending the wrong guy out for the job,' laughed Liam.

'You can always take my spot James,' offered Sienna. 'I don't even know why I bother making food these days, I might as well just starve by the amount of jobs I get given,' she said grimacing.

'Stop whingeing you two. Just go and get dressed, you're running out of time,' barked Caleb, James's Second in Command. Liam and Sienna hastily left the room while the others went back to what they were previously doing, as if nothing had interrupted them in the first place.

*

Tristan went back to his office to carry out another monotonous day of nothingness. Unless he was summoned *Upstairs*, or he had to be present on a mission to help his Nephilim, which was rare, his normal daily tasks were to sit around and wait patiently. So, when one was idle, the mind often becomes a place of torture. Memories of the past flooded his awareness intermittently and the one important aspect of his past was Elora, the three versions of her anyway. His heart missed many beats whenever he thought of her. He had found and heard nothing of her since her abduction a couple of weeks ago. Sometimes, even the smallest of rumours are leaked among the Fallen but not this time, at least not of her. All he had were his memories, no photos, no paintings, just centuries-old recollections. He swore at himself for not getting a photo this time around, especially since they now live in an age of technology. A knock at the rear door stirred him out of his dismal reverie.

'Come in,' he said. The door crept open with Sienna and Liam filing through one after the other, sitting down in the chairs in front of his desk.

'We followed the girl to Manchester Lane, till she just went *poof*!' said Sienna, holding both of her hands up and flicking her fingers out in a dramatic gesture. Tristan was not amused in the least. Turning his head to Liam, he waited for a better explanation.

'Yeah, pretty much exactly what Si just said. The girl just disappeared. We didn't see anything else, celestial or not, we even had the CCTV checked on either corner and out the front exit point of the underground parking, and nothing though there was a cat. Whatever it was, whoever it was, is good and probably the same as who took El. They didn't leave anything for us to find. Do you want us to go back and keep looking for other clues?' he asked, scratching his head.

'A cat? What did it look like?' he asked, his heart skipping a beat.

'Just like your normal everyday cat I guess. It was grey maybe? The video was too blurry. Why? Is that important?' question Liam curiously.

'No, I'll pass it Upstairs. If it is something intelligent enough to clean up after itself, it may well be too great a problem for us alone to handle. If they wish us to take point, we will, if not, we have other issues to sort out. Good work, both of you,' said Tristan trying to sound unconcerned while closing his report book. Both members of his team left him without question.

'A grey cat.' He repeated out loud. Conveniently Kingston entered the white office just as Tristan had spoken.

'There is only one grey cat that we know of who could portal a mortal.' Spoke Kingston.

'Balthazar.' Agreed Tristan. 'What does Balthazar want with El? Unless?' he froze.

'Unless it has something to do with Aurora?' finished Kingston.

*

Tristan stood alone looking at the grandfather clock in his dull office. It was the only thing that he owned, everything else belonged to the Gods. He had taken it with him on every mission, even to Paris where he had first met Elora then onto Germany stationed inside his headquarters. It was what helped to connect him to the mortal realm, something built by hand, by him. It looked different then, not washed in white. His very last memory of her at his barracks just outside of Paris, was when she had gracefully walked over to it and listened to its ostentatious chimes.

'It's dinner time gentlemen, hurry or we'll all be late,' he remembered her saying. He thought back to that very moment to see if he remembered the grey cat. But no, it was too deep within his past to be clear enough. He did remember her though. She was wearing that beautiful pale blue silk dress that she wore the first time that they had met. Looking at the very same clock again and hearing its gaudy chimes ring in his ears, he noticed that it was actually dinnertime again. A tragic smile spread across his face as he realised she was truly lost to him now. If she had indeed been taken by Aurora, then she knew his feelings for the girl. She was undoubtedly punishing him for his failure to protect her when she was taken by the Tyrant. He flicked a small tear away from his cheek, and left the office and headed to the common room for dinner.

Chapter Thirty-One

Family Ties

Aurora found Liz sitting in the drawing room. She seemed happy to be there now, in their company, unlike their last meeting in that very room.

'What is it that you have on your mind Liz?' she asked as she sat down on the chaise beside her.

'Oh, it's really nothing. Just, it's just, thank you. Thank you for, well, kidnapping me. Instead of taking me *from* my family, you have brought me *to* them. Does this mean that I have to sell my soul or something?' she asked nervously.

Aurora laughed slightly. 'No, that's not how it works. If you wish to stay with us and your family who remain with me in my service, then you just have to say that you're staying. Unlike others, I take a person's word as their vow. Just remember, if I still require you and your bloodline, you are still tethered to me till my task is complete, no matter how many years from now it could take, you need to sincerely take that into consideration,' said Aurora, looking into the hearth. 'We will need to find a job for you. It shouldn't be too difficult with your talents,' she finished, smiling at Liz.

'Can I ask you another question? One that you'll actually answer?' Liz asked anxiously.

'Go on, ask away. Though, I'll only answer if I choose to,' said Aurora.

'Why are you doing this? I mean, besides trying to rescue Lucifer from Hell, what are you going to achieve? Are we the bad or the good guys? I still have no idea why I'm here, why we're all here,' she said while clicking her fingernails together nervously.

Aurora took a moment to think about her response. 'Retribution,' she decided to answer with.

'Retribution for what?' asked Liz, truly interested.

'For the death of my mother, the imprisonment of my father, the downfall of every Angel loyal to them and for the life that I, and others, have been forced to live. Once my father is freed and has regained his strength, in mind and body, we will pursue the next phase,' Aurora answered confidently.

'And... the next phase is?'

'You don't think the Gods would allow us to just take their most precious prisoner right from under their noses without reprisal, do you? If I have to spell it out for you, you're not the girl I thought you to be,' said Aurora, slightly disappointed.

Liz paused, trying to think what the *next phase* could be. She couldn't think of anything besides one thing.

'War? You're going to war with the Gods?' she asked.

'Correct. Well done. Once we have him, they will stop at nothing to get him back and most likely, me too. It's not so simple as good or bad either Liz. There is no black and white only. Where there is light, there is darkness; where there is darkness, there is light. You cannot have one without the other. No one is simply good or bad, I know I'm not. The Gods, on the other hand, believe themselves to be above all of this. So, the only outcome for us is war. Do you think you're ready for something like that?' she asked.

'Ahh, I don't know. I mean, I'm not even twenty-one yet. Not sure I have the experience to even answer that question comfortably,' Liz answered apprehensively, looking away from Aurora.

'Age has nothing to do with being ready for war. Just ask your family members who have fought many throughout the ages. No one is truly ready, it is just one of those things that if it has to be done, you get it done. But don't think I would put you in the thick of it! That would be irresponsible of me. Not all who follow me are warriors you know. But, again, you do need to understand, that if we lose, I do not know what will become of us all. I hope, against all hope, that my mortal followers are spared but I cannot promise anything. We have and will continue to conceal everyone's identities to the other side, so that should help us by allowing you all to escape if the need should arise. In saying that, I assure you that I will do everything within my power to triumph over our enemy. That is my oath to you,' she swore.

'What did they do to you? You said, *the life they forced you to live*. Can I know that?' asked Liz.

'How about I show you instead?' Aurora instructed Liz to take her hand, as soon as she did, Liz was pulled into Aurora's mind. They stood within the church. It was cold and dismal. Liz looked at Aurora in shock.

'Whoa! How are you doing this, wait, never mind, you're an Angel, of course, you have magical powers or whatever. Where are we?' she asked a little excitedly.

'Where it all began for me as a child. A little church in a small village in Ireland. We are merely ghosts within my memory. They can't see or hear us, nor feel that we are here. Just watch and hopefully you will learn to understand why I am how I am,' Aurora instructed.

'Who's *they*? It's just us...' Liz stopped mid-sentence as screaming could suddenly be heard from down below. 'Whoa, did you hear that? Hey! What's that over there? The big cross thing, is there someone on it?' she gasped in disbelief. They moved closer to the large object, as it became clearer to them Liz doubled back.

'It's the priest. The Demon did this to him to intimidate my mother. It didn't work,' said Aurora. Evil resonated off it like steam from a heated spring. She could remember the feeling of what lay behind it, in the dark.

Liz was quiet now, to Aurora's delight. Unknowingly to her, they stepped back towards the portal for a better view. Aurora could sense the beady black eyes of the

Demon. It had walked out of the shadows and was showing itself to her mother and younger self. Liz watched the little girl intently, feeling panic rise up within her chest.

'Is that you? The little girl? You can't be more than three or four?' she whispered.

'Five, I was five years old and I had no idea what was happening,' said Aurora.

'So, they didn't prepare you for this kind of thing?' questioned Liz.

'No. They did not,' exhaled Aurora.

'Wow, just, wow,' stated Liz, not knowing what else to say.

Aurora could hear her younger self's thoughts, *If I run now, I would never see Mama again.*

She didn't move. Fear had frozen her younger self in place as she silently stared at the hideous creature before them. She remembered that her fear was not from the Demon itself, but from the thought of losing her mother. After finding out that her father was dead, losing the only other person whom she loved, and loved her, was devastating. The Demon's melancholic voice echoed throughout the tower. His tentacles swayed back and forth as if it were floating within the ocean. Aurora could see through the monster's projection of a human façade. All Demons want to look like mortals, it gave them a sense of power in a way. They could hide within the mortal realm without anyone knowing who or what they were. She remembered finding a book in her father's study as a child, it had magnificent miniature paintings on almost every page, with little handwritten descriptions below them. It was as if her father had captured her imagination and placed it inside this leather-bound book. The creatures of half man and half horse, some were tiny things with wings like butterflies and others were mischievous looking boys with horns on their heads. Then there was a section towards the end that felt foreboding. Like the creature before them now. The creature in the picture book was large, the colour of darkened blood and had small beady eyes beneath two gigantic horns in the middle of its head. *Evolution did not treat this one well*, thought Aurora.

Liz didn't know what to think when she saw the old man crudely attached to the makeshift crucifix. His eyes were wide open and silently screaming in agony. There was blood everywhere, a trail of it led directly behind them. She dared not turn around, she didn't want to face the monstrous creature that could do such a thing to a human being. The mother and child stood before the cross, also in a state of shock. *They knew him*, she thought. Then, she heard the voice of the creature, suddenly very close to her. She closed her eyes as it moved past her and into the vision of its soon-to-be victims. Liz couldn't believe that Aurora, a child, could have faced off with such a thing. She looked so innocent, with her vibrant emerald eyes and silver hair, identical to what it was now. Her mother was not at all like her, scarlet hair and fearful hazel eyes. Liz wondered what Aurora's birth mother looked like, and her father. She was still in shock to believe that she was hanging with the daughter of Satan. With all the stories about him, all being so terribly wrong. She couldn't fathom any of it. She felt as if she were trapped within a dream, even though she was literally trapped within a memory right at this very moment. She couldn't tell whether the child was frightened. She could see something like fear in her beautiful eyes, but she wasn't sure if it was there or not.

'Were you afraid?' she asked the real Aurora who was standing beside her. Aurora glanced at her younger self for a moment then answered.

'Yes, but not for myself. I'm afraid of losing Cora, my mother. She was all that I had left.' Liz left it there and watched the rest of the horrific scene in silence. Aurora stayed silent beside Liz and waited for it to end. She heard her mother scream, '*Aurora, run!*' to her younger self. The child hesitated for a moment and then sprinted towards them, towards the portal. As soon as she reached them, Aurora's memory faded away and the burning flames of the hearth crackled away in front of them again. Liz was deathly quiet. Aurora glanced sideways at her and noticed a slight build-up of tears in the corners of her eyes.

'He took me then. The last thing I heard was my mother's smothered screams and then everything disappeared. He had both of us in a hold, I had blacked out, but my mother, he had snapped her neck and hung her from the ceiling. He took me back to his lair, some dingy underground cave close to the Mediterranean ocean. Later I found out his orders were to kill me, but he had other plans. You see, he liked the taste of young *fleshlings*, as Demons call the children of mortals. He didn't know that I was actually an Angel, just not yet matured. I hadn't aged enough for my gifts to come into fruition at that stage. I could sense things, like spirits or people's emotions, but I had nothing that could help me then. He kept me in a cage for a time as he gathered child after child. He was hoarding us, until we were ready to be fed on. It was just my luck that Balthazar and Corvis located me in time,' said Aurora, staring into the flame.

'You said, he was ordered? Who gave the order?' asked Liz.

'The Gods,' answered Aurora. 'They had found out where Tristan was hiding me and sent the Demon to take care of me. That was after Tristan was demoted to a Guardian. He was lucky though. He could've lost his wings like the others who follow me. He could've chosen to Fall like the rest but he knew he needed to stay in their grace to be able to locate me and follow through on his promise to my father to protect me,' explained Aurora.

'You were just a child. That breaks my heart that they could even think of murdering a little girl,' she said, taking a breath before continuing. 'Is this the same Tristan that I have interviewed?' asked Liz curiously.

'Oh, my apologies. Yes. He trained under my father and saved me from the Pit. It was he who brought me to the Nephilim for protection. He is the key to all of this, unfortunately.'

'Oh, wait! Are you El?' she gasped.

'Yes. Well, I was,' said Aurora.

'What the? I assume that was part of your plan, I don't need to know. Wow, so much connects now and he's an Angel too! I thought he was just some weirdo who liked white an awful lot. You guys are everywhere! Wait, what's the Pit?' asked Liz, flabbergasted. 'And what happened to the Demon?'

'Oh, he's gone now. The Pit has many names, Hades or Hell it just depends what time you live in. It's getting rather stuffy in here don't you think?' said Aurora, feeling warm.

'I guess. I don't mind the fire though, especially in Melbourne's four-seasonal wintery days,' laughed Liz awkwardly.

'I haven't heard that before. It sounds delightful,' said Aurora as she opened the floor to ceiling windows with a flick of her wrist from the comfort of her chair.

'I'll never get used to that,' said Liz, uncomfortably grinning at Aurora.

Aurora rose from the chaise and walked over to the open windows. Closing her eyes, she felt the cool breeze brush past her face, she smiled.

*

The cool Melbourne breeze whisked itself through the stuffy nineteenth-century building. Liz could smell the eucalyptus from the gum trees as clearly as if she were standing outside next to them. Suddenly out of nowhere, a large black object came flying in through the open windows and perched itself on the arm of the chair Aurora was once again sitting comfortably in.

'Ah Corvis, I thought I sensed you. What have you brought for me today?' the abnormally large raven jumped up onto her shoulder and nuzzled into her neck. 'Good, that means we are in motion. Thank you, my friend, here you go,' said Aurora as she handed the black bird a dead mouse. 'I found this little guy only a moment ago on the window sill,' the bird stared at it a moment with its glossy grey eye, then in one swift movement, the mouse was gone, the bird too, straight back out the window. Liz had never seen a raven that big before, in her opinion it was almost the size of an eagle. The stunned look on Liz's face prompted Aurora to respond to her silent question.

'I understand that you follow the supernatural? Ghosts and witches and the like?' asked Aurora.

There she goes again, answering a question with another question thought Liz. 'Mostly just ghost hunting. I'm not really into the rest of it, the myth and such. Witches aren't really my forte,' answered Liz with a shrug.

'Well, do you know that in mythology witches and warlocks have some kind of animal, a kind of a pet if you will, that connects them to the Devil?' asked Aurora hinting towards something Liz believed she understood.

'Like a familiar? I think I've seen it on *Charmed* or something,' said Liz.

'Exactly, just like a familiar. Think of Corvis as my familiar. Of course, I'm no witch, but I believe everyone should be connected to someone or something during their lifetime, and Corvis is that something for me. He has watched over me for quite some time now, and I doubt he'll ever stop,' said Aurora leaning back into her sofa.

'Your grandfather has a little bird friend also. I'm not sure if you have noticed the leather glove he wears on his left hand? Well, I suppose you are smart enough to be able to guess as to what his pet might be,' said Aurora, smiling. 'Though, Corvis is much more than just your average raven. He was an Angel once but when my father was sent to his prison, Corvis, being a loyal friend, helped Tristan save me and was cursed into what you see now,' said Aurora.

'Will he change back?' asked Liz curiously.

'Perhaps. Xerxes is trying to figure out if there is a way but he believes that he and my father have been linked. So, in theory, if my father is released...'

'Then so is Corvis! Yes, familiar, connected to the Devil, I get it,' finished Liz.

'Exactly. One hopes anyway. In the meantime, he does what he can. One day I will be able to repay him,' sighed Aurora. 'Oh, I almost forgot to ask. How has your time been here spending it with your family?' asked Aurora.

'Unforgettable really. I never knew how much family actually meant to me before now. I think, even though I know you did it deliberately, I think they helped me in my decision. I think I'm going to join you. But on one condition,' said Liz, looking Aurora straight in the eye.

'Yes?' asked Aurora, already knowing the question after reading it in Liz's thoughts earlier in the day.

'I want to finish what I started with my project. Of course, I won't hand it in, well not the actual truth anyway. I just want to figure it all out. It's important to me and no I don't want you to help me, I want to do it on my own,' said Liz, confidently.

'I don't see an issue with that, as long as you don't break your word,'

'Okay, fair enough but what if it steps within the celestial realm?' she pressed.

'You can speak to Xerxes for guidance then, Balthazar will introduce you to him,' answered Aurora.

'I guess it's a deal then,' she said, giggling nervously.

'Good, but if have to say aloud that you will join me,' said Aurora.

'Oh! Sorry. I will join you Aurora, daughter of Lucifer. Is that right?' she asked.

'Good enough. Now go and find Balthazar and he'll show you to your permanent rooms,' said Aurora, preparing to leave.

'Wait! Could I please ask you one last question?' she asked hastily. 'Why here? Why this place?' she asked. Aurora looked around the grand room, and her face showed what looked like a mixture of sorrow and happiness at the same time.

'It reminds me of a time, long ago, when I was truly happy,' finished with the conversation, Aurora shook Liz's hand, welcomed her to the family, then graciously left the room.

*

Liz thought a moment about what Aurora had just said to her, about her moment of being *truly happy*. She wondered why that was. Then, she thought back to her pop and their conversation yesterday. Her mind was a flurry of conversations but this particular one repeated in her cluttered up head. Something that Aurora had previously said to her pop within his memory, '*They whisper into the minds of men.*' Over and over again, she comprehended it more and more. Aurora was doing a similar thing really, instead of whispering into her mind, she was putting things physically into play around her, like her newly reunited family in opposite rooms from one another. Liz didn't mind being manipulated though. She had lived her entire life, all twenty years of it, only knowing her mother, who unfortunately passed away from breast cancer four years prior. Now, however, there were so many of them, cousins, aunts, uncles, grandparents. She was over the moon. She was being distracted momentarily and realised quickly that she did have a task she needed to complete. She would get it done.

Her surname was now MacGregor after all. She had something to live up to and she would.

Chapter Thirty-Two

Light as a Feather

London

Aurora stood facing the altar within the Sanctuary of Westminster Cathedral,

silently splashing the recently re-furbished baptismal's *holy* contents to and fro with

her right hand as she awaited the arrival of her guests. A flicker of unease surged

through her just for a single moment, at the thought of seeing him. He had never

seen her in her true form before, not since she was a child, an image now a mere

shadow of the past. He would not be expecting to see *her,* however, but most likely

a Demon. That was one theory that had crossed his mind as to who could be the

Fallen's leader. Or perhaps, the child he once knew had lived and become that

Demon he was hunting. If only he had looked deep into her eyes, he would have

realised a long time ago who she truly was. *So, naive* she thought to herself, to fall

for all of her deceptions. But, it didn't make her love him any less. She had indeed

fallen for him, just as her advisers had predicted long ago, and he had become her

one and only vice. This was something she needed to rectify. Therefore, her only

plan, other than having him killed, was to win him over and have his people join

hers. It was the only way she could defeat her enemy, *their* enemy. *How could he trust me after everything I have done to him?* she asked herself. There was only one way to gain his trust back, or at least help her to break through the armour. This, she would have to keep to herself, as her people would not agree to it, especially Balthazar.

'Have the entrapments been cast?' she asked Balthazar.

'Yes, My lady, they will only be able to communicate with each other once they pass the threshold. The Valkyrie will not hear a thing, unless you allow it,' he answered. The candlelight within the cathedral flickered sending a chill down Aurora's spine.

'It is time,' she whispered and Balthazar slipped into the shadows to await their guests.

*

Tristan had followed the signs to El's and Liz's abductions and the connection El might have with Aurora, once his ward, now quite possibly the leader of the Fallen. With the help of Estelle's clever mind, they were able to link them. What she couldn't figure out was why they were linked. Estelle didn't have much evidence to go on, with the only exception being the Underground and the grey cat. They had found El, tortured by Demons within its even deeper underground catacombs, and Aurora had also been tortured by a Demon. Tristan remembered sensing Aurora's presence in the club. Later, finding out that a Nephilim had been murdered there, which reminded him of the prophecy that was foretold by the Elementals long ago. Not to mention her friend Liz had been taken by who he believed to be one of the Fallen's high ranking members. He knew he was grasping at straws, believing this particular murder was linked to Aurora and the prophecy but he knew she had been there. *She* had killed the Nephilim. Tristan believed she was the one the prophecy was talking about, the one '*born in ash, drenched in tears, she will destroy and conquer but only with your help. She will redeem seven in fire, bleed one, destroy another and drain the last, and reborn will she be again and again till she finds the key.*' Their main problem now, they still did not know if it was truly Aurora they were about to meet. They had, however, traced her to this very location, Westminster. The Valkyrie were waiting outside for the signal to enter, Celeste at the helm was not used to waiting, but was still ready to bring Aurora to her knees if she had to.

His only thought now was to rescue El. He knew somehow that Aurora had her, taunting him with her life. That she was using El against him because he had failed her and Lucifer so long ago.

He and his warriors moved silently through the nave of the cathedral, he forced his mind to be still and focus on the task at hand, shaking all thoughts of El from it, for the moment. He believed Aurora to be predominantly Demon in nature. So, he could not understand why a Demon could be in such a holy place such as this. It was understood that the Fallen could not touch holy soil or water. Both objects have been a great weapon against their dark brethren since the Fall. *So how could this Demon be here and why are they alone?* He thought. *It has to be a trap.* He saw the outline of a figure as they moved closer towards the altar. He signalled to his warriors to move forward. As they neared it, they could see it was shrouded in a cloak. Each of the Nephilim broke off into a v-formation and, in case of an ambush, Tristan had Kingston's hunting group of Nephilim waiting patiently within the hidden hallways above, watching. As they gained ground towards their enemy, the shadowy figure became more solid. It was facing the altar so Tristan could not see the Demon's face. He made the signal to halt and his warriors took their positions, even numbers facing inwards, odd outwards, aiming their angelic weapons towards the unmoving figure or towards a possible attack from behind.

'Do not move. We have you surrounded. If you have any form of weapon, disarm yourself now and slowly put whatever you have to the ground,' ordered Tristan to the silent statue in front of him. The figure did as he asked, it did not move.

'I said, disarm yourself now!' he yelled.

A woman's silky voice tiptoed its way out from beneath the cloak's heavy hood.

'I find this particular situation quite amusing,' Tristan shuddered at the familiar tone, but stood his ground not wavering at the strange comment, slightly curious as to what she had meant.

'I will not play your little games, no matter how hard you try to manipulate the situation,' he snarled. 'Comply with my orders and we can sort this out nice and easy.'

Giving him time to breath, she waited before speaking.

'Well, here we all are in one of the holiest of places in Great Britain and you, lore abiding citizens of the High Council, who protect the little *Unknown*s that worship here, move inside these walls with weapons! Threatening an uncertain enemy, that in fact, has none.' If there was anything uncertain about this particular scene, it wasn't that she was their enemy, it was because of the tension that now surrounded them. He could sense something was amiss.

'Slowly turn around, with your arms outward, I will not say it again,' he politely ordered this time. The figure did so, and as she slowly turned to face him, that uncertainty grew stronger. He shook it off and refocused on the situation at hand. 'Remove the hood, slowly.'

'Perhaps you should lower your weapon and then I will remove my cloak. Your warriors may stay as they are, but as you are so close, I'd prefer not to have that thing waving about in my face. I believe that is fair, do not you?' she asked.

Tristan looked to his warriors and gave them a nod to stand fast as he cautiously lowered his weapon to his side.

'Now you,' he said. Aurora slowly unclipped her cloak and as it fell to the marble floor beneath her, a wave of magnificent light shone over them all. Tristan then realised that this Demon was in fact not a Demon at all but an Archangel. He stood

in complete shock. The traditional custom of being in the presence of one of the

highest stationed Angels was to bow your head. This specific situation did not call

for that. No wonder she wanted him to lower his weapon. Once the glare had

diminished, he could finally see her face. Her beautiful silver hair tied back in a

braid displaying her almost godlike features, and those eyes, those familiar eyes.

'No, it can't be. You were human,' he stammered. Her gentle smile weakened his

heart once more.

'Yes, I was. Every time that we have met I have been human, with the exception of

when we had first met in my father's prison. I have lived and died a mortal being,'

she whispered.

He repeated the words in his head; *lived and died, lived and died.* He felt the air

around him transform, it was just her and him in their own little magical bubble.

She moved closer to him.

'Tristan, I have hurt you and I know that with all of the pain that I have caused you

I understand if you cannot trust me.'

He didn't move, didn't say a word, he couldn't. There was nothing he could say. He

couldn't even comprehend what she had done to him, let alone understand what she

was saying to him at this very moment. His whole body was numb, he was staring

blankly into nothing, his mind wiped of any feeling or emotion that he had ever felt

before in his lifetime. She was talking but it was incoherent nonsense. He then felt his heart rip in two, blood rushed from his chest and into his extremities in anguish. Finally, he sniggered, waking up from his stupor.

'Trust you? Trust *you*? You've got to be kidding me? Who are you, who in the hell of hells are *you*? Because you're definitely not Elora, Lora or El! She died! She's dead! They're all dead!' he choked as realisation grew within his mind. 'Oh my Gods, even the names are similar to yours! How did I not realise this before? Why was I so blind to it all? You are all of them and they are all you. You manipulated me into loving you... I don't understand,' he mumbled. Aurora could see the exhaustion take hold within his eyes. She struggled to hold herself back from him, to take him in her arms and comfort him. She knew her touch would not be welcomed.

'I'm such a damned fool,' he slumped to the ground.

Meanwhile, the Nephilim were powerless, stuck on the other side of their private bubble, not hearing a word of what was being said. They could see them both behind a haze but they could not get to them. James signalled Kingston who moved down to their location. He then attempted to contact the Valkyrie with no joy.

'Comms are down. Kingston have you got anything?' asked James. Their Guardian tried a different form of communication through the mind but couldn't get through to the outside.

'They must have put up some kind of barrier or entrapment spell. They have been ahead of us this whole time. We're alone unless Celeste figures it out on her own. I doubt Aurora came here without her own Guardians so there's no sending anyone out to fetch the Valkyrie. Not without a fight anyway,' said Kingston, taking a moment to look around trying to sense if they were not alone. 'All we can do is surround them and wait,' he finished, placing his weapon back into its sheath, the Nephilim all followed suit while keeping a close eye on Tristan.

*

Aurora thought about what she would say next before speaking it aloud. Looking down at his slumped figure on the ground, a part of her soul felt as if it were drowning in his pain with him. He wasn't alone in this.

'I used you, and I am not apologising for that. I am deeply sorry for the pain I have caused you but it was a necessary evil to achieve my mission. You know who I am, my true identity, you just don't want to believe it after everything we have been through together. That I had pulled the clouds down over your eyes for so many centuries and you had absolutely no inkling that I could be that little girl you once knew, that you had promised to protect.'

After what had seemed a lifetime, losing his self-control, taking his sword from the ground he rose to his feet and directed it at her throat, knowing full well it was useless against her.

'What are you playing at? What is your game here? Tell me! Tell me now! Or so help me, I will have the Three down here before you can blink an eyelid,' he

317

threatened. Gently, she raised her hand to the weapon pointing at her delicate throat and gracefully moved it away.

'Look around you Tristan. Open your eyes, can you see them?' He took her invitation and looked outside their little bubble, seeing dark figures hiding in the shadows.

'You believed that you had me surrounded, but in truth, it is the other way around. Understand, they will not harm your people, unless I am harmed which is why they are showing themselves to you now. Your friends outside cannot hear you which is why your own people have moved in closer towards us.' She freed them from their private solitude and stepped backwards towards the altar once more.

'I know you need time and I will give it to you. Finally, I have lifted this burden of truth from both of us but there is one more burden I wish to release you of,' she looked passed Tristan's saddened eyes and to his half-human, half-Angel warriors.

'Sienna,' she called. Sienna moved out from behind a pew and positioned herself behind Aurora.

'Sienna? What are you doing?' stuttered Liam.

Sienna looked lovingly into her boyfriend's eyes and said, 'I'm sorry Liam, it's nothing personal, I do love you. All of you will see this is a betrayal, but I love you all and, in time, you will understand why I did what I did.'

Tristan looked directly at her now. 'What did you do Sienna?'

'She did what she was tasked of her, by me.' Aurora raised her left arm and stretched out her hand. Sienna placed a rectangular trinket box into her commander's opened hand.

'When all of you were distracted by my abduction, locked away in your little laboratory or out searching for signs, Sienna stayed behind and found this for me.' Aurora opened up the box and lifted out a piece of delicate metallic-looking material in the shape of a feather. 'Finally,' she sighed with relief and placed it neatly back into its container and into a pocket inside her jacket.

'How did you?' stuttered Tristan, contorting his eyebrows into a confused frown.

'Oh, this?' Sienna pointed at the little box now in Aurora's hand. 'It was easy, well, easy enough for me anyway. Once her Ladyship had located it within your memories, after centuries of attempting to connect with you, she passed on the information to me. After Kingston and James's hunting parties left, post *El's* abduction and you, Estelle and Kai hid away in the lab, I volunteered to hold the base, as you know, and call for back up if you guys needed it. What you didn't know was that I also snuck around Tristan's office and located this little sucker, hidden behind the charming face of his treasured grandfather clock. As you were focused on locating El, you never thought to check it before we left for London. Assuming that's what you do on a daily basis. I've had it with me ever since and now, I return it to its rightful owner.' Tristan's face turned sour at the thought of Aurora showing Sienna his own private memories.

'Of course,' he thought aloud as he remembered the words of the Fates. '*Reborn will she be again and again till she finds the key*, it's obvious to me now as to why you targeted me because I held the key! I'm a fool,' he moaned, shaking his head. 'No, you were just in love with me Tristan. It is as simple as that. You cannot blame yourself for my deception. Thank you Sienna. You may join your grandfather now.' With a curtsey, Sienna turned and faced her former peers. Giving them a not-so-reluctant smile, she blew them a kiss goodbye and disappeared into the shadows behind Aurora to where Zachariah lingered.

*

Aurora, looking back towards Tristan, stepped closer. His warrior's reactions were swift, lifting their weapons out of their sheaths and aiming them in her direction. 'Calm yourselves Nephilim. Your weapons will do no harm here. I understand you are upset, that you believe you have just lost one of your own, but the simple thing is, she is not lost she is merely back with her true family. You are all more than welcome to join our cause.' As she spoke, she moved her hand in front of her, palm towards the Nephilim's weapons, then moved it towards the ground. An invisible force obliged the warriors to lower their weapons, their faces riddled with strain, as they reluctantly gave in. She then raised her hand upwards and gently closed it into a relaxed fist, a signal for her own warriors to emerge from the shadows, surrounding them in every direction.

'Look around you young Watchers, do you see my collective? What particular one stands out the most do you think? The mortals, the Angels or the Demons? Why is it that a Demon can step inside these holy walls you wonder?' she asked Tristan specifically. He merely stared blankly at her as he was writhing in anguish over what had just occurred.

'Your holy weapons do not work on my people, because they only work on true evil within this world. Angels, haven't you ever wondered why there are no holy relics within the Kingdom above? Why is it that no one is allowed to bring any outside object into their realm? I would think if I had created a species that I would show off my achievements to my fellow Gods.'

Liam spoke up then 'She has a point boss.' Tristan glared at his young warrior. 'Don't let her get into your mind Liam. We cannot trust a thing that she says or does.'

Aurora smiled slightly at this. 'Well, perhaps you should test my theory the next time you are summoned. Or don't, it is your prerogative. However, I would like to make a proposal. I would like to ask you to join us officially. You don't have to answer now of course, especially with your heightened emotions after these evening's events,' she said generously.

'We will not play your ridiculous games anymore Aurora!' he yelled, his frustration stealing itself away from him. Staring into his eyes, she gradually stepped towards him.

'I have something for you Tristan.' She took his reluctant hand in hers and uncurled his firmly gripped fingers. She could feel his unease at her touch, a mixture of rage and tortured love. Placing the gift within his hand, she wrapped his fingers back over it and leaned in closer, gazing into his perfectly steel blue eyes. 'This is no game Tristan. I know nothing I can say to you right now will make you understand who I am now or what I did. Except that a long time ago you took me from the blackest pits known to this world and placed me into the safety and care of loving parents. You saved me and I will do you the same courtesy. As soon as they find out you failed them, they will take your wings. I cannot allow that, you have suffered enough at my hands. What I have given you is my trust in you. If you are willing, meet me at the place that you believe you failed me in a fortnight, when the moon is at its highest. A feather for a feather.' Squeezing his hand one last time, she let go and vanished into the night, taking her warriors with her.

Aurora, he thought to himself taking in a deep breath to steady himself. He looked down into his hand and saw what he thought he had felt. A single pearlescent feather, belonging to her that was now his. The one thing that could end this war right here, right now. The Valkyrie appeared beside them as soon as Aurora had faded away, too late.

'About time you showed up,' spat Kingston. 'You missed, well, everything,' he finished glancing sideways at Tristan, who was still standing in the same position with his hand held out before him.

'What happened? We couldn't get inside. There was some kind of barrier that I've never seen before,' said Celeste in frustration.

'Never mind, we'll debrief you back at base. It's not a good time right now,' said Kingston, attempting to usher Celeste away from Tristan's view.

'Guys, pack up and let's head home,' he ordered and moved over to his friend. Tristan heard Kingston walking up behind him and closed his grip around the feather. He greeted him with a solemn smile as he placed the feather inside his armour. There was much to think about over the next fortnight and he needed to find solitude and scotch to help him do so.

Chapter Thirty-Three

Night Before the Dawn

Killedan Churchyard

"Darkness cannot drive out darkness; only light can do that."

Martin Luther King Jr

The commons that surrounded the derelict Killedan Churchyard were thick with green pasture and provided a magnificent view of the distant mountains that scattered themselves over the county. It was a stark contrast to the ghostly remains of what used to be the parish's most formidable of holy meeting places. The tower and bluestone shell of the main hall were all that was left after the Great Storm of 1839, known to the people of Ireland as the 'Night of the Big Wind'. After the great devastation that had occurred there, the townspeople believed that it had been cursed by the one and only ominous Devil. This was mainly due to the fact that the only deaths that had occurred that night, in this particular parish, were indeed within the burning remains of the church. After the parishioners tidied up their ruined village, they swore that no one shall ever again step a foot back into the Killedan Church, for they shall burn in Hell, or something to that effect. Aurora stared out across the commons and watched the sunrise, savouring the early morning dew as the wind brushed passed her. She smiled at the poor attempt of a barbed wired fence with warning signs that were half eaten away by years of neglect and rust. Making her way down the overgrown path, she stopped under the archway into the entrance where a wooden gate once stood. Glancing up into the blackened window of the still vertical tower, a chill swept over her. There were happy and cruel recollections of this place that still haunted her. Whoever said 'time heals all wounds', deceived the world.

She could see the remains of what used to be her little cottage, just over the rise. Memories of her Nephilim mother flooded her mind. How she missed her, even to this very day, centuries later. Walking over the entrance, she made her way through the many memories of her childhood. She saw her younger self playing 'Ring a Ring o' Rosie' with a couple of the other girls her age in what used to be the main hall. As she kept walking through the bluestone remains, it began to transform back into its original self before the storm. She saw herself once again, running down the hallway and decided to follow. Turning a corner, Aurora saw the ghostly girl holding a little ragdoll run up the staircase and into the tower. Still following her, she reached the top but the girl had disappeared. Her memory faded away and she could see the present-day ruins materialising around her. She walked forward towards the ledge and stepped on something. Looking down she found the little ragdoll. *Lucy*, she remembered. Kneeling down she picked up the tattered doll and stared at it in remembrance for a moment and then as she went to place it inside the pocket of her emerald woollen jacket, it turned to dust. Disappearing just like her memory had done moments before. She couldn't think about the doll now, not yet, as it would bring a flood of traumatic memories down upon her. Not when she was about to come face-to-face with Tristan, well she hoped she would be, if he showed. Thinking of Tristan, another memory entered her mind, this memory had only transpired moments ago, however. Xerxes, a loyal supporter and member of her inner circle of whom questioned her emotional attachment to Tristan on a daily basis, had a word with her before she left their sanctuary. His great methodical mind prevented him from understanding their profound connection, especially because it involved emotions, which he declined to think he had himself. His passion for scientific investigation and invention told a different story to Aurora.

'Do you think it's a trap?' he asked her.

'No, he holds my pledge and can do with it what he wishes. If he wanted to control me and bring me to the Gods, he would have done so already. He understands the power he holds right now in having a feather from my wing. He wants something from me. Perhaps it is just closure, perhaps some form of justice. Whatever it is, I will go and I will go alone, is that understood?' she glared at him.

'Of course, my Queen. I will ensure Balthazar and Corvis understand also. If anything untoward does happen though, we know what to do.' He nodded his head and the memory diminished.

Looking down into the building's remains she saw a glimmer of hope, Tristan had come. He immediately saw her and their eyes met briefly before he disappeared. Her heart fluttered nervously inside her chest. She could hear him ascending the stairs below, there were easier ways for Angels to travel but Tristan liked to do things in a more human-like manner these days. She took one last deep breath before he reached her and turned around to face him.

'I didn't think you would be here,' he exhaled. Aurora smiled at him and asked him why he would believe that.

'You may have thought it was a deception, a way for me to deceive you and have you brought to the Gods. Though, again that would be foolish since I can easily summon you with this.' He looked away from her and lent against the cold bluestone ledge, holding her feather.

'Even so. I believe I can trust you, though you do not trust me. I know you want to understand the complete truth which is why I knew and hoped, that you would come,' she answered. He stood facing away from her for a few moments while, she assumed, he was gathering his thoughts. After what seemed to be an age, he broke the deafening silence.

'I need to know why Lor.. Aurora. Why... why you chose death, over me,' he stared intensely into her eyes then. Her heart sank and she felt her blood drain from the rest of her body and filter its way into her pale cheeks.

'Where to start. You will say, at the beginning but the beginning was so long ago and you were there. So, I'll start with this place. There are certain events in my life that I have kept to myself since childhood. Not even Balthazar, Corvis or Xerxes know every detail of what I went through when I was taken from here.' Taking a breath, she continued. 'It is something that cannot be spoken, not by me. But I can show you if you allow me to?' she appealed.

Tristan merely nodded his response and she moved closer to him.

'Close your eyes, please.' He did as she asked and she cupped her hands around his face so that the tips of her thumbs rested on his temples. Closing her own eyes, she delved back into her past to this very spot in 1839 and relived her tragedy once again. Once she had shown him what was relevant to his question, she let go and took a step back from him, her fingers still tingling from the touch of his skin.

'Are you alright Tristan?' She looked at him with concern as his eyes were still closed.

'Yes, I'll be fine. I just need a moment,' he murmured.

He opened his eyes and turned back towards the ledge, as still as stone.

'I understand that you did all of this for your father, I get that. But transforming yourself into an *Unknown* only to go through the pain of death over and over again, to save a man you have never known is, it's senseless. You destroyed not only yourself over and over again but you destroyed me. You have broken me in two Aurora. One half despises you, while the other denies the truth and still fights to love you. You have put me at war with myself and I am lost. Now, seeing what you have just shown me, breaks my heart even more. I failed to protect you, I failed your father and in doing so, you have made me believe I was cursed. I can see how you truly felt, feel for me. I know you feel the same as I do and that you have suffered just as much. Perhaps that's all the truth I require to forgive you with, perhaps not. I cannot say just now. I need more time...to heal.' He was facing her now, trying to decipher her thoughts.

'I understand you need time Tristan, but after showing you what happened to me, I thought you would at least have questions about why your Gods sent a Demon to kill me. Or, are you still processing the fact that they are also not who you thought they were? I can feel your doubt even now!' she pressed.

'I know who they are, I always have,' he answered.

'So, you know they use Tyrants to spread their chaos across the realm? Yet, you still follow them like a loyal pet. How can you not see that we need to make a stand against them?'

He pointed to his heart as he answered her. 'You know why! Because we are tied to them. There is no way to break that bond without losing my wings, I will not Fall, not like the rest of them,' he said, digging his heels into the ground.

'What if I told you there was another way? That I can free you of your bonds. Your hollow oath holds no glory for you now Tristan. There is no honour in what they do or in what they make you do. Holding onto that only makes you a fool.' His eyes flickered and for a moment, she thought she had him.

'And what you have done is honourable? You have murdered mortals and celestials in your mission to save your father. You're just like them. Besides, there is no other way. I know you have newfound creations and unidentified powers, but there is no other way than stripping your wings to break the bond with our creators. We can hide from them temporarily but permanently, I don't believe you. I am better a fool than a traitor,' he responded. Her face saw red then.

'I am no traitor! I was born in death! The ashes of my mother and one tiny bead are all that I will ever know of her. My father fell in love, that was his crime, and hers, and they were both condemned for it! He fell into an eternal emptiness while she fell to her death. I was tortured in the filth of a Tyrant and then raised by the Fallen. I have lived in the wretched pain of knowing that my beginning caused my mother's end. I am the daughter of Light, but all I have ever known is this forsaken darkness. You are a fool to think that what you do and believe is righteous or just. To follow them will be your own undoing. What do I need to do to convince you that you're on the wrong side of this?' she pleaded.

Tristan placed his gentle hand on the side of her cheek as he spoke. 'Nothing my love, you can do nothing.'

Before leaving her, he placed the feather she had given him back into her hand and let go.

As he turned to go down the cold stone steps, she whispered into the breeze that followed him, 'I will see you at the gate then, my love.' After he left, Aurora stayed there for a while and watched as the sun slowly lowered itself into the distant mountains before her.

'What will I do now?' she asked the wind, as silent tears fell from her face and hit the cold pavement below. 'I really hoped he would join us after I showed him my truth. He has given me no other choice. He has decided to fight against me and I cannot allow him to get in my way,' she said.

'My Queen?' asked a voice from behind her.

'Xerxes is the weapon ready?' she asked him, knowing he was standing behind her.

'Nearly, I just require one or two more tests and then I believe it will be ready,' he said nervously.

'Don't *believe*, *know*. If it doesn't work, I will have to move to plan *B*,' she said regrettably.

'It will work. On my honour, it will work my Queen,' he swore to her.

'Good. I have faith in you my friend. Tell Balthazar I will return momentarily,' she said to him, still looking out onto the Irish moors. 'I need some time, alone.'

'Of course, my Queen,' he said and disappeared as quietly as he had appeared only a moment ago. Aurora contemplated her next move over and over again. She knew she could never be forgiven for what she had planned in the coming battle but Tristan had made it clear to her that he would stand against her, something she had feared he would do. Her heart was being ripped apart with the thought of

neutralising him, but it had to be done. Her father was her first priority, she owed

him that much, it was all that she could give to him for taking the love of his life

away. If she failed Lucifer, she could never forgive herself and neither could her

people. She had a choice to make, Tristan or her father? After everything she had

gone through to get to this very moment, there was no other choice to make.

She would always choose her father.

Chapter Thirty-Four

Tartarus Cries

The Pit

"Freedom isn't free at all, it comes at the highest cost."

Spartacus

'Where is he?' Aurora asked her Warlords.

'He is on his way Commander. Xerxes will be here, he just had to conduct some final tests to ensure the weapon worked correctly,' answered Balthazar cautiously, so as not to make his commander any more anxious than she already was.

'Shouldn't that have been finalised already? We are literally leaning on the edge between Earth and Hades, a breath away from battle.' The Warlords nervously looked at one another, silently hoping Xerxes would show up inside the war tent, and very soon.

'Perhaps we should start without him? He isn't really required for orders anyway. He will be here before it begins, you know he will Aurora,' Balthazar reassured her. He was the only one who would dare call her by her name instead of rank in front of others. He had earned it. After all, he was the one who had raised her. Aurora begrudgingly smiled and motioned for everyone to gather around the table covered in maps and mini chess figures, that if not fully

333

controlled by their master, would move on their own. They went over the specific details of the battle at hand. However, not all were meant to know each other's specific tasks, so each were discussed in private with their commander. This tactic was a normal process for them. This was how they had become so resilient over the centuries, testing their strategies on the minds of men over thousands of years of warfare. If everyone had known the entirety of Aurora's plans, someone or something would slip up. After everything she had gone through in her life, she was not about to trust just anyone, even those who followed her. There are spies everywhere, she would know, as she has her own working directly under the foul noses of her enemy.

'So, everyone is clear of what needs to occur?' she asked her Warlords. An echo of *Ma'am* in confirmation went around the table like dominoes, followed by a loud screech from Corvis who was comfortably perched on Styx's shoulder guard. 'Once Xerxes arrives with the weapon, you will move out to your positions. As soon as the first arrow hits, we begin. We cannot fail. We will not fail. After everything we have done to get to this point, we must not fail. Do not hesitate against the enemy, because they will not waiver against you. This is not our first fray and it will not be the last, but it is the most important battle we will endure together. We have only one outcome, and that is to release my father. Once we have achieved this, we fall back. He is our light within the shadows and we will liberate him no matter the cost. May the spirits of this realm protect you, so we shall meet again,' she blessed them.

'And also, you, my Queen, so, we shall.' There was only one Angel who called her this, Xerxes had soundlessly entered the tent.

'I have them, apologies for my tardiness, I just wanted to triple check everything. Don't want to accidentally kill anyone, do we?' he smiled at Aurora as he graciously handed her the newly formed weapon he had been studiously working on for a number of decades. 'No, we do not,' she grinned back. 'Ladies and Gentlemen, to arms!' In response, her Warlords beat their right hand in the form of a fist over their heart and left the tent, with the exception of one. Aurora took Balthazar's hand before he had the chance to move outside, 'I wish to add one more task to your list of things to do this night my brother.' She asked him, a sound of desperation in her tone. Facing her, he took her hands in his, 'the shake in your voice gives you away my darling sister, you need not ask. I will take Tristan before the Gods do. Will you speak to the men before we begin? They are eager to hear you'. She nodded in response. Balthazar reached both of his hands up and clutched her face between them, 'may your mother's spirit protect you, and may you bring your father's wrath down upon them all.' He turned and left her alone within the war tent. As he disappeared, she let out the breath she had been holding with a great sigh and looked at the weapon she held in her other hand, took another breath and placed it into the quiver positioned on her back. She stepped outside to look upon her battleground. Breathing in the rancid air she signalled her warriors to turn inwards and face her, they moved with such ease the ground beneath barely rumbled. Balthazar was not wrong when he said they were eager to hear her, their eyes spoke his truth. 'Warriors. I do not use this term lightly.' Pausing slightly while looking into the eyes of her people, she continued. 'You honor me here with your presence today. For you chose to be here, to stand by my side and fight for what is just and true. Your valor will not be seen out there on the battle ground, but right here, in this very moment before we take our first step into the light. We are at the very precipice we have yearned for. For centuries we have bled for one another, for centuries we have wept for our fallen. It has been a difficult journey for us all, and it will continue to be so. Because this is not the end, this is just the beginning.'

'My friends, you are not merely warriors, you are more to me than that. You are blood, my blood. The blood of my father runs deep within us all. The very reason we are here this day. For he is locked away deep within the damning pits below. Freedom will be his once again, and we will be the ones who grant that freedom!'

'Darkness will fall this day, because we will tear it from the skies. The creatures beyond the shadows will fade into nothing! The Archangels will burn in the Flame, and we will go on and rise once more from their ashes!'

'Warriors, are you with me?' a thunderous roar erupted from the mass of immortal and mortal alike. Aurora smiled at their answer. Signaling them to once again face their enemy, she made her way to her position.

'Then let the first arrow see the dawn of day.'

*

The mist wound its way up the path where the Nephilim stood, anxiously awaiting the battle to begin. The tension between the allied warriors sent some into dizzy faints, while others watched for movement in the far distance before them. Tristan stood behind them with the Archangels Gabrielle, Uriel and Raphael, who were deliberating the magma battleground ahead. Watching them intently, Tristan noticed that Gabrielle seemed amused.

'Are you going to share your reveries with the rest of us? Or do we have to entertain ourselves while we wait for the bloodshed to begin?' he asked her. Turning her angelic head towards him, she had the most devious of grins spread across her face.

'Well Tristan, commander of none, except for children. Since you asked so politely, I'll let you in on our little conversation.' Beckoning him to move closer with a slight wave of her hand, she informed him of their discussion.

'My dear sister Uriel was merely pointing out the fact that they have *Unknowns* fighting with them! How absurd is that? How are they going to put a dent in our armour with mortals? It's pure chaos over there with the assortment of beings they have. I can't see any self-control working out for them at all. What is it your Nephilim say? *We have this in the bag?'* Tristan looked over at Uriel, she was not smiling but shaking her head at her sister Gabrielle for her small-minded naivety.

'With respect Gabrielle, I wouldn't underestimate them. They are the truest of warriors. I actually wouldn't put it past them if they were born in the middle of battle! Aurora has gathered them over the past centuries and kept them alive somehow. I don't know the exact intricacies of it all yet, but if we can get a prisoner of war, we might be able to figure it out,' said Tristan, attempting to enlighten Uriel's dim-witted sister. Gabrielle was not astonished nor pleased at his difference of opinion.

'So, she has been collecting humans like little toys and now she finally gets to play with them. How charming and yet, quite against the law,' she mused.

'Gab, I think there is a little more to it than that,' retorted Uriel, starting to look frustrated with her sister.

'Oh? And what is that my dear sister?' asked Gabrielle.

'I believe they have formed some kind of agreement, a deal as you would say. If they have done so, and both parties are willing, she has done nothing against the law. It is interesting however, how she has kept them hidden for so long.' With a sense of achievement in her tone, Uriel had finally put her ignorant sister in her place.

'Michael wouldn't agree with you,' Gabrielle responded quickly.

'Well Michael isn't here, is he? So, tough luck Gab.' Tristan thought this was a good time to change the subject.

'Where is Michael anyway? I thought he would want to be a part of the action?' he asked. The sisters and their silent brother Raphael looked indifferently at each other. Finally, the brother responded. 'He was ordered to stay up there,' was all he gave.

'Right. I guess they have their reasons. Anyway, I better leave you and return to my position.' With a slight nod to his superiors, he turned and headed towards his men.

'Welcome back brother,' a cheerful Kingston greeted him as he returned. 'So, did they have anything relevant to say? Or was it just wishy washy idiocy as usual?' he asked Tristan.

'The latter really. You know officers, all talk and no muster. Gabrielle finds it amusing that the enemy have Unknowns fighting with them. She believes they have no chance against us,' he informed his most trusted friend.

'I assume you told her they are actually brilliant warriors in their own right?' Tristan nodded. 'I take it that nod means *yes, but she still wasn't listening.* Lovely, just lovely. Well, hopefully we can win this one. With the Three on our side we should be in with a fighting chance,' said Kingston confidently.

Tristan kept his eyes front as he answered. 'Well actually, Uriel spoke up about Aurora's warriors. I was not surprised she was against her sister again. Anyway, all we have to do is just hold the line, the Archangels will do the rest. Though I'm not so sure that I have your confidence brother. With what we have witnessed Aurora do, I believe we may not be the winning side at the end of this. My main question is, where are her Nephilim? We know she has a number of them as allies.' Searching the enemy's ranks, both Guardians could not see any of the children of the Fallen.

'Actually, now that I look at her warriors, there doesn't seem to be an awful lot of them. Yes, they have enough to go against our numbers today, but from what we have traced over the past week, there should be more of them,' Kingston pointed out.

'Well, we don't have all of our warriors present, so why should she? I believe it is just another one of her strategies. Why have all of your jewels in one box, she's thinking beyond this battle,' Tristan assumed, looking beyond the wall of Fallen Angels and men.

*

'What are you doing Caleb?' whispered James. Caleb had his head tilted slightly towards their two officers in charge.

'I'm trying to hear what they're saying, be quiet,' shushing James, he turned back toward Tristan and Kingston. Caleb had decent hearing, better than most other Nephilim, but he had to focus.

'Well? What are they saying?' asked Liam, joining in on the action.

'Wow! You're actually interested in something beyond your deep despair, are you?' sniggered Caleb. Estelle gave him a great whack over the back of the head.

'Ow, what'd you do that for?' he stammered.

'For being a dick, that's what,' responded the fair-haired Estelle. She giggled, as she too tried to listen in on what was going on.

'Well Caleb? Please do tell us what it is that is so interesting beyond our own conversations,' spoke Kai, for the first time tonight.

'They're talking about Aurora and if she will fight Tristan or not. Something about the Three stopping her and that we might have a fighting chance.' He stopped.

'And?' asked Estelle impatiently.

'There's movement ahead,' he responded. At this they all looked forward towards their enemy and saw a number of different golden-clad armoured, what they assumed, Warlords moving out into position.

'It must be that time,' said James, glancing over at Liam, who was again lost in his own thoughts, looking as if he was searching the enemy for someone they knew.

'Are we ready?' he whispered to his fellow warriors.

'As ready as we could ever be I guess. It still doesn't feel right us targeting the *Unknowns* though. Yes, it is fair but, since when does the enemy play fair?' responded Estelle.

'They're our orders, so unless told otherwise that's just what we have to do. They are not completely mortal remember? Most of them have been alive for over a century. They will be a good match for us,' stated her brother. 'If not, better,' he added bleakly.

All of a sudden, the sound of something cutting through the air ceased their conversation.

'Tristan!' gasped Estelle as she witnessed him fall to the ground.

The Nephilim broke formation and ran directly to their leader. He was desperately gasping for air as blood leaked out of the wound beneath the arrow's puncture.

'His heart! Who did this?' bellowed James as he leaned down towards his mentor. Kingston held his friend tight, trying to comprehend the situation.

'She did,' he murmured, tilting his head towards Aurora. The others followed their officer's gaze and saw her standing proud, scythes in her hands motioning her warriors to begin the battle.

'We have to move him to the back, we need a healer to stop the bleeding! Wait! He's bleeding! Why is he bleeding?' questioned James, as he never knew Angels to bleed, not unless the weapon was made from Featherstone.

'I doubt the arrow tip was anything made from the mortal or even the celestial realm. It disintegrated into the wound.' Kingston had pulled the arrow out of Tristan's chest. Looking up towards the fray ahead, he began to stand, lifting his wounded friend with him. 'I'll take him to the healers and be right back. James, you're in charge until my return. Hold the line, no matter what,' he ordered as he headed towards the healer's tent.

'Yes Sir. You heard him, back into formation. Guys, I know this is rough, but we have to focus on what is in front of us, not what is behind us. Hold strong and stand fast.' The Nephilim moved back to their battle position, ready to do their part as a fearless anarchy of legionaries stormed towards them.

*

The battle strategy that Aurora had planned was a simple one. Take down the decoy target, rush the enemy with her legions of brutal warriors, cause chaos, trap second to fourth targets, take them down individually, then retrieve the prize. She wasn't sure how she would get to her prize yet, or if the traps would actually work. So far, her plan was working though. The Archangels had placed themselves at the head of their troops, making them easy targets for Aurora's plan to be successful, it was as if they had never fought a battle before. Using one of Xerxes many fabulous trinkets, they trapped each Archangel within their very own, temporary prison. According to Xerxes, Aurora had approximately twenty-five minutes to disable each one individually. However, that calculation was dependent upon the individual strength of each Archangel, so she may have less time to deal with them.

She could do that, she just couldn't face them all on her own at once, especially if the Valkyrie joined in on the fun. Balthazar and Styx's legions would stop them in their tracks for as long as possible. Their warriors were a mix of previous members of the Guard and Valkyrie, all they lacked were their wings but they could still take them on. Giving Aurora enough time to focus on the Three alone, her three Archangel family members.

Raphael would be the toughest, so he would be first, then Gabrielle. Uriel was an interesting one, very cunning and she never undervalued her enemy. Aurora had also heard rumours that Uriel might actually be sympathetic to her cause but she needed to hear that from the horse's mouth to believe it. She would leave her to last. After that, all she needed was free access into the Pit, which she knew she would get if her plan worked. It was time to move in and start putting it into action. As soon as the first Archangel was in the right position, three mortals aimed and released a number of arrow barrages in their direction. These arrows had a specific kind of rope attached, that when linked, created a force field that no Angel could escape, a new and improved Angel trap. Raphael and the others were now trapped, sending a surge of nervous energy throughout the God's forces. Aurora went straight for him, aiming low and hitting hard. Hand-to-hand combat for an Angel was easy, so Aurora took out her favourite weapons of choice, her golden war scythes. Raphael matched her and removed his double-edged sword from its sheath. As they fought, the battle around them continued. Maintaining their fortitude, Aurora's warriors fought until their bones turned to dust. A number of the enemy were going down too, not a desirable outcome for either side but it was necessary. Her legions were closing in on them. The unexpected appearance of her own Nephilim warriors flanking the enemy, led by Sienna, struck a blow to Aurora's enemy's morale but they didn't quit. Tristan's Nephilim held their line, not wavering in the clash of weaponry.

After several minutes of difficult combat and a number of hard blows to her golden armour, Aurora had outmanoeuvred Raphael. Blood dripped from her forehead as she trapped his right arm and left leg together with her scythes, a move she had used on Balthazar many a time in training. She might have at least fifteen or so minutes maximum till Raphael figures out how to release them. Time enough to take out her next target, the beautiful Aphrodite that was Gabrielle, as vain as she was stupid. She just stood within her prison waiting for it to disappear. Aurora decided she wasn't worth the energy and removed her bow from her back. Grabbing an arrow and aiming quickly on point, right at her aunt's ugly heart, slightly off to the right, she let it go. Wonderfully, it hit its target, who in utter shock fell to the ground in agony. Aurora walked up to her and smiled, then ran to her final target, Uriel. Who was waiting patiently with her weapon in hand, a bronze warhammer. Aurora was fresh out of weapons now, with exception of her bow but she had no chance against a hammer like Uriel's. The best she could do was hand-to-hand. All she had to do was get rid of the weapon. So, aiming another arrow, this time at her target's hand, she shot and missed. Running directly at Uriel, she aimed another, glancing the side of her target's shoulder brace, a distraction for her next arrow, which she aimed yet again at the hammer, hitting it where Uriel held it. She dropped it. With her final arrow, Aurora used it to move the warhammer as far away from its owner as she could. The prison faded and Uriel was straight onto Aurora, using her magnificent wings as extra power to push her into the ground.

'Two can play that game, aunt,' said Aurora with a grin, releasing her own far more resilient wings she pushed herself back into Uriel, forcing her backwards as she lost her balance. They grappled each other repeatedly, both becoming exhausted.

'Why are you doing this?' gasped Uriel, trying to catch her breath.

'For my father, my mother, and for myself,' she said proudly. 'How could you watch them destroy my family, your family?' she asked through gritted teeth, landing a blow across Uriel's face.

'We had no choice,' she attempted to justify.

'There is always a choice!' screamed Aurora, finally taking control and bringing Uriel into a headlock. 'Right now, I have a choice, to break your neck, to suffocate you or to let you go, I know none of these actions will kill you, but they will remove you from the action,' she said.

'Do it! You've won then. Isn't that what you want?' Uriel yelled back, giving into her niece.

Aurora let go of her and stepped back.

Unsure about what was happening, Uriel unnervingly stood. 'What is this?' she asked.

'I made my choice. Hopefully, not regrettably, I let you go,' she said exhausted. 'I only ask one thing of you in return.' Curious, Uriel raised an eyebrow and asked her what it was she wanted.

'Just take me to him, that's all I ask,' she said, sincerely. 'And all of this will cease,' she vowed.

'You're saying, that if I take you to Lucifer, that is it. You will end this bloodshed?' questioned Uriel, looking doubtful.

'Yes. You have my word, on my father's life and my mother's memory,' she vowed again. Uriel stood for a moment, looked around to see if eyes were on them and thought about it and agreed. Without sending word to anyone, she took Aurora through a portal and down into the Pit. Uriel led her through a passageway, past fire-lit torchlights and heaving spider infested walls. After what had seemed like hours, they finally reached the threshold, the gates of Hell as some would put it. Hecate's beautiful but terrifying hounds guarded the door into the Pit. Uriel walked up to them and waved her hand over their heads, each of them fell to the ground into a deep sleep. Taking out a small dagger from a hidden gap behind the hounds, she reached down and nicked the flesh of the closest canine, stealing a drip of its blood onto her finger. She then pressed the bloodied finger onto the centre of the gate and they graciously opened before them. This was something that Aurora had no knowledge of. You required approval from Hecate herself to enter the gates into the Pit, and with the help of an Archangel they walked straight through the gnarly door and into the great prison. Aurora followed Uriel quietly, trying to think of what to say to her father when they met. She thought of her warriors that still fought above. She had looked better, now battered and bloodied, but that didn't matter. After a maze of tunnels and many other prison cells filled with Greater and Minor Demons, they finally reached the one she had been waiting her entire life to see. The creature inside was curled up in the corner, asleep, slightly shaking from its weakened state.

'Your father. I am sorry you have to see him like this but I can't do anything about that, it is our creator's orders that he be left weakened. I wasn't able to help him when he fell, or your mother, as the Gods and the Valkyrie outnumbered us. If this is all that you wanted, I am grateful I could help,' she said, shame in her voice.

'Yes, you may leave us now,' said Aurora and she did, leaving no trace of her treachery behind.

'Father. Can you hear me?' she asked the dishevelled creature in the corner. It moved slightly, then lifted its head and looked in her direction. Her heart broke for the thousandth time.

'Father. It is I, Aurora, your daughter,' she said, hoping he would recognise her name.

The creature stirred. 'Aurora? Is it really you? Am I not hallucinating again?' he whispered.

'No, you are not. I am real. Please, can you move? Come to me, I need to give you something,' she pleaded, ushering him with her hand to move towards the bars. Slowly, reluctantly he got up. Limping, he moved towards her, his wings dragging on the ground behind him. She took his hand and placed the petrified feather, a vile of purple liquid and a whistle into his hands.

'Destroy this,' she said of the feather. 'And drink this, I promise you it will help. Do you remember how to use this?' she asked, pointing at the whistle. He nodded *yes* and she begged him to drink. She could see tears forming in his eyes.

'What's wrong father?' she asked.

'You, you have your mother's eyes,' he choked at the thought.

'Father, please, you must drink it. Drink it now!' she begged again, as she could hear guards approaching from afar. Finally, he sculled the potion and it took effect immediately, giving him life again. It wouldn't make him strong enough to fight but it would help him endure portal travel. He crushed the feather in his hand and watched as it disintegrated into the air around them. The gate into his cell opened and he took Aurora into an embrace that he had been waiting centuries to do. With teary eyes, Aurora whispered her love to him and their embrace tightened. After a short moment of pure happiness, she realised the Sentinels, the guards of the Underworld were right on their heels.

'Now, father, think of Corvis and use the whistle! It will take you where you need to go,' she said, pointing at it in his hand.

He looked at her. 'But what about you?' he asked worriedly. Deja vu consumed Aurora's mind as she remembered being in this exact same situation before as a child with her Nephilim mother Cora.

'Don't worry about me father, I have a plan. Balthazar will help me get out, but you need to use the whistle now! The Guard is coming, please I'm begging you! I'll be right behind you. I promise,' she pleaded. He took her hand in his and placed the whistle into his mouth with the other. Looking at her with trusting, fatherly eyes, he blew it and disappeared. Her hand empty. Only one could use a whistle portal and it was only him that needed to get away. Now, it was her turn to be incarcerated. If the Gods had her, they might not try too hard to look for him, for a time. She felt around her pockets to ensure her mother's bead was still there. Finding it beneath her armour, she hid it within a crack in the ground, she would use this at a later date, for as long as it took her to remember again. That should be enough time for Balthazar to hide her father. Taking out her very own vial, the last of the blue-hued liquid from another pocket, she sighed a breath of relief and consumed every last drop. Dropping the vial to the ground, she glimpsed sideways, seeing the Sentinels had surrounded her. She fell to the ground in pain contorting and changing into an *Unknown*. The guards watched in shock as she transformed.

After years of colluding, planning and tragic heartbreak, she had finally completed her task, she had saved her father. She knew Balthazar would do as she had asked and save Tristan from the God's wrath. He had failed them after all, giving the enemy the key to their greatest weapon. She was on her own now, and just as her mother had done before her, she had made her choice.

This time, however, she chose to save them both.

Meg Wilson, the daughter of a police officer and aged care nurse, grew up with her

nose in many books. Her love for Classical Mythology steered her to study Ancient

History at Macquarie University in Sydney, graduating with an Arts degree.

Working fulltime in the Australian Defence Force for over a decade, she decided to

devote her spare time to creative writing.

What began as a pastime, turned into a novel.

Follow her on Twitter @megdwittle

Or Instagram @megwilsonauthor

9 780648 480723